Rytuał

Rytual

Chloe Elisabeth Wilson

PENGUIN BOOKS

UK | USA | Canada | Ireland | Australia
India | New Zealand | South Africa | China

Penguin Books is part of the Penguin Random House group of companies whose addresses can be found at global.penguinrandomhouse.com

Penguin Random House Australia

First published by Penguin Books in 2025

Copyright © Chloe Elisabeth Wilson 2025

The moral right of the author has been asserted.

All rights reserved. No part of this publication may be reproduced, published, performed in public or communicated to the public in any form or by any means without prior written permission from Penguin Random House Australia Pty Ltd or its authorised licensees.

Penguin Random House values and supports copyright. Copyright fuels creativity, encourages diverse voices, promotes free speech and creates a vibrant culture. Thank you for buying an authorised edition of this book and for complying with copyright laws by not reproducing, scanning or distributing any parts of it in any form without permission. You are supporting writers and allowing Penguin Random House to continue to publish books for every reader. Please note that no part of this book may be used or reproduced in any manner for the purpose of training artificial intelligence technologies or systems.

This is a work of fiction. Names, characters, places and incidents either are the product of the author's imagination or are used fictitiously. Any resemblance to actual persons, living or dead, events or locales is entirely coincidental.

Cover design by Josh Durham, Design by Committee
© Penguin Random House Australia Pty Ltd
Cover photograph by Oleg Iandubaev/Alamy Stock Photo
Author photograph by Giulia Giannini McGauran
Typeset in 12/17 pt Minion Pro by Midland Typesetters, Australia

Printed and bound in Australia by Griffin Press, an accredited ISO AS/NZS 14001 Environmental Management Systems printer

A catalogue record for this book is available from the National Library of Australia

ISBN 978 1 76134 669 9

penguin.com.au

MIX
Paper | Supporting responsible forestry
FSC® C018684

We at Penguin Random House Australia acknowledge that Aboriginal and Torres Strait Islander peoples are the Traditional Custodians and the first storytellers of the lands on which we live and work. We honour Aboriginal and Torres Strait Islander peoples' continuous connection to Country, waters, skies and communities. We celebrate Aboriginal and Torres Strait Islander stories, traditions and living cultures, and we pay our respects to Elders past and present.

For Jillian, and Helen before her

Prologue

Hers was the second dead body I'd ever seen, not counting my mother's. My mother doesn't count because when people died in nursing homes or hospital beds or a worn lounge chair they had 'passed away'. *Dead* was bright-red blood – striking even in almost complete darkness. Hers was the second dead body I'd seen in as many months, and it was, if I'm honest, two too many for someone with my gag reflex.

'What the fuck?' I kept saying. Over and over, like a chant. 'What the *fuck*?'

'I can explain,' Luna said, wiping the knife on the leg of her cargo pants, as if it were paint or chutney or nothing at all. 'But first we need to move her body.'

She said it as though it was something I'd already agreed to – as if I'd known this was where we'd end up. And at first it made me mad. But I was tired. In my body, yes, but also in a grand, spiritual sense. And because I was tired, and I'd already sunk so much of myself into believing that this was the right place and the right time, I said, 'Okay.'

One

The cycle studio was called Ride On!, and the exclamation mark was compulsory. It was located in Richmond; a neighbourhood of Melbourne that most resembled a kind of Corporate Disneyland – everything in Richmond was designed to meet the needs of ambitious young professionals. As I stabbed the studio key towards the lock in the freezing dark of early morning, so hungover I was probably still drunk, I was reminded of the fact that I was neither ambitious nor professional, and even my youth felt questionable.

When the lock finally sprang open, I bolted up the stairs, the shadow of four consecutive negronis prodding at the back of my throat. When I made it to the landing, I ran my fingers over every light switch and snatched up the heating remote. The heater clicked on, then off, then on again, then it stalled. I stared it down, my right eye twitching in time with the machine's little ticks, and eventually heat flooded the reception area. I leant over the desk to steady myself. I was not going to be sick. I checked the time: 5.41. Technically, I was supposed to open the door to clients at 5.45, but anyone who arrived a full fifteen minutes early to a 6 a.m. weekday cycle class was probably dangerous. The instructor and studio owner, Steffani, was also yet to arrive.

Ride On! was essentially a hallway with a collection of rooms that ran down the left-hand side. First, there was the Pilates studio. A woman called Freesia taught reformer Pilates four nights a week, and I often caught her taking photos of herself on the equipment before and after class. I say 'caught', but she rarely flinched when she met my gaze in the mirror. She was a micro-influencer as well as a fitness instructor, and also a floral designer. Anyone with under 100,000 followers apparently qualified for the title of micro-influencer, which seemed depressingly inclusive to me.

The second room was the cycle studio – the main event – which held thirty stationary bikes and an intricate lighting rig. The instructor's bike was presented on a raised platform, which most of the instructors were fine with given they were also actors or failed actors. Classes took place in a lighting state you might describe as 'in the club', which tricked people into thinking that 45 minutes on a stationary bike was a fun and rebellious thing to do after populating spreadsheets all day. Behind the cycle studio were a small kitchen-cum-staffroom and two oversized changing rooms. The changing rooms were demarcated by gender, although the clientele at Ride On! was almost exclusively wealthy women.

When I started my role at Ride On! I thought that working there could fix me. But, just over a year later, Steffani was really on my case about signing up for the Ride On! teacher training, and I realised that any hope I had for transformation had vanished.

Rytuał

I couldn't stop making glib jokes about Ride On!, which meant that it really was all over. I had a habit of chasing belief with scepticism, but never scepticism with belief again. My pattern was: belief, scepticism, something new. I'd told Steffani I was considering the teacher training, but I was considering it about as much as I was considering moving to Norway. It was a year since my mother had died, and I was still bumping around in the dark, trying my best to make out the shapes of people and places. I wanted to keep this a secret, but the smell of grief was thick in my hair, like a bonfire or last night's vomit.

After I'd prepared the cycle studio – powered up the club lights and selected a playlist titled 'Empowering Weekday Wakeup' – I did a sweep of each of the changing rooms to make sure no one had forgotten their sweaty underwear the night before. When I returned to the reception desk, I heard knocking. 5.52. I ran down the stairs and unlocked the door. A woman who came to class most days stared back at me, her skin bright with little flushes of pink. She had long, dark hair and an angular body, the kind of body the early 2000s tried to strongarm women into believing was the only possible body – that is to say, despite her sharp edges, her frame also carried a pair of enviable breasts. The pace at which these thoughts appeared to me was truly shocking. The call was definitely coming from inside the house.

'Hi,' she said, smiling expectantly. I smiled back. After a moment, she added, 'Can I come in?'

'Of course! Sorry.' I pulled the door towards me, which only left her with a small gap through which to enter the studio. She wore a fragrance I'd smelt before but couldn't place. It was floral, but also somehow woody. Herbal, maybe. I followed her up the stairs.

'I'm Rose,' she said, when we made it to the landing. 'Rose Liu.'

The computer screen was dark, but I fiddled with the mouse beside it anyway. 'What size shoe?'

'Eight.'

I handed her a pair of worn riding clogs. Steffani called them 'clip-ins', but the only way to describe them on an aesthetic level was a velcro clog. Rose smiled again and walked towards the changing rooms. She moved as if she'd never slept through an alarm, or perhaps never needed to set one in the first place. I flopped into the reception chair and pressed the computer's power button. As the screen lit up, I picked at the balls of fabric that lined the inner seam of my leggings.

'Do we have tea, Marnie?' Steffani said, bounding up the stairs. 'Where's the tea?'

She dropped her duffel bag on the floor beside me and slid a sweaty can of Red Bull from the side compartment. She stared at me as she chugged from the can.

'I'll make some now.' I made a feeble attempt to stand up, but my heart wasn't in it.

'No! Don't bother. The stampede will be here any minute.'

I nodded.

Steffani was six foot one, blanketed in lean muscle, and had a perpetually hoarse voice. Her hair was long, thick and bleached blonde, but she got her roots done so often I never discovered what her natural colour was.

Steffani lumbered towards the cycle studio, and I counted the seconds between 5.58 and 5.59. At 5.59, twelve women would clamber up the stairs and each profess that they 'Couldn't find a park!' despite the fact that I knew where they lived, and where they lived was around no more than two corners. Like clockwork, three women trundled through the entrance, in varying volumes of goose down. A searing pain hit the centre of my skull, and I was reminded of the negronis. I checked their names off the list, threw them a pair of shoes each and waited for the second wave. Then the third. Until each checkbox was marked, all puffer jackets accounted for, and Steffani's hoarse voice was booming over the speakers.

When I plucked my phone from the pocket of my Ride On! branded hoodie, a new message stared back at me.

> You were right – were
> practically neighbours!! walk
> home was so quick lol. here
> are my bank details:
>
> BSB: 655-849
> Account Number: 1066948
> Account Name: Justin Langfield
>
> I think it was $60 but just
> transfer me 25 :-)

The number was unfamiliar, but Justin's leathery cologne still clung to my skin. This was not the first time I'd arrived at Ride On! with a blistering hangover, which did make me feel as if my life were marked by a series of clichés. It was comforting, in a way – slipping into the persona of 'geriatric party girl'. I was twenty-nine, but when I overheard groups of young women in line for the bathroom at a club I felt about one hundred and five.

It all started when I met Kahli, through a Facebook group called Popping Candy Real Estate. Kahli had advertised a room for rent in her 'Two-Bedroom Mid-Century Oasis', which should have been listed as a 'Cramped but Impeccably Renovated Two-Bedroom Thornbury-Adjacent Apartment'. There is a vein that runs through the city of Melbourne called the 86 tram, and it strings together the city's most desirable neighbourhoods like beads on a necklace. Fitzroy. Collingwood. Fitzroy North. Clifton Hill. Northcote. Thornbury. Preston. As the 86 climbs north, the rent gets cheaper, although not as cheap as you'd expect. Kahli's apartment was on the border of Thornbury and Preston, but the postcode was Preston. Preston is not at all close to Richmond. It was deeply inconvenient for me to live there, but I wore my commute like a badge of honour.

Kahli was two years older than me, but her life was worlds apart from mine. For one thing, she owned the apartment we lived in, but given how much money she spent on ketamine, I was starting to suspect that a hefty inheritance had been thrown at its asking price. Kahli was a consultant at a firm called Wallenheimer, and she was the kind of person who never arrived at a location with the objective of making friends. Our relationship was my favourite hobby.

I pocketed my phone and traipsed down the hall to the kitchen-cum-storage room. Even with a wall between us, Steffani's voice was grating. While I prepared tea for the clients, I also downed the juice of three off-brand Nespresso pods and a GoProtein bar. I looked at my phone again. The message from Justin stared me down. We'd met at a bar called Education State. As I ran my coffee-coated tongue over my top teeth, memory bubbled to the surface.

'Some people cave when they get keto breath, but that's just your body going into ketosis,' he said. 'You just need to eat more protein.'

'Keto breath?'

'Yeah, your breath smells like faeces for a few weeks, but it's actually not that bad.'

I stared at his bright gold watch, my brain soaked with gin and Campari.

'Do you work at Wallenheimer?' he asked.

'No, no, I'm just here with my friend.'

I looked for Kahli, but everyone in the bar had merged into a uniform blob. I couldn't tell if it was because they actually were all dressed the same, or if the gin and Campari had betrayed me.

'Oh, sick. You work at Left Field, then?'

'No. I work in a bar,' I lied. 'Not like this one. The people who do coke in my bar can't afford it.' He stared at me, blankly, which was a waste of a perfectly good joke. 'I'm becoming a spin instructor,' I added, for some pathetic reason.

'Oh. Cool. I love cycling.'

I smiled, tense, and looked to his shoulders. They were solid, sensible. His body looked like a funnel. I was bold enough to reply, 'You would.'

Five minutes later we slipped out of the bar, in search of an Uber and something to talk about.

The reason Justin had sent me his bank details was to pay him back for my share of the ride home. Apparently, it was surging. I couldn't work out if I was supposed to feel empowered by this sense of hook-up parity, or furious – either way, when he'd suggested it all I could think to say was, 'Okay.' I gave the message a thumbs up and returned to the boiling kettle, but just as the switch moved from boiling to boiled, a figure appeared in the doorway. I jumped. It was Rose.

'Do you have any spare towels?' she said, catching her breath. 'I forgot to bring one.'

I mumbled something between 'Of course' and 'Sure', and turned away from her towards the shelves stuffed full of Ride On! merchandise. As quickly as I handed her the towel, she was gone. I didn't have time to tell her that it cost $49.

When I returned to the reception desk, I positioned the teapot beside the stack of small white cups that Steffani had artfully arranged the night before. The class had nineteen minutes left, and although I could have been completing the stocktake or cleaning the toilets or crafting passive-aggressive replies to client reviews, instead I typed *Rose Liu Melbourne* into Google's thin, indifferent mouth. The first result, as always, was LinkedIn. Rose Liu – rytuał cosmetica. It was not unusual to discover that the women who attended Ride On! worked for aspirational startups, ad agencies that specialised in hocking sneakers, or companies leading the charge when it came to new media. It meant the women were always wrapped in expensive, airtight lycra, and en masse they resembled a family of seals. My own worn, bobbly leggings made the divide between client and employee crystal clear. rytuał cosmetica was one such company, although they weren't dealing in podcasts so much as lip gloss.

From the search results, I clicked the image tab and scrolled through row after row of press shots, event photos, product campaigns. The images often featured Rose and the brand's founder and CEO, Luna Peters. I returned to LinkedIn. Her profile picture looked as if it belonged in a modelling portfolio. LinkedIn told me that if I wanted to keep perusing the employees of rytuał cosmetica, I would need to log in, and obviously I would have rather drunk bin juice through a straw than notified anyone of my sleuthing. Instead, I had the rare urge to examine my own digital footprint. 'Marnie Sellick' returned a small collection of photos: two pictures from my personal social media profiles, a pixelated close-up linked to a local newspaper feature, and a group of five people smiling, herded together by a publicist, with the headline *Most promising young screenwriters announced for Fifth Act film fellowship*.

My face was softer, as was the rest of my body. But my hair was still honey-blonde, landing apathetically just below my shoulders. My eyes were grey-blue. I zoomed all the way in, waiting for some sense of recognition, but the girl in the photo stared straight through me. I edged the zoom over the man standing next to me. He was much older than the rest of us. I could only look for a moment before a wave of nausea clamped down on my stomach. I closed the browser window and stood, motionless, trying to decipher whether this was a false alarm or the Campari really was making a comeback. As quickly as the thought had formed it became very obviously the latter, and I ran down the corridor towards the men's changing rooms. I barely had enough time to flip the lid before hot, sour liquid flooded my mouth. I watched the red-tinted foam infect the pristine toilet water. Once I was sure it was over, I leant my chin on folded arms. *Never again*, I thought, but my conviction was slippery.

From the cycle studio, I heard Steffani yell, 'Only *you* can change your reality, riders. It's time to level up.'

Two

My shifts at Ride On! were segmented into morning and evening, which left me with the hours of ten until four to myself. Steffani could occasionally manage without me in the evenings, but I had agreed to this top-and-tail schedule at my interview without really considering how restrictive it was. On my days working for Ride On!, I would arrive at the studio before 6 a.m. and leave at 7 p.m. having only done seven hours of paid work. My work day being one hour shy of what was standard irked me, as if I were living inside a cheap, plastic dupe.

Despite craving something greasy and full of garlic, at 10.15 I descended the stairs and found myself face to face with a large plastic bucket full of lettuce. The walls of the salad bar were tattooed with peppy advertising copy; phrases such as *Lettuce do all the work!* and *Better than a soggy focaccia at your desk, guaranteed!* Spending time in Richmond made me think about death more than I'd expected. Not because I was depressed, but because everyone I encountered in Richmond gave the impression that they were actively not thinking about death. I never asked any of them, of course, so my reasoning was imprecise.

'What are we in the mood for today?' the salad bar attendant chirped. His name tag identified him as Logan and described him as a Salad Master. I selected a Thai chicken salad, and Logan smiled as if I'd made the correct decision. 'So awesome. That'll be twenty-two dollars.'

As I waved my phone over the payment terminal, I considered the fact that my financial wounds were largely self-inflicted. Logan kept his eyes on the screen.

'Excuse me,' he said, as I walked towards the pick-up station. 'I think it was declined.' A small queue had formed at the till, each person staring at me dead-eyed, having been at their desks early enough to warrant a 10 a.m. lunch break.

My phone buzzed as news of the declined transaction appeared on screen. It was the pointy end of the pay cycle, but I was sure I'd seen $65 in my account the night before.

'Sorry, I thought that card had enough on it,' I said, my cheeks red-hot. I expanded the list of transactions and tried to make sense of the $5.60 in available funds. At the top of the transaction list sat a charge from Uber. $59.40. *I* had paid for the ride home, and Justin was right: it had been surging. I considered tapping the terminal again to buy more time, but the pantomime of it all made my palms sweat.

'Could we cancel that?' I said, but as the words left my mouth, the man at the front of the queue dipped his phone towards the screen. He smelt like burnt wood and whisky, with a hint of soap. When I turned to face him, his features aligned in a way that made my stomach drop: grey hair swept to the right, stubborn pockmarks just visible beneath a tasteful layer of stubble.

But this man's eyes were bright blue and he was too short. My pulse settled as I thanked him. He mumbled something unintelligible and took a step closer to Logan the Salad Master. I was not his charity case – I was an inconvenience.

I opened the text thread with Justin again. His breezy tone made my blood boil. I couldn't work out if his shonky accounting was genuine or if it came from a worse financial position than mine. I remembered us comparing screens, making a show of who was brave enough to press *Request ride*. But my memories were linked by dodgy wiring.

I collected my cardboard bowl and took a seat at the window. With a mouth full of chilli and lettuce, I typed:

> Hi Justin, I've just checked my account, and it looks like I paid for the ride home?? If you needed $25, you could have just asked. Your breath smells like shit, by the way. Calling it faeces doesn't change anything. Good luck with the keto! Marnie

I hovered my finger over the send button without any real conviction. As I backspaced, a new message appeared:

> Hey :-) how's your day?

I closed the thread and locked my phone. The simplicity of men astounded me. I had a tendency towards what was referred to as 'heteropessimism'; that is, I felt pessimistic about the state of affairs between men and women. The word had only entered the cultural conversation a few years prior, but broadsheets were already commissioning thousands of words on how most women were sick of hearing about it. I longed to meet these women. I often wondered if they were men.

I finished my salad and returned to the studio. In the corner of the Pilates room sat a pile of perky yoga bolsters. I dragged three from the stack and arranged them into a makeshift bed by the reformer machines. As I settled into my lumpy nest, I opened a podcast app and typed *Rose Liu rytual cosmetica* into the search bar. I did this whenever I met someone I found impressive, because everyone who was anyone had been interviewed for a podcast. Often, the sound of their voice as they danced around 'um's and 'like's was enough to put me off – enough to assure me that they weren't as impressive as I'd once thought.

The search results spat out a distinct lack of Rose's name. Instead, each interview featured Luna Peters. Luna was the kind of public figure whose story permeated your awareness without you ever seeking her out. We'd all seen her house tour. We knew exactly where the house was. rytuał was the same – its identity was intrinsically tied to its presence in Melbourne. It was the Melbourne-based cosmetics brand that had cracked the international market, and its success belonged to all of us. I had overheard Ride On! clients saying things like, 'I would literally let Luna Peters hit me with her car.'

Luna was petite, with olive skin and long, chocolate-brown hair that unravelled like devil's ivy. Her eyes were so green I wondered if they were contacts. Her arms were dotted with the right kind of tattoos. But I'd never met her. Never really looked at her, intentionally. Everything I knew about her, I'd absorbed via osmosis. There was a specific corner of my brain where information on Luna and her contemporaries was meticulously filed, categorised, archived. As if it might one day prove itself useful.

I selected an episode of a podcast called *Hysteria*, the show description of which read *An interview series with women at the helm of businesses that aren't afraid to make a scene!*

Ride On!, I thought.

'Hello, and welcome back to *Hysteria*. I'm your host, Carmel Patterson, and today I'm live from the Sydney Opera House with Luna Peters, founder and CEO of rytuał cosmetica.'

The audience cheered.

'Thank you, Carmel. It's an honour to be here.' Her voice was playfully husky; void of any twang and yet still quintessentially Australian. Warm, authoritative.

I closed my eyes for a moment, hovering just behind their voices. I imagined the audience staring back at me, their eyes wide and hungry. No one dared take a breath. They teetered on the edge of their seats as Luna mused, 'Well, our desire to view women at the helm of successful businesses as some kind of avatar for the brand is just a product of late-stage capitalism.' When they laughed, it was violently enthusiastic. Their bodies convulsed as they performed the act of understanding. It was kind of scary, actually, and as that thought unfurled, I imagined them all covered in blood, staring up at Luna as if she had the power to shape and break the course of their lives.

'Marnie? What are you doing?!'

The bolster beneath my cheek was soaked with saliva. I opened my eyes and scrambled to sit up, my neck and shoulders frozen in a stiff knot. Steffani was standing over me, clutching another can of Red Bull. 'It's four-thirty.'

'Sorry,' I said. 'I must have fallen asleep.' I stood up and made an attempt at fluffing the bolsters. 'Sorry.'

'I need you to wipe down the bikes before five,' she continued, ignoring my apologies. 'I have to do my Wim Hof.'

She left the Pilates room without further discussion. My headphones had fallen out of my ears at some point, and as I collected them from the floor I heard a tinny voice say, 'Our products don't change the way you look, they pull your natural beauty into focus.' My phone was fifty minutes deep in a completely different interview with Luna. So much information, filed away for later; categorised and metabolised, on the off chance I'd one day reach for it.

~

When I arrived home that night, Kahli's duvet had migrated from her bedroom to the couch. The apartment was dark, aside from a voluptuous red candle that flickered angrily from the kitchen bench – the wax had completely liquefied, which placed Kahli's presence in the living room at three hours or more. The voices of Real Housewives blared from the TV, and as I emerged from the hall, Kahli's head jolted towards me. 'Fucking hell, you scared the shit out of me,' she said. Kahli had wild caramel hair flecked with blonde, which fell to just below her shoulders. In my mind she was tall, but in reality she came up to my collarbones.

'Sorry!' I went to fill a glass of water. The carcasses of two separate food deliveries covered the marble countertop. As I guzzled from the glass, one of the Housewives said, 'I'm down a tooth and anxious as hell. How do you think I'm doing?!'

Kahli hit pause on the remote. 'You can turn on the lights if you want.'

She said it with a faux sweetness that implied she really wanted me to turn on the lights, so I did. The apartment was a modest 1970s cream brick, on the second floor of a block of twelve. It was a smart investment, Kahli said, in the tone people often used when investing solely their parents' money. Her ex-boyfriend had attempted a renovation of the kitchen and living spaces, but abandoned the project after Kahli cheated on him with an entrepreneur from Dubai who affectionately referred to her as his 'little blowfish'. She hired the host of a famous TV renovation show to finish the job. That's what Kahli had told me, although Kahli collected these kinds of stories, and they often turned out to be more air than dough.

'How was your night?' she said, a tuft of her hair static-ed to the wall behind the couch like an antenna. 'I was so cooked. I barely did anything at work today.' Beside the couch, on a small wooden stool, her work laptop was still open, the screen dark.

'It was good. I went home with this ad guy. He tried to convince me that hot dogs with cream was a good high-fat, high-protein snack.'

'Gross.'

My pulse quickened as the story's conclusion presented itself. 'Yeah. He asked me to transfer him my share of the ride home, but get this: *I* paid for the ride home. If I hadn't checked, I would have actually sent him the money.'

I waited for Kahli to share my outrage, but she was uncharacteristically flat. 'That's so weird, are you sure you paid for it?'

'Positive.' I scuttled over to the couch and perched myself opposite her. As I handed Kahli my phone, open to the charge in my banking app, she shuffled just a few centimetres closer. I watched her fix her eyes, quizzically, on the screen.

I lived for this subtle shift in Kahli's body language. It was somewhat of an addiction. I don't know what it was about Kahli, except that I do: she possessed so many traits that felt impossible to me. She approached conflict like an army that knew it was going to win. She was all of the limp literature on not giving a fuck, repackaged and brought to life. Which was why whenever she sent me a text that said *Free tonight?*, I made myself available. The itinerary was always the same: we'd get rip-roaring drunk, spilling out of the apartment and into whichever restaurant, bar or club Kahli swore would change my life. They never did, but I kept coming back for more – buying in over and over in the hope that eventually she'd rub off on me.

'Was the sex good?' she said.

'It was fine. It was good, yeah. I think.'

Her right eyebrow crept up her forehead. 'What does that mean?'

'It was good! I was pretty drunk.'

She nodded, carefully examining my face.

'What?' I said.

'Did you like him?' Her lips teased a smirk.

'I don't know.' My face burnt bright red. What I was really embarrassed about was how hard I found it to decide if I liked him, what I liked, what I was supposed to say next, where to go, what to do. There was a time, not too long ago, when my own appetite had set the ground rules for everything I did. But I had since become a mystery to myself.

'Okaaaaay then. I'm going to bed,' Kahli said, blowing a kiss. 'Night.' She turned off the TV and dragged the duvet with her across the glistening floorboards. When the door to her room thumped shut, I returned to the text thread with Justin. As I stared down the flaccid three-piece smiley face, I couldn't imagine his eyes. The living room's steely quiet set off an itchy panic just below my sternum, so I took the phone to my room and closed the door.

My bedroom was furnished, for the most part, by Kahli. When I'd interviewed to rent the room she stipulated that I could bring my own furniture as long as I promised not to bring MDF within one hundred metres of the building. Otherwise, she was happy for me to use her furniture for the duration of my tenancy. I had to look up what MDF stood for on the way home. Thanks to Kahli, my room was decorated with 'pieces' (a word she used to describe both vintage furniture and long-sleeved tops) that clashed spectacularly with my grubby lifestyle.

The bed frame was made from sleek untreated timber and could be disassembled in five minutes or less. On the far side of the room, a large window revealed the communal garden's three trees. It was the beginning of winter, and two out of the three had lost their leaves. The third tree's leaves shivered beneath the glow of the streetlight. On the left side of the window, a full-length mirror leant haphazardly against the wall. It took me four weeks of living there to discover that it was held in place with silver brackets and wire – made to look haphazard, although I knew Kahli would have laboured over the exact angle to best showcase the room. On the right side of the window, a black leather armchair with chrome bones collected dust. It was horrendously uncomfortable, but all of Kahli's friends had the same one. There was also a built-in wardrobe, left open to reveal all of my polyester.

Rytual

Beneath my jackets and dresses, I could see three plastic storage tubs stacked up against the wall. I'd put them there a year ago, in the hope that it would mean I never thought about them, or their contents, or the woman they had once belonged to. The sight of them still hit me square in the chest. I slid the wardrobe closed and paced the length of my bed. It was only 9.30. It was a Friday night. I watched myself compose a reply to Justin.

> Day was boring, nothing to report. Come over?

I couldn't imagine him saying yes, which was why I sent it. I still couldn't remember the colour of his eyes. He replied straight away.

> Why not lol!! What number Mansfield r u again?

> Just check Uber xx

I held my breath as I stared at his side of the conversation. The promise of vindication lit up my brain like I was one of those rats on cocaine. Or, a human on cocaine. The three dots appeared. Disappeared. Appeared again.

> Shit, it's not there. I think u paid for it after all! So sorry Marnie

I smiled. But the high was synthetic, and it didn't last – he didn't offer to transfer me his share of the ride home, or even $25. I also didn't ask him to.

83 Mansfield. Unit 3 xx

I threw the phone on the bed and went about making myself as desirable as possible, which is to say I brushed my teeth and took off my bra. The simplicity of men astounded me.

Three

In the light of sobriety, Justin's torso still looked like a funnel. His shoulders were hard and the veins that snaked their way around his forearms caught me off guard. His curly brown hair was full of product and looked better maintained than my own limp waves. As he unbuckled his belt, the sound of metal against leather brought my body to life.

'This is so crazy,' he said as he stepped out of his jeans. I found it hard to believe this wasn't something he did all the time.

'Is it?' I said from the bed as I wriggled out of my leggings. Beyond my bedroom wall, I heard Kahli's feet making their way to the bathroom.

We lay face to face. His eyes were blue, after all. He raised a hand to my cheek and tucked a strand of hair behind my ear. 'I can't stay the night,' he whispered. 'CrossFit at eight.'

'Totally,' I said, and although this wasn't grammatically correct, it solidified the terms of our engagement. I rolled to sit on top of him; he was already surprisingly hard. As I lowered my lips to meet his, I let my hips rock back and forth along the length of him. As we kissed, our tongues found the same rhythm, dancing around each other in perfect time. He pulsed beneath me. When he flipped me over, I tugged at his underwear. He let out a little laugh as he sat all the way up and shimmied out of them. I did the same.

'You're really beautiful,' he said as he crawled on top of me again. His earnest tone made me claustrophobic. I pulled him closer although I could feel my desire withering; something was beginning to rot. He kissed down the length of my torso, and as his tongue made contact with my pussy I felt nothing. I closed my eyes and tried to drag myself back to the belt buckle. I reached for his veiny forearm, but it didn't touch the sides. And here is where my physical and mental worlds divided: I had spent the past year of my life churning through men like Justin, in the hope that – like working at Ride On! and obliterating myself with Kahli's roster of Party Friends – they could wipe the slate clean. But when it came to sex, I was stuck wanting someone who didn't exist, and no matter how much mental energy I threw at the problem, my body was tuned to the wrong frequency.

As he slid a finger inside me, I gave in. I let myself fall into the memory of another time and place, and a different body altogether. Justin's forearms lost their muscular veins. His brown ringlets turned grey. I imagined him sitting up, one hand still skilfully manoeuvring its way in and out of me. His skin was creased by laps around the sun, but as he said, 'You know you're an attractive woman, Marnie,' it hit the room in the right key. He was never really earnest, never completely present, but the chase set me on fire. Justin's fingers sped up, which meant he was expecting me to finish. I exhaled. I had sworn to myself that I'd stop using the fantasy, but it was so much easier than directing

Rytual

Justin, or whoever was in his place. *This is the last time*, I thought to myself. Then I remembered his cool hands as he bent me over crisp hotel sheets. As he grasped the back of my head and pulled it back towards him. As he said, 'I find you very attractive.' I came. Justin popped his head out from between my legs and smiled. The comedown was immediate. I rolled over and bit my tongue to stop myself from crying. That was the last time.

~

On Saturdays Freesia taught the cycle classes, despite only being qualified to tell women where their pelvic floor was located. She was an old friend of Steffani's, and her 60,000 followers were good for business. There were also no evening classes on Saturdays, so I was free to leave before lunch. After I'd cleaned the toilets and made another pot of tea, I allowed myself thirty-five minutes of screen time at the reception desk. I scoured the usual: Instagram (using the browser on a real computer was so highbrow), Pinterest, Reddit. I watched a few videos of the middle-aged actress with whom I had recently become obsessed. When I woke up to myself scrolling through the *Daily Mail*, I made sure to pre-emptively clear the browser history. From the cycle studio, Freesia squawked, 'Honeys, we've got just three songs left. I challenge you to really push it, push it *good*,' as the playlist transitioned to 'Push It' by Salt-N-Pepa. I paused for a moment, observing my body from somewhere just above the reception desk. Maybe it was my cumulative lack of sleep, but for a moment I did think, *Is this it?*

I pulled my phone from my pocket. I'd been paid overnight. As I began a new transfer to Kahli, the door to the cycle studio slid open.

'Do you have any water?' The colour had drained from Rose's cheeks. She threw her head between her knees. 'Sorry,' she said, her face inverted. 'I'm feeling a bit dizzy.'

I ran out from behind the desk and ushered her towards the seating bank where clients often applied their riding clogs. As she sat down, I caught a whiff of her fragrance again: rose, something woody, something herbal. 'I love that perfume,' I said, before remembering the circumstances. 'Sorry, I'll get the water.'

When I shuffled back from the kitchen-cum-storage room, Rose looked suspiciously healthy. As I handed her the glass of water, she said, 'The music was so loud, I thought I was having a panic attack.'

'Oh, that means you're doing it right.'

Her laugh was neat and contained. She took a sip of water and wiped the back of her hand across her forehead. 'I didn't sleep much last night. Sorry, I don't know why I'm telling you this.'

'Rose, before you walked out of that class I was browsing the *Daily Mail*. I think you were sent to save my soul.'

She laughed again. 'Good memory.'

'What do you mean?'

'You remembered my name.'

'Of course I did,' I said, without thinking. Then, 'I remember everyone's names. I'm a freak like that.' This time, she didn't laugh. I felt my cheeks prickle.

She drained the glass. In the studio, Freesia told the women that they were approaching their last hill climb. She made a 'Wooooo' sound into the microphone, but her voice broke mid-woo, which made her sound like a wooounded animal.

'My boyfriend. We're having some problems. Well, I'm having problems. With him.'

I nodded. She didn't elaborate. I let the silence pool around us, until eventually all I could think to say was, 'Men are disgusting.'

'I couldn't agree more,' she said, a hint of mischief in her eyes.

She handed me the empty glass and set off down the hall. I tried to think of something witty to call out after her, but I'd used up all my material. As I returned to the reception desk she spun around and said, 'It's rose, sandalwood and vetiver. rytuał *She*. The fragrance.'

'Oh, right. Thanks.'

She disappeared into the women's changing room. Immediately, I typed *Rytual She* into the browser's search bar. Eight thousand product reviews, with an average rating of 4.7 out of 5. I clicked the link to the rytuał website. At the top of the page, the brand's logo – the outline of two sets of lips, interlocked like a chain – was centred above the site's navigation. The fragrance was packaged in a frosted white glass bottle, with a chrome cap stamped by the same lips.

'Great work today, ladies! If you have any questions, feel free to let me know, otherwise give the bikes a wipe down and enjoy your Satur-yay!' Freesia chirped. Seconds later, she burst through the sliding door and sped past me to the stairs. 'I need to vape,' she said, already halfway down the first flight.

When I looked back at the computer, Rose was waiting at the edge of the reception desk. 'Do you want to get a drink sometime?' she said. Behind her, a horde of women exited the studio, bringing with them the stale air that had built up over the course of the class. It smelt like feet. 'A real drink,' she added, her eyes on the empty water glass.

'Sure,' I said, swallowing my elation. 'Sounds fun.'

She handed me her phone with the Instagram search page already open. When my face appeared, I hesitated. My profile was bland – a collection of sunsets, the backs of other people's heads and the occasional 35 mm photo Kahli had taken of me on a night out. I didn't post very often, and I'd scrubbed the grid of anything that alluded to my life before its current incarnation. When I passed the phone back to her, she was smiling.

'I'll message you,' she said. 'Thanks for the water.'

She disappeared down the stairs, where she would inevitably discover a strung-out Freesia sucking fervently on her jewel-encrusted Hello Kitty vape pen.

I practically threw myself at the computer. I added rytuał *She* to cart so quickly I couldn't remember the specifics of the process required to do so – I just arrived at a total of $150 and a prompt to enter my email address to receive exclusive offers. I flew through to checkout and agreed to pay for the bottle over four interest-free payments.

'Bye,' one of the clients said as she passed the reception desk. A string of sweaty women followed, and I smiled, nodded, even added the occasional, 'Thank you!' But my mind was elsewhere. My phone buzzed with an email confirming *rytuał cosmetica order #8837421*.

'I love that perfume,' a voice said, from behind my left shoulder. I turned to find Freesia guzzling from a white cardboard cup. She was staring at the order summary on the desktop screen. 'My boyfriend's housemate has it. I always steal some when I'm there.'

'Yeah. Same. It's my favourite.'

My phone vibrated in my hand. A message from Rose.

Tonight? Caroline's at 8?

Rytuał

'Have you ever done keto?' Freesia said, as she cupped a hand to her mouth. 'I think my breath stinks.'

~

That afternoon, from my bed, I gorged myself on Rose's social media presence. Her Instagram grid made Rose out to be either a very successful model or some kind of culinary tastemaker. There were so many pictures of food: slices of glistening peaches, a pastel-frosted birthday cake, oysters glinting in the sun. There were floral arrangements and bottles of natural wine. There were photos of Rose and Luna off duty. There was one picture of an anaemic-looking man in a vintage T-shirt, which I assumed to be her bad boyfriend.

Holding my phone above my forehead, I opened the camera app and took a picture of myself staring cooly into the screen. It was unflattering and useless, but as I zoomed in on my cheeks, my eyes, my forehead, I found some comfort in knowing how each square centimetre of my face could appear to a third party. I often thought that this was what we were all obsessed with: discovering everything we possibly could about the way we looked and the way we were perceived, rather than enjoying the gratification that came with sharing it. We were pursuing a PhD on ourselves, and the phones were our primary tool for collecting data. How depressing.

I opened my wardrobe and began sifting through its contents, creating a pile of potential outfits on my unmade bed. As I stared at the pile and willed an appropriate combination to present itself, my phone buzzed violently against my hip. I pulled it from my pocket and glanced at the unfamiliar sequence of numbers on the incoming call. I imagined a world in which Rose had asked Steffani for my number, because she'd been locked out of her Instagram account and desperately needed to speak with me – which is to say, I answered.

'Hello?'

'Marnie! Hi! How are you? It's been so long.' I lowered the phone from my ear and considered the numbers again. It wasn't Rose, but it wasn't spam either.

'Who is this?' I asked, returning the phone to my ear.

'It's Lily from Fifth Act.'

My stomach dropped.

I froze. I didn't hang up, but I didn't say anything. I just stood there, in the middle of my bedroom, staring out at the one tree that still had grey-brown leaves attached to it.

'I've been thinking about you a lot lately.'

I hung up and threw the phone on the pile of clothes. I recoiled, as if I'd exposed myself to some horrible virus, and went to the bathroom. In the mirror's soft light my skin looked grey. I traced my fingers over the dark circles that shadowed my eyes, remembering what someone, somewhere, at some point had said about facial massage or drainage or tenderising yourself for skin health. I pressed a little harder on the circles, before dragging my middle and index fingers down my cheekbones to my chin. I had no idea where things were supposed to be draining from or to, but the repetitive motions were soothing. I kept rubbing, dragging, kneading the skin, watching it move like plasticine. My heart rate lowered as I focused on the cool blue of my irises. I hunched over the vanity and pressed even harder, my biceps jumping away from the bone to sustain the effort. I could see red marks forming on my cheeks, but I kept going.

From the hall, I heard Kahli call out, 'Are you doing a wardrobe cull? Can I borrow a top?'

By the time I opened the bathroom door, Kahli was already inspecting the pile of clothes. 'Actually,' she said, grimacing at an oversized business shirt, 'I don't know if we have the same style.'

Four

Caroline's was an unassuming cocktail bar, tucked away on a residential street in Collingwood. I took the 86 tram down its familiar vein, emerging onto Smith Street. From there it was a short walk downhill, past a bagel shop that also sold a curated selection of vinyl, and what was once an underground sex club, but was now a graphic design studio. Kahli and I often laughed about how Melbourne had become a parody of itself, but we never did anything in protest. I spotted Rose on the footpath before she saw me. She was wearing a black slip dress over a pair of pants with childlike flowers seemingly spray-painted on the knees, but as I got closer it became clear that the flowers were dyed into the fabric. A boxy black puffer jacket hung from her shoulders. On my body I'd hung a pair of black suit pants and a black boat-neck top. Fashion had always felt like a mystery to me.

'Marnie!' she said as she looked up from her phone. Her hair was slicked back into a severe ponytail. 'I love your pants.'

'Oh, thanks,' I said. Rose made a beeline for the entrance. I followed, thankful for her lead.

From the street, it looked as though Caroline's was made up of two small rooms. Once inside, I discovered that the bar extended much further into the building than I'd initially thought. It was like stepping into an optical illusion. A tall bartender with a thick, wiry beard ushered us towards a booth.

'Would we like still or sparkling water this evening?' His body was wrapped in a black leather apron, but it was pulled too tight – the outline of his torso made me feel uneasy.

'Sparkling,' Rose said, without so much as a glance in my direction. The bartender gave a reverential nod and went about procuring a carafe of sparkling water. When he was gone, Rose finally smiled. 'I know the owner,' she said, as if she was confessing a secret. 'We used to date. A million years ago.'

'Awesome,' I said, still grasping for an interesting response. The jovial version of me Rose had met at Ride On! was otherwise engaged.

'It's a great bar,' she continued, undeterred. 'I couldn't give it up.'

When the bartender returned with our sparkling water, he positioned a brown card in front of each of us. Before he could explain anything, Rose said, 'Two gin martinis. Dirty.' She looked over at me, suddenly concerned. 'Is that okay?'

I gave a nod. The bartender praised Rose's choice and retrieved the brown cards.

'So. What's your story?' Rose said, crossing her arms. 'Have you worked at Ride On! for long?'

'A year. But I think it's time for me to move on. I'm considering a few different things.'

'Like what?'

'I don't know. Moving overseas, maybe? Norway.'

'Why?'

Rose's blunt curiosity reminded me of Kahli, but she was softer. Kahli would fire off a series of questions without waiting for the first answer, but Rose seemed genuinely interested in weaving her way to the truth.

'Something to do?'

The bartender returned and deposited our drinks on red cardboard coasters embossed with a swirling pink 'C'.

Rose plucked her martini from the table and raised it to eye level. 'Cheers!'

'Cheers,' I said, weakly. We drank. It tasted like $25.

'How long have you worked for rytuał?' I said, returning the glass to the coaster.

'How did you know I worked for rytuał?'

It was impossible to remember which facts were given to me and which were pilfered from the internet. Before I could formulate a response, she said, 'I'm kidding. We're not very subtle about it. Us rytuałists.'

'rytuałists?'

'rytuał employees. We're a bit omnipresent, aren't we?'

'Everyone knows someone,' I said, as if it was something I'd said before.

'Who do you know?'

'Oh, no one. It just feels like everyone in Melbourne knows someone. At rytuał.'

'Does it?' She drank. 'I heard you write films.'

'How did you know that?'

'You won a prize. You're not the only one who knows how to use Google.' She stared at me with a sheepish grin.

I sucked at the rim of the glass. The alcohol wasn't working fast enough. 'Ha. Right. Yeah, I wrote a screenplay. The award was funded by a production company. I worked for them for a while. I'm just trying to figure out my next moves.'

'You already said that.'

'Sorry—'

She threw her hands up to shoulder height. 'I've been spending too much time with Luna. I didn't mean to cross-examine you, you don't have to explain anything.'

I was reminded of Luna's voice in my tangled headphones. 'What's she like?'

'Luna?'

I nodded. 'She seems . . . intense.'

'She is. She's brilliant.' Rose reached into her pocket and pulled out a small plastic bag. 'Do you want an edible?'

'A . . . weed edible?'

She nodded, brusquely, as if the conversation had suddenly exhausted her.

'Sure,' I said. She grinned as she handed me a pair of red gummy lips. The sharp herbal taste seeped out of the gelatine onto my tongue. I chewed it four times, then swallowed. Rose watched, her eyes fixed to my face.

'So, why'd you quit?'

'I, uh . . . It was a weird time. I worked for that company, and then . . .' I trailed off. I really hated telling the story, which was why I so aggressively avoided it. Every time I told it, it sounded false. I couldn't muster the tone of voice to explain it properly.

It didn't sound like my story. Rose just waited. 'Bad boyfriend. And my mum died.' I pulled a face. 'I'm fine, though.'

'Why was that the first thing you said? "I'm fine, though." You don't have to be fine.'

'Kind of feels like I should be,' I said. I plucked the toothpick from my drink and slid the skewered olives into my mouth. When I'd swallowed, I added, 'I don't know that I was ever really that good. At writing. I'm still . . . trying to work it out.'

She frowned. 'What do you want, Marnie?'

From the hours I'd spent listening to women pontificate on How to Be a Boss Babe, I knew that this question was almost always at the heart of their prescriptions. *Get clear on what you really want*, they said, as if it were that simple. As if there weren't layers of other things in the way, things that shifted what it was you were allowed to want and when. The question played on repeat in my mind like elevator music.

'I think I'm just'—I paused—'sick of asking myself that question.'

She let out a breezy laugh. 'Touché.'

'Why are you interested in what I want?'

Rose leant across the table conspiratorially. As she brought her face closer to mine, I caught a glimpse of a scar that ran from her left cheekbone to her ear. It was faded, and concealed beneath a layer of foundation. I hadn't noticed it before. 'I don't know yet. But I like you.'

I slunk back into my chair, desperate to change the subject. 'What happened with your boyfriend?

'Tom? Oh, I won't bore you with the details.'

'It's not boring. The other morning, when I let you into the studio, I'd just slept with this ad guy who asked me to pay for my share of the Uber home. But then I found out that *I'd* actually paid for it.'

The mischievous look I'd seen at the studio returned. She grinned. 'Men,' was all she said.

As she said this, I felt something squirm against my leg. I imagined a family of cockroaches crawling up and out of my handbag, but it was just my phone. I stuck a hand inside and retrieved it. My fingers were starting to tingle.

KAHLI HALE
Free tonight?

'I think he's seeing someone else,' Rose said. 'I work a lot, so it's hard to carve out enough time. When we first got together he found me so exciting. He liked that I worked a lot.'

I locked the phone screen and returned it to my bag. 'What does he do? For work.'

'He's a writer too. Kind of. He can't seem to finish anything. But what he does write is great. I don't know – we met at a time when I was feeling a bit lost, and being with him helped me feel like myself again. Now it's like I don't even know him. I think he woke up one day and decided he resented me, but instead of ending it he just drifted off to somewhere else.'

'Why stay with him?'

'I just keep hoping it'll go back to how it was.'

I nodded.

'Have you ever thought about copywriting?' she asked, changing the subject with precision. 'I could chat to Luna, if you'd like?'

'What?' The room was starting to spin, but it wasn't unpleasant.

'We're always looking for like-minded individuals to join the team.'

'At rytuał? Me?'

'It's much more about a culture fit for us than anything else. Do you like working at Ride On?'

I laughed, but my mouth closed as it came out. 'It's not really a passion of mine,' I said. 'And I can tell you said that without the exclamation mark.'

Rose started to giggle. Suddenly, everything about this situation was so funny I could barely catch my breath. I doubled over on my right side and slid down onto the cool leather of the booth.

'It's nice, isn't it,' Rose said.

'It *is* nice.'

The bartender returned and asked if we wanted another round, but Rose answered so fast I couldn't tell if it was a yes or no. Her phone rattled on the table, and the man in leather circled back with the bill. She was swift to hand him a black credit card before returning to her phone. 'I actually have to run, but let's get you in for a chat with Luna next week?'

'Oh, no, seriously, you don't have to do that,' I mumbled.

'It's no trouble. Everyone starts in Customer Service, so you'll have time to—'

'No, Rose, I mean it. Don't worry about it. I'm not ready.'

'For what?'

I didn't have an answer. The EFTPOS machine let out an enthusiastic beep.

'Receipt?' the bartender said, staring intently at Rose. She shook her head, and he scuttled away.

'One meeting. A chat, really. Super casual. Just you and Luna.' Rose smiled, hopeful. 'What's your email?'

~

As I lay in bed that night, the ceiling became a swirling vortex. I sat up, did a lap of my room and chugged the glass of water I'd left out on the bedside table. I could taste dust particles as they danced down my throat. I plucked my laptop from beneath the bed frame and crawled back into bed. I'd replied to Kahli's text when I got home, but it was too late – the house was empty, her room dark.

I opened two browser tabs: The YouTube homepage, and a Google search for my name. I found the picture from the Fifth Act fellowship again and zoomed all the way in on my eyes. I flicked back to the other tab and typed *Luna Peters* in the search bar.

Her house tour was the top search result. It had 9.3 million views. I couldn't remember when I'd first seen it, but you didn't actually need to have seen it in order to think you had – it was that kind of video. Luna opened the door to her inner-city treehouse and flashed a smile at the camera crew. 'Hi, I'm Luna Peters, CEO and founder of rytuał cosmetica. Welcome to my home.'

She turned to walk down the hallway, before returning to the camera and gesturing for its operator to hurry up. I knew how tightly rehearsed these kinds of things were in order for them to appear completely spontaneous. I looked up at the ceiling again. Still spinning.

'I bought the house two years ago, but the renovations took a full year. I'm a bit of a control freak, so I'd like to formally apologise to my builder on the record.'

From the hallway, Luna ushered the camera towards a sunlit lounge room. It had a sunken floor, with two black leather couches positioned opposite each other. A coffee table made from purposefully misshapen marble sat between them. On it, a stack of books resembled an untouched game of Jenga. I paused the video and tried to focus my eyes on the titles. The most I could make out was *Home: The heart is home*, which didn't seem right.

'I bought the couches second-hand and had them reupholstered in black. I have a thing for black leather.' She winked at the camera, which from anyone else would have seemed misplaced, but from Luna it was thrilling. She skipped down the stairs and plucked a book from the pile. 'My team at rytuał had this book made for me when we opened our new office space last year.' She rotated the cover to face the camera. There was no text, only a photo of a dark-pink tube with the rytuał logo: two sets of lips interlaced like a chain. 'Our first product was the lip oil. This shade is called *Lust*, and yes, it is my favourite, thank you for asking.'

Watching Luna, I saw so many of Rose's mannerisms: the nonchalant shrug she'd given as she told me she couldn't give up Caroline's; the wicked smile when I'd told her about Justin. As Luna danced from the living room to the open-plan kitchen, I unbuttoned the top of my pants. I didn't consciously think about what I was doing – for whatever reason, it felt like the obvious response. I unzipped my fly as Luna said, 'My publicist would prefer that I told you it's vintage, but fuck that.' She covered her mouth. 'Am I allowed to swear?'

I traced my index and middle fingers over the worn cotton of my underwear as Luna explained that she'd commissioned a local artist to design the kitchen's wallpaper. In the meticulously landscaped courtyard, sunlight hit her hair at the exact right angle to send a little burst of magic off into the sky. I pushed my fingers inside myself as Luna said, 'It's not much, but on a sunny day when I'm up to my eyeballs in emails, I just camp out here until I feel as though I have enough space to breathe again.' As she tiptoed back inside the house, I pulled my fingers out and began to rub them over myself. She opened a sliding door to reveal a mood-lit bathroom, and smiled as she said, 'Now, this – this is my favourite part of the house.' She opened the mirrored cabinet above the sink to reveal what must have been hundreds of glass bottles, jars and pots.

'This is where the magic happens,' she said, and I began to press harder, rub faster. I imagined Luna stepping out of the shower and opening this cupboard to begin her day, each morning a fresh start. I thought about the frictionless life she lived, the way things just seemed to work out, although I didn't really know if this was how she lived, and maybe the question mark was what made it all so irresistible. As I closed my eyes, I imagined my head in her lap. I felt her hands segment my greasy hair into three equal sections. I let the scene unfold; the glow of the red gummy lips made everything so inconsequential. While she was braiding my limp, oily hair, Luna leant down to my ear and whispered, 'You're an attractive woman, Marnie.' I came, but as pleasure rippled through my body I heard my phone buzz against the timber bedside table. I snatched it up reflexively. A new email. From luna.peters@rytual.co. I choked on my spit as I struggled to sit all the way up.

Dear Marnie,
Good evening.
Please join me for an employment pre-screening at 10.30 a.m. on Tuesday 6 June.
No need to bring anything, just your radiant self.
Let me know if you have any dietary requirements.
Warmest,
Luna

It was 11.05 on a Saturday night. I looked around the room, searching for eyes or ears or a credible witness. But the cold, empty apartment was still, and as I focused on the stillness a faint ringing noise emerged. When I returned to the computer a few minutes later, a teen pop star was sullenly walking through his Los Angeles mansion. He turned a corner and said, 'This is my Twitch streaming room.' I closed the laptop.

Five

When I woke the next morning, my right hand was still wrapped around my phone. I couldn't tell if I'd fallen asleep with a rigor mortis claw or I'd found the shape from somewhere below conscious thought. Either way, it wasn't good. Despite this, I returned to Luna's email.

No need to bring anything, just your radiant self.

I locked the screen and opened it again. And again. I could hear Kahli conducting a symphony of pots and pans in the kitchen. I slid out of bed and down the hall, my hand still clutching my phone.

'Hey,' I said, from the entrance to the kitchen and lounge room. 'What did you get up to last night?'

Kahli was sullen faced, wrapped in her silk robe (as opposed to her faded pink fluffy robe, which she wore exclusively when she wanted to dissolve into the couch). The kitchen's entire collection of pots and pans was stacked on the counter, the cupboard doors agape behind her.

'Hung out with Tom,' she said, barely looking up. 'Where were you?'

'Oh, I had drinks with a friend. Sorry, I didn't see your message until I got home—'

'It's fine.'

I watched her try to slot a colander into a saucepan half its size, until the name Tom attached itself to another memory. 'Which Tom?'

'That guy I've been seeing.'

I nodded. All I could remember about him was a story in which Kahli jokingly called him a softboy, but when he tried to google what it meant he typed *Milkboy* instead. 'What's his story again?'

She gave up on the colander and moved on to the frying pans. 'Writer. But he works in a bar.'

My senses sharpened. 'Coffee?' I said.

She stacked one pan inside another and returned them to the cupboard. 'I just have to finish this first.'

'No pressure.'

'I'll come, I just have to finish this first.' She exhaled forcefully as she struggled to find the right lid for a mid-sized saucepan. I could see it on the bench beside her, but I said nothing. Instead, I went to the bathroom and sat under the flow of the shower until my fingers crinkled. When I emerged, Kahli was dressed, made up and waiting for me on the edge of the couch. I pulled on the clothes I'd just wriggled out of, ran a brush through my hair and presented myself to her. 'Did you sleep in those pants?' she asked, as she slid her sunglasses over the bridge of her nose. She didn't wait for an answer before she stood up and walked towards the door.

~

'Tom has a girlfriend,' she said, fifteen minutes into our excursion, as we collected our cardboard cups from the cafe's takeaway window. 'I've seen her name on his phone before but now I know for sure.'

'How?' Without discussion, we walked towards the European grocer that sold an overwhelming variety of large olives and tiny fish. I sucked at the lid of my coffee cup.

'His bathroom is full of skincare. Makeup. It was stacked. Do you know rytuał?'

I stopped dead in my tracks. 'He had rytuał in his bathroom?'

Kahli shot me a judgemental glare as she stepped out of the flow of pedestrians. 'What? Why are you making a face?'

'I'm not. It's nothing. How did you . . . meet him?'

'At the bar he works at. I told you this. Why are you being weird?'

'I'm not being weird! Did you . . . confront him?'

'He said they're in an open relationship, but I don't believe him.' She drank from her cup and wrinkled her nose in disgust. 'This is gross. How's yours?'

For whatever reason, it felt important to lie. 'Gross. Same.' I feigned revulsion.

'Classic.' She continued drinking anyway. We stopped at a pedestrian crossing. I leant against the traffic light pole, assuming the position of someone whose amygdala was not running in overdrive.

'Why didn't you grill him?'

'I don't know,' she said, dismissively. 'I couldn't be bothered.'

'Sorry, just checking I'm still speaking with Kahli Hale?'

The lights changed. Kahli hurried across the road as I struggled to keep up.

'I'm not, like, some robot, you know.'

'I know you're not. You're just so . . . you're Kahli.'

She made a face. 'What does that mean?'

'You're good with conflict. It's impressive.'

When we'd reached the other side of the road, she exhaled and said, 'It's different with dating. Like, I can't find the words, or I feel like a different person. Absent dad, blah blah blah.' It was the first time I'd ever seen her squirm. We walked a few paces in silence.

'Do you see much of your dad now?' I asked, carefully.

'He's dead,' she replied, unfazed. 'That's how I bought the apartment. I told you that.'

She hadn't, but I wanted Kahli to see me as someone who could handle this level of classified information. 'Will you see him again?'

'I already told you, he's dead.'

'I meant Tom.'

She shrugged. 'Not my monkeys, not my circus.'

'What does that mean?'

'I mean, I'm not the one with the girlfriend. That's a *him* problem.' I swallowed any further questions. Kahli's shoulders were creeping towards her ears. She stopped at the entrance to the European grocer. 'I want some good cheese.'

'Let's go to rytuał,' I spluttered. 'The store. If she can have it, so can we.'

Rytuał

'I thought you were broke.' She crossed her arms at her chest, but she didn't turn. I'd piqued her curiosity.

'I just got paid. Yesterday.'

Kahli's eyes narrowed. 'Okay,' she said, eventually, abandoning any desire for cheese. 'Why not.'

~

The rytuał flagship store was set between an art gallery and a gastropub, at the intersection of Collingwood and Fitzroy – which is to say that the store's location had been selected for its proximity to new money and old architecture. The building had begun its life as a post office but was now rendered in light-pink cement and branded with the rytuał logo. A woman in a red cotton drill set waited patiently at the front of the store, armed with an iPad and an excess of gold jewellery. As Kahli and I approached, she caught sight of us and smiled. Her chestnut hair was woven into two braids that had been pinned across the top of her head as if she were a von Trapp child. Through the store's oversized windows, another staff member stood behind the point of sale, her eyes glued to the computer screen. As the scent of sandalwood and rose wafted out into the street, Kahli perked up. 'I know her,' she said, staring through the window to the woman at the register. 'That's Clea's sister.'

'Cool,' I said, as we approached the entrance to the store. I had no idea who Clea was.

'Good morning, ladies. Welcome to rytuał cosmetica.' The woman at the entrance gave us each a solid dose of eye contact before consulting her iPad. 'How can we assist you today?'

'Just browsing,' I said, before Kahli could interject.

'Perfect,' the woman replied. 'Have you shopped with us before?'

'It's a shop, I think we can handle it,' Kahli said, before barging inside. I blushed on her behalf, irritated but still impressed by her ability to discard anything that didn't directly benefit her.

The woman in red smiled sweetly. I apologised profusely, but she was cheery. 'You don't need to apologise,' she said as she tapped at her iPad.

'I'm Marnie,' I added, on some pathetic whim. Perhaps news travelled fast.

'I'm Juno,' she replied, simply and without any sense of recognition. Perhaps not.

Inside the store, Kahli was already hugging Clea's sister – whose name, I would learn, was Isabel. She was dressed in the same blood-red two-piece as Juno, and had a red pixie cut to match. Watching the two of them, it dawned on me that I'd suggested we visit the store on the off chance that someone was waiting for me to do so. When I approached Kahli and Isabel, the exact opposite feeling came over me. I hovered beside them as Isabel mentioned something about Mykonos and the year 2017. Eventually, Kahli said, 'This is my housemate, Marnie.'

To Isabel's credit, she broke eye contact with Kahli to smile at me; said it was lovely to meet me; asked me how my weekend had been. When the conversation returned to Mykonos, I excused myself. I wandered around the store, drinking in the smell of rytuał *She* that was somehow everywhere. I looked around at the collection of bottles, pots and tubes that lined the shelves. The walls were tiled in a pattern of beige, peach and pink, and at the centre of the room sat an impressive collection of testers, along with various application paraphernalia. A brass sink was connected to the tester bench, with a pile of fluffy white towels folded beside it. There were four other women in the store, each of them on high alert, trying desperately not to break anything.

I hovered beside the sink, searching for an instruction card, but it was unencumbered by anything other than towels. As Kahli let out a throaty laugh, I reached for a bottle of facial cleanser and turned on the tap. It was the first time I'd held a rytuał product. The bottle was made of plastic, but it had the weight of glass. The packaging itself was pearlescent, with a pale-purple pump affixed to the top. On the side of the bottle, it said CLEANSE – *your hands, your sins, your face. The purpose of art is washing the dust of daily life off our souls.* As I pumped a small amount of golden gel into the palm of my hand, the scent of honey and cinnamon overwhelmed me.

'Marnie?'

I dropped the bottle into the sink. It made a rattling sound as it clattered around the brass. When I turned my head, I was relieved to find Rose emerging from what I assumed was the storeroom. 'Isabel, come with me,' she said, her voice sharp. Isabel's body language changed as she followed Rose to the sink; she shrank two inches beneath Rose's disapproval.

'Did Isabel give you a sink demonstration?' Rose asked, knowing full well she hadn't.

I went to answer, but Isabel beat me to it. 'I was just about to,' she stuttered.

'No time like the present.'

Kahli continued to hover by the point of sale. Rose turned off the tap and indicated for Isabel to shuffle in next to me, while she prepared a towel on the lip of the basin.

'Tell me about your routine,' Isabel said, suddenly nervous. 'Skincare, makeup, SPF.'

I looked to Rose for an answer. She gave me nothing. 'I, uh. I don't really have one. Just whatever I have at home.'

Isabel nodded as she wiped a hand over my palm and collected the cleanser. She turned on the tap for just a moment, lathered the cleanser between her palms and returned it to my right hand. Her movements were rigid. 'How would you like your routine to feel?'

'I don't know,' I said, as she massaged the back of my hand. The figure-eight patterns were mesmerising, but Rose was unimpressed. She pre-emptively turned on the tap, and Isabel positioned my hand under the flow of water.

'Okay. How would you describe your skin?'

'Sorry, I'm not very good at this. I don't know,' I admitted. It was this response that prompted Rose to intervene.

'Isabel, can I step in for a moment?' she said. Mortified, Isabel retreated. Somehow, among the movement, Rose managed to drape the white towel over my hand. Isabel watched from the right side of the sink, her jaw clenched.

'Marnie, I'm going to show you our daily moisturiser. It has a lightweight cream consistency, but the finish is matt. We use tocopherol, a form of vitamin E, to keep the skin hydrated. How does that sound?'

'Great,' I said, but she was already massaging the cream into my skin. It smelt like orange peel and warm spice. The jar from which she'd scooped a white dollop was glass, with a pale-green lid. Each product had its own unique design, but it was the use of gentle pastels that drew a through line. On the side of the jar, I could make out the words HYDRATE – *replenish and soothe. The tree that grows beside running water bears more fruit.*

'Isabel, could you please ask the other customers if they'd like a cup of tea?' Rose said, frustration bleeding through her professional mask. As soon as Isabel had disappeared, she leant towards me and whispered, 'I have to let her go today. Not quite the right . . . fit.' She handed my right hand back to me. 'How does that feel?'

I traced my left thumb over the skin she'd just massaged. It felt as if it belonged to someone else. 'Amazing.'

'Great,' she said. 'Let's take a look at some makeup.' I followed her dutifully to the tubes of lipstick and mascara. At least thirty shades of foundation were laid out in the shape of the rytuał logo beside them. 'Did Luna reach out?'

'She did,' I said. 'Last night. Thank you so much.'

Rose just smiled. She plucked a baton of lip gloss from the table and handed it to me. 'This is our Glazed Lip Oil in *Lust*. I think you'll like it.' I went to wave the tester's wand over my hand, but Rose opened a compartment beneath the bench and presented me with a small cardboard box instead. 'Take it. Our treat.'

She watched as I fumbled with the box, bending it out of shape as I slid the hard plastic into my palm. The tube made a satisfying click as I loosened the lid from its body. I noticed a faint tingling sensation as I coated my lips in the dark-pink syrup.

I returned the product to its packaging as Kahli appeared on the other side of the tester bench. 'I should get going,' she said, somewhat surly.

Rose looked her up and down. 'I'm Rose,' she said. 'You look so familiar to me. Have we met?'

Kahli crossed her arms at her chest. 'You don't look familiar to me at all. No offence.'

Rose laughed. 'None taken.'

'I should go, too. Thanks Rose,' I said, cutting in.

'It's my pleasure. We'll see you soon, Marnie.'

As Kahli and I trundled out of the store, Kahli gripped my left forearm. 'That's her,' she said, practically spitting. 'I've seen her on his phone.'

~

Kahli and I climbed the stairs that afternoon to find a small pink box waiting at our doorstep. It was addressed to me. I retrieved it from the welcome mat as Kahli fished around in her bag for keys. Inside the box, I found my bottle of rytuał *She*, propped up by a large volume of textured white paper.

'When did you buy that?' Kahli asked as she fed her key into the front door.

'Friday,' I said, and as I pulled the last sheet of paper out of the box, I discovered a handwritten note:

> *I can't wait to meet you, Marnie.*
> *Luna. X*

Six

When I arrived at the address Luna had shared in her calendar invite, I wondered if she'd made a mistake. The red-brick facade reached three storeys high, without windows or signage. In tiny lettering beside a cast-iron door was a phone number. After pacing like a constipated labrador for long enough, I keyed the numbers into my phone. A voice answered on the third ring.

'Welcome to rytuał cosmetica, how may I assist you?'

'Hi, my name is—'

'Oh, Marnie! Welcome. My apologies, I'll come and collect you.' Was this Luna? Her voice was tighter than it had sounded in my headphones. Seconds later, a short woman with bright-blue eyes and delicately rouged cheeks appeared in the doorway. Her curly blonde hair bounced off her shoulders. I recognised her from the website; she modelled the lightest foundation shade – P1.

'Good morning, Marnie. Welcome to *Emma*. Please, come in.'

'Hi! Thanks.' I caught the familiar aroma of rose and sandalwood on my way past her. 'Who's Emma?'

Her face collapsed into a knowing smile. 'That's the name of this office. We're at 25 Emma Street, but we call her *Emma*.' The door slid into place behind us.

'Cool. Great,' I said, as my eyes adjusted to the dark wood-panelled hallway. An iPad was presented on a side table, lit by a curved chrome standing lamp. The floor sloped gently uphill.

The woman tucked a tendril of golden hair behind her ear. 'I'm Eva,' she added. 'I'm the Head Office Experience Coordinator. If you could just sign yourself in, I'll give you the full tour.'

The screen of the iPad was sparse, with a list of names printed in the signature rytuał sans-serif font. Next to each name was a box that read *Present*. I tapped my right index finger gently on the box. A screen appeared with a series of statements:

> I agree that I am in full health, both of body and mind.
>
> I agree that I am well-intentioned in visiting the rytuał cosmetica office, whether for the purposes of business or pleasure.
>
> I agree that I will protect the interests of rytuał cosmetica both for the duration of my visit and subsequent to it.
>
> I agree not to disclose confidential information shared within the walls of the rytuał cosmetica office to anyone not present today.

A small empty box sat beside each phrase. Eva watched intently as I selected each of them. After the fourth tick, a new screen appeared:

> A warm welcome to you, Marnie Sellick. This agreement is legally binding.

Below this statement sat a checkbox and the word *Okay*. The only option was to accept. A chime rang out from the iPad as the list of names returned. As if activated by the chime, Eva walked past me to the end of the corridor. 'This way,' she chirped, holding the door open from the other side.

Stepping into the reception area was like stepping into a cone of fairy floss. There was pink, everywhere, in every shade. Sweeping skylights left the space drenched in natural light; a stark contrast to the sombre mahogany of the hallway. I imagined people saving images of the foyer to Pinterest boards titled *Office Goals*. Standing in it felt unreal, as if I could look but would never be able to touch this level of aesthetic perfection.

Eva marched over to a polished concrete desk, collected another iPad and tapped purposefully. 'Help yourself to tea,' she said, without looking up. A tray of the same pink ceramic cups I'd seen at the store was waiting on the coffee table, beside a large white teapot. I poured myself a cup.

'It's our house blend,' Eva said. 'Lavender, chamomile and rose. Great for the skin.'

'It's delicious, thank you.' I hadn't tasted it yet.

'This way,' Eva said, and as I jolted towards her half the cup's contents flew to the floor.

'Don't worry about that,' she said, before I could actually worry. 'I'll get someone to clean it up.' She tapped at the iPad again. 'Luna is waiting.'

I followed her through the doors to the left of reception as footsteps hurried to clear the puddle behind me. I didn't look back.

~

A grey tablet on the door to the meeting room read *Jean*. As I passed it, I saw the text at the bottom of the screen change from *Available* to *Occupied – Luna Peters*. Eva ushered me through the door and closed it behind us, revealing a long, dark glass table. At the end of the table sat Luna. It was shocking, seeing her in three dimensions. She was the same as every image I'd ever seen of her – small frame, olive skin, glossy, coffee-coloured hair that fell to just below the line of her nipples – but at a higher resolution. My heart jumped over itself when her green eyes looked up.

'Luna, this is Marnie Sellick,' Eva announced.

'Thank you, Eva.' Luna's voice – her real voice, not the one I'd absorbed through my shitty headphones – filled the room. Eva nodded and left without another word. And then we were alone.

'Hi, Luna, it's so great to meet you,' I said, flicking my eyes from the ground to the table to Luna's eyes – only for a second – before returning them to the ground. While I did this, Luna got up out of her chair and walked the length of the table to meet me. She was wearing a cropped white business shirt with a pair of structured brown suit pants. My underarms were already damp. Without saying anything, Luna pulled me in and hooked her arms around me: one over my shoulder, one around my waist. I held the tiny cup of tea away from her body. With my nose pressed up against the side of her neck, her scent was overwhelming. But it wasn't rytuał *She*. It was something else. It was smoky, but not like cigarettes; a stick of incense, with citrus and spice.

'It's a pleasure,' Luna said, her head still perched on my shoulder. I released her body, assuming we'd hugged for the correct amount of time, but when she felt my arms slacken Luna gripped me tighter. I returned my hand to her back and tried to relax, which only made my armpits damper.

She took a step back and smiled. I put the teacup down on the table.

'Welcome to our home.'

She turned to offer me a seat. As I lowered myself onto the cool leather, Eva appeared at the door holding a wooden platter. Luna nodded for her to enter, and she unloaded the spread in front of us. There were two cheeses – one hard, one white like vanilla slice – a pile of dried figs, dark, salty almonds, thick slices of bread and a white ramekin of butter, a pile of strawberries, a few sheets of lavosh crackers and an open tin of sardines. It was at least six times too much food for the occasion. Eva rushed back to the door and retrieved another teapot from a metal trolley. We sat in silence as she presented the teapot to us, swiped my original cup from the table and promptly left.

When we were alone, Luna slid into the seat opposite me.

'This is incredible,' I said. 'Wow.'

'Go on, then.' She gestured to the food but my hands remained pinned to my sides. She caught my hesitation and reached for a slice of bread, slathering it with butter. 'I have a confession to make,' she said as she chewed. 'I have a really good feeling about you, Marnie. I don't want to jinx things, but I think you could be really great here.'

'Wow, that's—'

'I don't know how interested you are in joining us, but I hope you'll consider it. Even if you're not sure what kind of role you're interested in, we've got a killer HR lead whose modus operandi is to help our people pave their own road to success.' She placed the bread back on the platter, shaking her head with a smile. 'You don't remember me, do you?'

My fluttery heart took a dive all the way down to my stomach. 'I don't know—'

'I wouldn't expect you to. It's a me thing. I'm an elephant.' She took a bite of the bread.

I clawed at my memory, but Luna's face was only familiar from through a screen. 'Where did we meet?'

'Aren't you going to eat?' she said, suddenly serious.

'Sorry. I didn't want to . . . ruin it.'

She poured two cups of tea as she said, 'You don't need to apologise, Marnie. Ever.'

'I don't know about that.' I chewed on a small handful of almonds as she slid a cup across the table. 'I've got a few overdue ones on the ol' conscience.'

She shook her head, smiling. 'You really don't remember me.'

'I don't. I know you said not to apologise, but I'm sorry, I only know you from'—I gestured to the room, the office, the fragrance I'd spritzed on my neck that morning—'this. I think.'

She rolled her eyes. 'School! North Park Primary School. I'm a few years older than you, but I remember you from after-school care.'

'Oh,' I said, sitting up a little straighter. 'Right!'

'You had this bright-blonde bob. It was almost radioactive. People pay thousands for that as adults.'

'I know, I say that all the time. I looked like I was born into a weird doomsday cult.'

'Were you?'

An uneasy laugh escaped me. 'Of course not. Well, it's nice to see you again.'

'You too.'

She reached for one of the figs and took a bite. 'Please don't think that this is any kind of interview. I want the conversation we have today to be about you as a person, not you as a few dot points on a résumé. Can we promise that to each other, please?'

'Of course. I don't even have a résumé.' I wanted to hold my breath until I passed out, or potentially until I died.

'That's great.' She picked up her cup of steaming golden water and gestured for me to do the same. 'Me either, by the way. This is all I have.' She looked around the room. 'Well, this and Caroline's.'

'Caroline's? The bar?'

'Mmm-hmm.' She nodded as she reached for another fig. 'You really should eat some more, Marnie. We pride ourselves on our catering.'

I carved a slice of cheese from the block. It had a faint black pepper taste. It was exactly what Kahli had meant when she said she wanted 'good cheese'.

'So, what do you know about rytuał?'

'Ahh . . . I went to the store and tried some of the products. I bought rytuał *She* online. I have the lip gloss. I've listened to a lot of interviews with you, and—'

'Lip oil. Glazed Lip Oil. Which shade?'

'Oh, it's, ah'—I reached for my bag and raked my hand through its contents until I found the smooth, glass-like tube—'*Lust*,' I said, reading the label triumphantly. The air in the room suddenly felt stale. I returned the lip oil to my bag.

'Product is of little concern at this stage,' she said, although just mentioning that there was something to be concerned with, at any stage, made me panic. 'Do you know much about our ethos?'

'I know you're all about skin health. The no-makeup makeup look. Except for eyes and lips, of course.'

Her mouth quivered on the edge of a smile, but it didn't eventuate. 'We're all about women. We're disrupting the way the beauty industry does business. Do you understand that, Marnie?'

'Of course,' I replied. 'I knew that, I think it's really important.'

'So do we.' Luna crossed her legs beneath the table. 'How do you feel about women?'

I laughed. 'In general?'

'Or specifics,' she mused, straight-faced. She crossed her arms. I watched the conversation hurtle away from me at breakneck speed.

'I love women. Obviously.'

'Is it obvious?' She raised an eyebrow. 'And how do you feel about yourself?'

'What do you mean?'

'I think it's quite a straightforward question.'

I crossed my arms, mirroring her. 'How does anyone feel about themselves?'

'I'm not asking "anyone". I'm asking you.' She uncrossed her arms, then her legs. The urge to do the same itched like lice.

'I'm a person. I'm fine. I'm kind of tall.'

Luna nodded, looking down at the floor with wide eyes. She waited a minute before she said, 'That's all?'

'How would *you* answer that question?'

She leant forwards, across the table, and stacked her forearms on top of each other. 'My physical body is just a vessel for everything I want to do in this life. I'm smart, I'm great with a crowd and I have impeccable taste in most things. I find it challenging to reconcile my true self with the version I share with the world, but I try not to be too hard on myself because it's insane to have as many people invested in the minutiae of my life as I do. I think I'm fair, but I find it hard to let go of things.' She slid back in her chair. 'Would you like to try again?'

I chewed on the inside of my cheek.

'These are just stories, Marnie. Mine and yours. I'd like to help you turn the page.'

'I don't need you to do anything—'

'It's not a case of need. Do you *want* it?'

There it was again. The list of things I wanted followed me like a shadow: I wanted a new pair of runners. A car. To know what to say when people asked, 'How are you?' I wanted my mum back, and a glass of water, but mostly I just wanted to know how everyone paid for things.

'I think I do,' was all that came out.

Luna stood up from her chair. 'It was wonderful to meet you, Marnie. You've got something really special about you. I'd like to offer you a job, if you'll take it.'

I stood hastily, levelling our eye lines. 'That's it?'

'That's it! But please, take your time to think about it. You're welcome to start as soon as you're ready. I can see you excelling in our Creative department, but everyone starts in the trenches at rytuał. You'll see what I mean. People move fast. I'll have an offer sent over in the next hour or so.' She walked towards the door. I followed her on the other side of the table.

'Do you need my references or anything?'

'We've spoken with Steffani at Ride On!. She was very complimentary.'

I snorted. 'That is truly shocking to me.'

Luna stared at me, quizzically. 'You deserve the world, Marnie. I want you to believe that.' She smiled. It was the kind of smile people went into debt for.

She opened the door and stepped out into the hallway. I followed, and as the door clicked shut behind us I watched the message on the grey tablet shift from *Occupied* to *Available*. 'I'll see you soon,' she said, as she turned away from reception and strode off down the corridor towards another room with her name on it.

Seven

'This is for you,' Eva said as she pulled a wallet-sized pouch from behind the reception desk. Inside it, four tubes huddled together like candy-coloured sardines. I recognised one as a miniature bottle of the facial cleanser.

'Oh, thank you.' I took hold of the pouch and smiled. It felt unexpectedly silky. I was coming to learn that rytuał was obsessed with making plastic feel like anything other than plastic.

Eva left a lengthy gap before responding, 'No trouble.'

'Eva, are we in *Britney* or *Jean* for the product update?' a familiar voice asked from behind me. As I turned, Rose's eyes lit up. 'Marnie!' she said. 'What a lovely surprise.' Her hair was blow-dried to fall obediently on either side of her face – even a single flyaway was out of the question.

'The product update is in *Britney* this morning,' Eva interjected, reading off another iPad that had materialised in the seconds since I turned away from her.

'Wonderful, thank you so much, Eva.'

'It's no trouble.' I wondered if there were specific questions that Eva found to be troubling. I watched her stow the iPad behind the desk, presumably on top of a stack of iPads that would each be removed and returned multiple times before the end of the day.

Rose took a step towards me and whispered, 'How did it go?'

'Good! I think. Luna is . . .'

But before I could work out what Luna was, Rose offered, 'Amazing?'

'Yeah.'

She rubbed a hand over my upper arm and smiled sweetly. 'I've got a great feeling about this.'

'Me too,' I said. My cheeks were heavy – I'd been clutching at the same smile since I'd left the meeting room.

'Rose, they're ready to start,' Eva said from behind the desk.

'I'll see you soon, Marnie.' She released my arm and walked towards the row of meeting rooms. As Rose disappeared down the hall, Eva returned her attention to my presence in the reception area.

'Thank you so much for visiting us today, Marnie. If you could record your exit time on the way out, that would be most appreciated.'

'Sure. Thanks for having me.'

'No trouble,' she said.

I turned, clumsily, and walked towards the exit. 'See you soon!' I yelped as I pushed the door open. The low light of the entryway was a relief. I found myself on the list of names and tapped *Depart*. A new screen appeared with a timestamp: 11.15 a.m. I tapped *Accept*.

Bon Voyage, Marnie Sellick.

Rytuał

~

The grey sky coated Collingwood in a lacklustre glaze. Despite this, I had a spring in my step. I pulled a tube of lip oil from the plastic pouch and waved its wand over my lips. The colour was called *Appetite*. I would have called it *Dark Red*, but there was nothing aspirational about the truth. As I waited for the tram, my phone vibrated in my palm. An email from cleo.henning@rytual.co:

> Dear Marnie,
> Good morning.
> We're pleased to share that your application for the role of Customer Service Consultant has been successful.
> Please find your official offer of employment attached. If you could sign and return this to us as soon as possible, it would be most appreciated. If you have any questions at all, feel free to let me know.
> Thank you, Marnie. Wishing you a fabulous remainder of your day.
> Cleo Henning
> HR Lead
> rytuał cosmetica

Cleo Henning was just one of countless characters I imagined I'd meet inside the walls of *Emma*. Armed with only her name, I imagined a woman who owned a series of silk suits, had her curtain bangs trimmed every six weeks, and made natural wine in her backyard. I loved Cleo Henning.

High on the promise of my new social circle, I dared myself to peek at the attachment. The now-familiar rytuał sans-serif font outlined the rules of engagement meticulously. The design of each page made it look less like a contract and more like a pitch deck – rytuał was pitching for my new life.

The text under the heading *Hours of Work* on the fifth page read:

> *You are employed in a full-time capacity, with an expected weekly schedule of 40 hours per week. You may be required to work upwards of these hours in the event of any international meeting requirements, social gatherings, intensive periods of business growth, new product launches or other tasks as required by rytuał cosmetica.*

Below that, the next clause read *Remuneration*:

> *You will be paid a salary of $49,000 per annum, less applicable taxation. In addition to this, you will be provided with thirty complimentary rytuał cosmetica products per year.*

My heart sank at the sight of $49,000. The way the numbers collected made me think of tinned tuna and rice, and bobbly leggings with a constant string of holes in the crotch. $49,000 was less than I made at Ride On!, albeit not by much. With the exception of the year I was paid for my potential, I'd been broke my entire adult life. I'd naively assumed *something* would happen *at some point* in my creative life to change this, but I didn't have a creative life anymore. *Something* seemed further away than ever. And $49,000 was right there.

Rytuał

The tram arrived. I climbed the stairs. In the distance, a woman shouted, 'You make me want to vomit!'

~

When I arrived at Ride On! that afternoon, Steffani was halfway through her own workout. When I poked my head through the studio door, she didn't look up. Her eyes were fixed on the screen between the handlebars. Her headphones spiralled around her ears like miniature black ram's horns.

'Hey,' I said, waving my arm at her like an attention-starved Sim. Steffani kept pedalling. I tried to pick the soundtrack to her workout, but Steffani's taste in music was wildly eclectic. There was also a chance it was just white noise. I took a few steps towards her and waved again.

This time she looked up, and I saw a drop of sweat roll into her eye. 'Marnie,' she said, pulling one of the ram's horns from her ear. 'Oh, fuck, you scared me.' She held the headphone between her fingers, and I caught the sound of heavy metal music.

'Sorry,' I said. 'I waved.'

She tapped her phone and dismounted. 'Just getting in a sweat before emails. How was your lunch?'

'Good, I actually wanted to talk to you about that.'

'About lunch?' She pulled a towel from the handlebar of the bike and shuffled to sit on the edge of the instructor's podium. As she removed her shoes, I caught a whiff of her hot, vinegary feet.

'No. I actually . . . I should have told you. I went to an interview this morning. But you'd already know that.'

'Good for you, Marnie! Getting back into film?'

'No, it was for rytuał cosmetica? The beauty brand? You gave them a reference, I think.'

'You've met Rose, haven't you?' Steffani said, ignoring my question. 'She's a Warrior. She does something there.' Club Warrior was what Steffani called the group of clients who'd taken at least one hundred classes at Ride On!. If you bought each class separately, it would mean you'd spent at least $3500 at the studio, and in return you were gifted a plastic drink bottle.

'Yes,' I said, finally. 'She introduced me to Luna.'

'You met Luna?' Steffani said, perking up. She crossed her legs in a lotus position and stared up at me with wide eyes. 'What was she like?'

'Amazing. So cool. Shorter than I imagined.'

'I did a yoga teacher training in Bali with someone who works there. Can't remember her name. Eva, maybe?'

'Yes! Eva!'

'Small world.'

Steffani seemingly forgot that this encounter with Luna would have any repercussions for Ride On!. Eventually, I said, 'So, obviously I need to resign.'

She exhaled. 'Actually, I'd been meaning to talk to you about that. This all feels a bit serendipitous.'

'What do you mean?'

'Take a seat,' she said, which in this case meant the floor. I sat in a cross-legged position, and she shuffled off the podium to sit opposite me. 'Marnie, I think you're great, but I don't think Ride On! is the right place for you. Which is perfect, if you've found something else.'

'What?'

'You're hilarious, don't get me wrong, but I just don't think you represent what Ride On! is about. This is a place for people to become their best selves. It doesn't seem as if that's something you're . . . interested in.'

'Yes, I am,' I said, my body suddenly stiff. 'It is.'

Steffani winced, tilting her head from side to side. 'You're always taking the piss out of things, and I can smell . . . I mean, you're hungover. A lot. When I hired you, I thought maybe I could help? But it's just . . . I don't think I'm qualified to be that for you. You know? Maybe it's time for you to see someone. Professionally.'

A cold laugh escaped me. 'It sounds as though you've made a pretty professional assessment of the situation.'

'Babe, I was a mess after my mum died. I feel you. But you've got to look after yourself. And I have to look after the business.' She reached for my hands and gripped them with her sweaty palms. 'Hurt people hurt people. It took me a long time to realise that. You're in the driver's seat.' She reached back over the podium and pulled another can of Red Bull from her duffel bag. 'I hope you find what you're looking for,' she said, as the can made a hissing noise.

'Is that really part of being your "best self"?' I said, staring at the can. She smiled maternally, as though I was a child mid-tantrum. 'Do you want me to stick around for next week, or can I get out of your hair sooner?'

'I don't mind. Whatever works for you. Do you need me to give you a reference?'

'You already did.'

She cocked her head to the side as she took a sip. 'Did I?'

'Yes. I said that before.'

She shrugged. 'If you say so. I black out when I look at the screen for too long.'

I didn't know how to end the conversation, so as Steffani continued to drink from the can of Red Bull, her legs knotted around each other, I walked out of the room and down the stairs. And I never went back.

~

The house smelt like lasagne. I'd killed the rest of the afternoon at the pub closest to Ride On!. It was unrenovated and uncool, and at two in the afternoon the only other patrons were those who'd been there since eleven. It was a relic of Old Richmond, and it likely wouldn't last another year. I drank three flat pints and scrolled my phone like a demon. I thought of the thousands of hours I'd spent poring over videos titled *How to become That Girl*. I wondered if there was someone, somewhere, who might like to become *this* girl. I re-read the *Remuneration* section of my rytuał contract, scanning desperately for new information. When I saw the corporate drones emerging from their offices, I packed it in for the day and joined them on the train, then the tram.

When I emerged from the hall to the lounge room, I found Kahli sitting opposite a man on the couch. The man was facing the windows, so I could only see the back of his head. They were speaking softly. Some kind of action movie was paused on the TV. When Kahli saw me, she sat bolt upright. 'You're home early.'

The man turned to face me, and he was very obviously Tom. Skinny, kind of anaemic-looking, a level of facial hair that toed the line between edgy and scruffy. 'Hi,' he said, none the wiser. 'I'm Tom.'

The oven's alarm screeched. Kahli sprang up from the couch and skipped to the kitchen. I'd never seen her move like that. 'I'm Marnie,' I said, eventually.

'Lasagne?' Kahli said, as she pulled the steaming tray from the oven. I was starving, but I didn't know if I was supposed to decline.

Rytuał

'I don't want to intrude,' I said, looking from Kahli to Tom and back again. Kahli's intense stare gave nothing away, and because I was starving and didn't have the energy to decode her, I agreed. Tom moved from the couch to the small dining table and waited to be served. I tried to catch Kahli's eye as I rummaged through the cutlery drawer, but she kept her gaze on the lasagne. The plates. The salad bowl. When we were all sat at the table, Tom finally said, 'This looks amazing.'

'I got a new job today,' I said, to the room, but mostly as a reminder to myself.

'What do you do, Marnie?' Tom asked, but he was easy to ignore.

'At rytuał. I got a job at rytuał.'

Both Kahli and Tom looked up from their food. 'What?' Kahli said. 'You didn't tell me you applied.'

'I didn't. They . . . well, they kind of scouted me.'

'To work at rytuał? What, in the store?'

'No,' I said. 'The office.'

'Customer service?' Kahli said, at high velocity. 'Is it, like, customer service?'

I took a bite of the lasagne. It was too hot. I chewed it anyway. When I'd swallowed, I said, 'Everyone starts in customer service, but people move fast.'

'I know someone who works at rytuał,' Tom interjected, and both of us turned to look at him.

'Who?' I pried. Kahli kicked my ankle beneath the table. 'What's her name?' Kahli kicked me again.

'Rose. Rose Liu.'

Kahli and I stared at Tom, incredulous. 'Isn't that your girlfriend?' Kahli said, before correcting herself. 'Your primary partner.'

'Oh, yeah,' he said. He ate his lasagne, unbothered. 'I forgot we had that discussion.'

'Surely that's, like, the number one rule of polyamory? Telling people about your girlfriend?' I said.

Tom just shrugged. After a moment of silence, he said, 'I don't believe in love as ownership. I think it's important to remain untethered.'

Before I could kick Kahli back, my phone buzzed against the marble countertop. I hopped away from my seat and flipped the screen to face me. Unsaved number.

> Hey Marnie, it's Lily again.
> I'd love to catch up – let me
> know if you're around next
> week. Hope you're well!

'Have you met Luna yet?' Tom asked from the table, but I was elsewhere. I deleted the message. 'She's fuckin' crazy.' When he realised how it sounded, he added, 'Not because she's a woman. It's not about gender. She's . . . intense.'

'Some people are just crazy,' Kahli mused.

Another message appeared on my phone. Another unsaved number.

> You haven't signed your
> contract yet – everything
> okay? Love to get the ball
> rolling. X L

'I like crazy,' I said, as I toggled to the email attachment and waved my finger over the signature box. 'Crazy is good.'

Eight

The weekend took forever to end. My phone told me I'd spent six hours and seven minutes staring at the screen on Saturday, and five hours and fifty-five minutes on Sunday. I bought a banh mi from the Vietnamese bakery around the corner. I read an article on Luna's morning routine. I watched a TED Talk on the power of visualisation. When my hips started to ache from sitting for too long, I went on a walk. I came back and tried to watch a movie, but got distracted by the light of my phone. I kept the movie paused until my laptop died.

After I'd returned the signed contract to Cleo, Luna was quick to suggest I visit *Emma* for an induction on Monday morning. On Sunday night, my phone buzzed.

> **LUNA PETERS**
> Can't wait to have you join us tomorrow. X

> I don't know if I'll be able to sleep
> tonight, ha ha! Really excited xx

Try progressive muscle
relaxation, have you done it
before? I'll send a link. X

A link arrived with an image of a woman lying peacefully on a beach.

Her voice is dull, but the
pacing is great.

> Thanks so much!! Wow you didn't
> have to do that, really grateful! xx

That or you could always
pleasure yourself, works every
time. X

I looked up from the screen. The ring of the empty room returned. I kept the message thread open and placed the phone on my bedside table. I stared it down. This was the kind of thing women spoke to each other about all the time. We were normalising pleasure, and breaking taboos. I had consumed so much literature – Instagram tiles – on the subject. I collected a glass from my bedside table and filled it with water from the bathroom. When I returned to my room, the screen was dark.

~

There were seven other people waiting outside *Emma* when I arrived. We stood separately, dotted across the pavement, our chins glued to our chests as we stared intently at our devices. Somehow, we'd all managed to dress in black and white. As I readjusted the collar of my oversized business shirt, I wondered what Luna would be wearing. When Eva appeared at the door to the office, dressed in a blue velvet jumpsuit, we snapped to attention.

'Good morning, eight. Please, this way.'

She held the door open and we moved cautiously inside. As I brushed past her, I noticed the same scent Luna had worn to my interview. Smoky, spicy, a hint of citrus.

'I love that fragrance,' I said, once inside the wood-panelled hallway. 'Is it new?'

Eva's eyes lit up. 'It's in the final stages of testing. Top secret, but a new release for Q4. You'll notice quite a few people wearing it around the office today.'

'Cool,' I said. My cheeks were tight.

Eva took hold of my arm. 'It *is* cool, isn't it?' Her tone was thankful, as if she'd been waiting for someone to say this for a very long time. She released my arm and trotted down the corridor.

I queued for the iPad. It only occurred to me then that the people in front of me had also been here before. To think of them eating cheese and sourdough with Luna felt like betrayal. When my turn arrived, I ticked the box beside each pledge hastily, eager to keep up with the group.

> **A warm welcome to you, Marnie Sellick. This agreement is legally binding.**

'This is the last time you'll need to sign in on arrival, how exciting,' Eva said as she whisked past me into the foyer.

The rest of the group had made their way to reception, and I heard one new recruit say to another, 'Do you know when our employee discount goes into effect?' I wanted to tell her to keep her voice down, but perhaps it was better for me if she'd only come for the discount. I shook the thought out of my head and followed Eva towards the foyer.

'Welcome, eight.' Eva made her way to the front of the group. I joined at the back, shuffling for a position to make eye contact with her as she spoke. Activity hummed from beyond reception as people went about their days.

'We're so pleased to have you here. Today is day one of your induction training, and we have a lot to get through. I'll just ask that you hand in your mobile phones, as we want this to be a productive day of learning.' She approached the reception desk and collected a rectangular pink container. 'If you could please deposit your phones inside this crate, I'd be most grateful.'

Whispers moved through the group.

'Why?' a person with pink hair asked. Eva's right eye twitched ever so slightly.

'We want this to be an immersive experience, Austen. We promise to return them to you at the end of the day.'

Austen said nothing in response. The crate made its way around the group, met with varying levels of enthusiasm from each recipient. I added my phone to the pile and handed it back to Eva.

'Thank you, Marnie.'

A woman I hadn't seen before walked over to Eva and collected the crate. It dawned on me that I was yet to spot a man inside *Emma*.

Rytuał

'We'll begin the day with a tour, followed by a talk from our founder and CEO, Luna Peters.'

My pulse began to race. I pressed my thumbnail into the pad of my index finger.

'If you could all follow me, we'll begin our tour this way.' Eva walked towards the corridor. As we filed through the door, I turned to Austen.

'Did you meet with Luna when you had your interview?' I asked, hushed.

'No, I had mine with, ah, Rose? I think that was her name.'

'Oh, right, yeah, Rose. Cool. Thanks.'

'No problem.' Austen walked ahead of me. I smiled to no one. I stuffed my hands in the pockets of my pants. I'd thought my white shirt and black pants were utilitarian chic, but once inside *Emma* I felt like a waiter. The rytuałists didn't wear clothes, they wore *outfits*.

Eva stopped a few doors down the corridor. She waited for the rest of the group to arrive.

'Here we have our meeting rooms. As you can see, they're located closest to the entrance, so that when we're hosting visitors we can get right to business.'

Austen raised a hand.

'Yes, Austen.'

'I was just wondering, this might be a stupid question, but—'

'There are no stupid questions here. Unless the question is where to get the best iced latte, to which the answer is obviously Calooh.'

'Right. Well, I just wanted to know, is it pronounced rye-tual? Or ritual?'

The activity around us came to a momentary standstill. The look on Eva's face said this was a question with world-ending repercussions. 'Well, the spelling is Polish, in honour of Luna's grandmother. Technically, it's ri-tooh-al, but we say ritual.' She smiled with only the bottom half of her face. 'We do explain that on the website.'

Austen nodded solemnly. The exchange had been brief, but had left a permanent mark on Austen's record. There were definitely stupid questions.

'Are there any *other* questions?' Eva continued, back to her perky self.

'What's the story behind the names of the meeting rooms?' a woman at the front of the group, wearing knee-high white boots and a white sweater dress, asked.

Eva exhaled with glee. 'I'm so glad you asked, Coco.' She tucked her hair behind her ear, as she'd done tens of times already, and continued. 'We named these rooms after women we believe to have been unfairly treated in the public eye. It's a tribute to the fallen women, if you will.' Eva offered up this information as if she'd practised it in the mirror, in the shower, in front of anyone who would listen. She pointed to each of the rooms as she named them: 'Billie Holiday, Jean Seberg, Amy Winehouse and Britney, of course.'

It was the first time I'd thought any part of rytuał was somewhat on the nose.

'Are there any other questions?' Eva repeated, chuffed with her own performance.

The group shook their heads with conviction. Without thinking, I responded aloud, 'No.'

A few people turned to see where the noise had come from.

Their eyes made fleeting contact with mine before they returned to Eva.

'All right, let's continue,' she said, moving down the corridor.

Eva zipped past the remaining meeting-room doors and followed the curved hallway around to the right. After *Britney*, the corridor opened to reveal a light-flooded open-plan office space. The building was sandwiched between two other converted warehouses, so the source of the light was always up; giant panels of glass lined the ceiling. The floor was polished concrete, but a pink tint left it warm. Inoffensive instrumental music played from a speaker – or a collection of speakers – somewhere in the walls.

'This is our Global Head Office space. As you may well know, we launched in the United States and China last year, and we're working on a European launch. We have a local team on the ground in each region, but the bulk of our logistics and strategy happen here.'

A woman passed us with a tray of figs and smoked almonds, and four cups of black coffee. She walked to the desks closest to us and handed the cups of coffee to the women working there.

'What about Australia?' Coco asked.

'Another great question, Coco.'

Austen stared at the floor.

'We have a separate space for our Australia and New Zealand team. We'll get there shortly.'

We continued past the desks to another corridor that began on the far left side of the room. It was mood-lit, and the walls were painted red. After a few metres it was hard to remember we'd just walked through so much light. A metal door appeared on the left. Eva stopped in front of it and waited eagerly for the group to catch up. I heard someone towards the back of the group say, 'I was a sustainability consultant at DeRoix, but I wanted a change.'

'This is where the real magic happens: the Lab.'

We all looked at the door. No windows, no indication that there was actually anything going on behind it. The grey tablet at eye level read *The Lab – Occupied – Testing in progress.*

'We're working on a number of exciting advancements at the moment. We try to be innovative rather than reactive – the beauty industry moves so fast, it's impossible to capitalise on trends without compromising quality. Maybe that makes us the trendsetters.'

Long before I'd hastily purchased rytuał *She*, I'd heard about their product releases. People set alarms, pre-ordered, begged, borrowed, stole. rytuał had managed to stay on top of reinventing beauty. In recent months they'd garnered a number of copycat brands, smaller companies using their aesthetic like a template, but it never took. There was always something missing.

Without further discussion, Eva continued down the corridor. The deeper we moved into the building, the dimmer the lighting became. When we arrived at our next destination, the corridor felt like a warm cocoon.

The grey tablet by the door to Eva's right read *ANZ Team – Open Work Session*. Beside it, the steel mouth of a small elevator.

'To answer your question from earlier, Coco, this is where our Australia and New Zealand team works.'

We all looked at the door. Again, there was no indication of anything happening behind it. It could have been a prop – we were none the wiser. This time, however, Eva swiped a fob beside the doorhandle and the lock granted us entry. She pushed the door inwards and we followed her inside, where a spiral staircase began immediately after we crossed the threshold. The air was thick with floral incense. Beneath us, two pods of ten desks filled the space, and all were occupied bar two. People worked diligently at their stations.

'Good morning, Team ANZ. I have our new starters here for a tour.' The women hunched over their desks jolted to attention as we descended the stairs. One face remained glued to its screen, a look of concern plastered from brow to brow. The face belonged to Rose.

The room was much smaller than it first appeared, and the desks took up most of the space. On the right side of the room, a long sideboard presented the full rytuał product collection. On the left, a small refreshments station held a baby-blue espresso machine, a pile of sliced figs and a mound of smoked almonds, and a small jug of water beside a collection of little pink cups. Rose finally looked up from her computer.

'Marnie!' she cried, although I couldn't discern if my face had caused her excitement or stress. Two of the other team members greeted women in the group: *Hello, so nice to see you, I would die for your hair/eyes/mohair cardigan.*

'How's your morning going? It's pretty incredible in here, right?' Rose's mascara had bled onto the skin below her eyes. She looked markedly more tired than she had pre-dawn at Ride On!.

'So good! It's great, really wonderful.'

The lack of natural light in the basement was stifling. Still, similarly to Kahli's house, if you took a photo from any angle it would come up practically perfect.

'If anyone needs the bathroom, now would be a wonderful time,' Eva said, as she turned to indicate a door tucked behind the staircase. The elevator's below-ground counterpart sat beside it. 'We'll be here for five minutes, so please, take your time.'

A few women moved to form a line at the bathroom door. Rose inched closer to me, the same spicy citrus fragrance hovering around her.

'I really like that new perfume,' I said. I meant it.

Rose took hold of my enthusiasm. 'I have a spare tester if you'd like to take it home. Just be sure to keep it under wraps; it's top secret until the release later this year.' She walked back to her desk and pulled an unlabelled fragrance bottle from the top drawer.

'It's called *We*.'

I paused to make sure I'd heard her correctly. '*We*?'

'Yes! Our first fragrance was rytuał *She*, and this new addition is rytuał *We*. Much more inclusive. For all genders.'

She handed me the bottle, which indeed read *We Eau de Parfum*. The only other text on the bottle read *50 ml*.

'Oh, of course. Thank you so much.'

'Rose, we were wondering if you had the final product blueprint for *We*? The website copy is just a placeholder at the moment—'

'Laura! Shhh.' Across a pod of desks to my left stood three identical women: flat brown hair that stopped abruptly just below their shoulders, gentle facial features, the orange sheen of a light fake tan. I ran my eyes across them, scanning for a foothold. The only thing that clearly differentiated them was their eyes – one had dark brown eyes, one green, and one bright blue. The blue-eyed one blushed as the brown-eyed one shot her a punitive stare. 'We must remember to always be risk-aware,' she added, glancing over at the new recruits.

'I'll send it through in a moment,' Rose replied. All three of the women smiled. 'Oh, sorry. Marnie, this is Laura, Laura and Laura. From Marketing.'

They looked over at me, still smiling. The one in the middle – the green-eyed one – gave a tiny wave.

'What are the chances,' I said. They returned to their desks.

'We call them The Lauras,' Rose added, which seemed superfluous. 'Have you seen Luna today?'

'Not yet, I think she's speaking to us after this. I'm excited to'—Rose's eyes darted between mine—'see her again.'

Right on cue, the door at the top of the stairs opened. 'Good morning, everyone!' Luna launched herself through the door wearing a pair of red-tinted sunglasses. Her arms were bare, showing off her collection of fine line tattoos. Eva snapped to attention from the refreshments station.

'Luna, what a delightful surprise! We were just about to come and find you.'

'My calendar says we were scheduled to meet at ten-fifteen.'

Eva blushed, hard. 'Yes, my apologies, we'll be up in just a moment.'

'I'm here now, aren't I?'

Luna descended the stairs. I felt Rose wrap her arm around my shoulders, her hand coming to rest on my left triceps. When I looked for her eyes, they were focused on Luna.

'Marnie! It's so lovely to see you again,' Luna said as she stepped off the last stair. Rose lifted her hand as Luna kissed my left cheek. I started to feel faint. 'How are you this morning, Rose?'

I wiggled my toes for something to focus on.

'Good. Busy. Just working on the new training plan. Marnie, you'll be one of our guinea pigs! We're changing our Induction Learning Pathway. It's very exciting.'

I looked over at Rose and tried to nod, but my vision blurred. There was too much perfume and not enough air. I caught Rose's concerned expression, but it was too late. Was I falling forwards or backwards? It didn't matter. The room went dark.

Nine

I opened my eyes to blinding light. I was lying on a red velvet couch. Floor-to-ceiling windows with black iron frames stretched out in front of me, overlooking a small courtyard. Luna was sitting at a glass desk to my right. A large silver monitor obscured her face. I shuffled to sit up, releasing my neck from the vice grip of my shirt's top button.

'What happened?'

She slid out from behind the desk and drifted towards me. 'Any excuse to get out of a dry office tour.' She winked. 'You fainted. Are you a fainter?'

'I was really hot. It was hot in there. Sorry.' It was hard to look directly at her.

She sat beside me, resting a hand on my left thigh. I flinched, and she returned it to her lap.

'No apology necessary. It worked out well for me, too. I hate those induction talks. I'd much rather get to know people one on one.'

'Cool.'

'I like your pants,' she said, her eyes on my lap.

I blushed. I was wearing the same pair of pants I'd worn to meet Rose. They were black and high-waisted, with an oval-shaped silhouette, which made them look more expensive than they actually were. 'Thanks. I wear them all the time.'

I looked around what I assumed to be Luna's office. rytuał products were scattered across most surfaces. Three framed magazine covers adorned the wall behind her desk. In one, Luna stood in front of a red backdrop with her hands on her hips. She looked beautiful – of course she did – but there was something so unfair about a still image. Those who had only seen her in two dimensions had barely seen her at all.

'I hate that one,' she said, noticing my interest. 'Eva had it framed without asking me. They didn't provide any wardrobe options, so I had to wear what I had with me. The photographer kept calling me "Lena". And I had a UTI. A real trifecta.'

'That's awful,' I said.

'No, it's not,' she replied, swatting my comment away. 'It's fine. Would you like some water? Tea?' She walked over to a robustly stocked drinks cart, continuing with her back towards me. 'I also have gin, but something tells me that wouldn't be the wisest choice.' She spun around to face me, a wry grin forming. 'But, then again . . . I'm game if you are?'

I returned her smile. 'Tea would be great, thanks.'

She poured from a small white teapot. It was steaming hot; it must have been prepared minutes, or seconds, earlier.

'What time is it?' I asked.

'Two-thirty,' Luna replied, carrying two pink teacups back to the couch. 'You came to, then fell asleep. I've been keeping an eye on you.'

She sat opposite me, with her back against the arm of the couch. There was enough room for both of us to extend our legs. After she handed me the cup, she slid off her loafers and let her toes tap the rubber soles of my Doc Martens.

'I should take my shoes off,' I said, nearly spilling the tea as I threw my weight forwards.

'Not necessary, please. Unless you want to. My couch is your oyster.'

'I hate oysters,' I said. 'Phlegm of the sea.'

Luna's eyes sparkled as she laughed. She put her cup down on the coffee table and laughed for longer than I expected. I gave an encouraging smile. When she caught it, she said, 'You look just like your mum when you smile.' It knocked the air out of me.

'How do you know . . .'

'Jean. Her name was Jean, right? How fitting.'

'Yes, but—'

'I was so jealous of the girl with the cool mum. She was young. Much younger than my parents.'

I nodded, but I was starting to feel faint again. Luna must have noticed, because she placed a hand on my shin and said, 'Life is fucking cruel.'

'Yeah.' My mouth was dry.

We sat in silence. Luna stared at me, her green eyes like a spotlight. Eventually, I said, 'When were you and Rose together?'

Luna tossed her hair over the arm of the couch and laughed again. 'Oh, god, ancient history,' she said. 'Did Rose tell you that?'

'She said she . . . dated the owner of Caroline's.'

'Cheeky Rose,' she said. 'What do you think of Tom?'

I took another swig from the teacup, but my mouth was still dry. 'Rose's Tom? I've never met him—'

'Uh-uh-uh,' Luna tutted, raising her index finger. 'Let's not build a relationship on white lies.'

'I've only met him once. Kahli didn't know about Rose. How did you . . .?'

'I'm a very loyal friend, Marnie. I did some background on Kahli. Small world! They broke up, by the way. Tom and Rose. Over the weekend. Thank god, I couldn't stand him.'

'Oh. Right.'

She fluttered her lips as she exhaled. 'Anyway, boring! Have you been writing much?'

'No, I don't really write anymore.'

'Why not?'

'How did you know I was a writer?'

She scrunched up her face as if she'd bitten into something sour. 'Really, Marnie?'

'I didn't expect that you'd—'

'Why did you stop?'

'Writing? I can't . . . I don't enjoy it anymore.' It was a hard and shiny phrase, popularised among my peers in the years after we'd finished university. Some wanted more stability, physiotherapy, central heating, but if you admitted that things hadn't worked out as you planned, you left yourself open to pity. In my case, it was the truth – or, it was as close to the truth as I could get without losing my first layer of skin.

'This company is a place for people with big ambitions to thrive. I can see you thriving here. If you can go within and heal whatever is blocking you, you'll be unstoppable. I want you to be unstoppable.'

I chewed on the inside of my cheek. 'I wasn't ever that good. I got lucky.'

'So?' she said.

'So, I just did it because people told me to.'

'People who?'

'I wanted the feeling of being chosen, then I was chosen, so I just kept going. Like a dog.'

'Who specifically chose you?'

'I won a prize. But you already know that, don't you.'

She nodded. When I didn't elaborate, she returned a hand to my shin and patted it twice. 'All in good time.'

Luna collected her cup of tea and wandered over to the window. 'I know the salary for our Customer Service team is . . .' She paused. 'Look, it's pretty abysmal. But we have to weed out those who only want to talk the talk from those who want to get up and run. You know?'

I nodded.

'You'll be on probation for your first month here, after which the sky's the limit. I think your chances of progressing straight away are very high.'

She spoke as if this was something that would be decided by fate, rather than something she could directly control.

'Thank you,' I said, which wasn't quite the right response – it felt as if it had been rinsed through Google Translate one too many times.

Luna stared down at the courtyard. 'It's quite isolating,' she said, 'being successful. I have to separate Luna Peters the brand from Luna Peters the person. When they're glued together, things get messy.' She poked out her tongue and mimed dry-retching. 'Even the truth sounds trite these days.'

'I can imagine. Well, I can't imagine, exactly, but I have an idea. I can guess—'

'Which is to imagine.'

I blushed.

'I'm just teasing,' she added. 'Shall we get back to the group? It's afternoon tea time.'

'Sure. Of course. Sorry.'

'You don't need to apologise, Marnie. For anything.'

She walked over to the couch and placed a hand on my shoulder. The pointed tips of her dark-red nails dug into my skin as she squeezed it twice.

~

I followed Luna through a maze of stairs and hallways. 'This building was originally a boot factory, but they were also cooking heroin on the side,' she said, as a hall became an open-plan kitchen. Five long blond-wood tables filled the space. The new recruits were seated at the furthest one.

'Good afternoon, nine,' Luna said. 'My apologies for missing our introduction, but the good news is Marnie's feeling much better now.' I swept my eyes across the group, smiling feebly. The women stared back at me like hungry wolves. Except for the one named Coco, who nodded enthusiastically from the end of the table. She had a round face with two symmetrical dimples at her cheeks, and it looked as if it took a lot of effort for her to relax them.

'We had a lovely chat,' Luna said. 'I hope to chat with each of you very soon. For now, you're in capable hands with Eva.

She lives and breathes rytuał's values.' Luna collected a handful of almonds from the platter closest to her – brushing her arm against Austen's shoulder – and bounced off.

'Oh,' Eva said, deflated, as she watched Luna leave. 'I thought she might stay for afternoon tea.'

The long dining tables were flanked by timber benches. I sidled up to Coco, claiming the only available seat.

'Hi,' she said, wiping crumbs from her hands. 'I'm Coco. That was crazy in there, you looked like you were dead for a second! Are you okay?' Her voice shot through punctuation as though it were only a suggestion.

'I'm totally fine, just a bit embarrassed.'

She stared at me. 'Was Luna your person?'

'My . . . person?'

'It turns out everyone was recruited by a rytuał employee – we all know one person. You must've got lucky to be chosen by Luna.'

It took me a second to piece together what she was saying. 'I wasn't chosen by Luna. I don't think.'

'I know Fatima from Global Marketing, she invited me to apply,' Coco continued.

'Oh, right, no – Rose invited me to apply. From Training.' I said this as if I understood the job description of someone who 'worked in training'.

'Oh! Rose is the sweetest.' Coco looked relieved.

I stared at the others. I hadn't paid much attention to the rest of the group until now. I wanted to match each with their recruiter, although my understanding of the rytuał org chart was limited to Luna, Rose and Eva. Coco must have seen me jumping from face to face, because after a moment she said, 'That's Sarah M., Sarah R., Shami, Minnie, Alissa, Tamara, and Austen you probably remember. I'm Coco. I already said that, didn't I? Classic me.'

'I'm Marnie.'

'I know.'

I looked at Coco properly. Her skin was arrestingly clear – I wanted to ask her how she achieved such an understated, dewy glaze, but I was worried it involved acids and a facialist and a designated beauty fridge. She had deep-brown eyes and a sharp, jet-black bob.

'All right, eight, we've got quite a bit to get through before we finish up today, so let's keep moving?' Eva's voice squeezed itself inside the question mark. 'Follow me and we'll head down to IT, where we'll take your staff portraits and you can collect your phones.'

'Why would our phones be held by IT?' Austen asked from the other side of the table.

'Well, where else would it be appropriate to store a phone?' Eva laughed, slightly too loud, and turned. 'Let's go,' she said.

~

As Eva swiped her pink fob over the sensor, another room drenched in natural light was revealed.

'Good afternoon, Eva. Hi, everyone.' A woman dressed entirely in apricot linen walked towards us. Behind her, there were more computers. More outfits. More perfectly made-up faces.

'Eight, this is Priya. One of our senior service desk analysts.'

Priya's large round glasses gave the illusion of her eyes bulging out of their sockets. 'It's a delight to meet you all, truly,' she said, without blinking. As Priya took us in, Eva cleared her throat.

Priya continued to stare, smiling as if we were the cast of a very successful sitcom.

'Priya? Do you have the final results?'

She jumped to a start, collecting yet another iPad from a desk behind her. 'Here you are,' she said. But Eva was already scanning the screen.

'We'll proceed to staff portraits in just a moment, but before we do—' Eva took one final glance at the iPad, perplexed. As she zoomed in on something at the bottom of the screen, Priya collected the phone crate from a shelf to our left and presented it to the woman I thought was Sarah M., but could also have been Tamara.

'Sarah M., Sarah R., Alissa, Minnie, Tamara, Shami and Austen,' Eva recited from the iPad. The only people she hadn't named were Coco and me. My heart sped up. 'Can I ask you all to wait here for a moment? Everyone else, please proceed to the portrait studio.'

From my right, Coco took hold of my hand. She squealed. I looked to her, then back to Eva.

'Just Coco and me?'

'Yes, that's right,' Eva confirmed.

'This is my favourite part,' Priya said. 'This way.'

Coco let go of my hand and bounded after Priya. That was the last time I saw Austen, Sarah M., Sarah R., Alissa, Minnie, Tamara and Shami. Or whatever their names were.

~

When I heard 'staff portrait', I'd imagined a passport photo, but the studio nestled into the nook of two red-brick walls indicated something entirely different. A light-pink cyclorama extended to the ceiling. In front of it stood a DSLR on a tripod, wrapped in a ring light. On the left, below two round rytuał-branded mirrors, were two perspex side tables. Both were covered in rytuał products.

'Think of your staff portrait as a way for other rytuałists to get to know you. We want to see who you really are,' Priya said as she pressed a button on the camera. 'We're more than just colleagues here, as I'm sure you're aware.'

Coco darted over to the product table and began applying a lip oil.

'Will the others be joining us?' I asked Priya.

Priya smiled and looked to the floor. 'You should ask Eva.'

I joined Coco at the table beside her.

'I can't believe they're letting us use all of this.' She reached for a cheek tint. 'This goes for sixty-four dollars. Forty in the US, but there's the exchange rate, and tax. Have you tried it before?' She presented me with the little glass pot.

'Oh, thanks.' I removed the silver lid and dabbed at the pink putty. The pigment was strong. At first, I looked like a clown.

'You have to really work that one into the skin,' she said. 'It's worth the extra time. I use my ring finger, and just keep tapping until it blends with your foundation.' Her instant warmth made me suspicious, which in turn made me frustrated. This resulted in me not really knowing how to arrange my body, or where to place my eye contact.

'Thanks,' I said.

Coco leant a little closer. 'Do you think the others were fired?' she whispered. Before I could reply, Priya's face appeared in the mirror behind us.

'Who wants to go first?' she said.

Coco raised a hand to shoulder height. 'I volunteer as tribute!' she said, skipping towards the backdrop.

As I returned to the table of products, Eva appeared holding two phones, one in each hand. I took mine as she handed me a small pink fob. 'For tomorrow,' she said. 'Congratulations!'

'Can I ask . . . what happened to the others?' I said.

'You can ask,' she replied, watching Coco move enthusiastically from pose to pose.

'Oh, okay, sorry—'

'I'm just kidding!' she said. 'They weren't quite the right fit. We're a very specific business and we have a strong sense of when things aren't going to work out.'

'Didn't they sign a contract?'

She cast her eyes down to Coco's jewel-encrusted phone case. 'Everything is discretionary.'

I tapped at my phone screen. It had been switched off.

'Your turn, Marnie,' Priya called.

Eva moved her hand to pat my upper back, and I walked towards the backdrop as if possessed. Priya fiddled with the tripod, adjusting its height to meet the line of my eyes.

'Ready?' she said, as she stared intently at the camera's display.

I tried to smile, but my face was too tight and my eyes were too wide.

'Marnie, smile!' Eva coached from the sidelines. 'With your eyes, just smile with your eyes. Casual.'

I looked to the floor, then back up at the blistering ring light. The smell of rytuał *She* was thick in the air. I thought about what it might feel like to have more time. Or to be able to buy time. I thought about a vanity covered in rytuał products. I thought about Luna's red nails against my skin.

'Got it,' Priya declared.

Ten

On Tuesday mornings at rytuał, a company-wide event took place in the meeting room called *Britney*. Between nine and nine forty-five, everyone's calendars were blocked out for an event called THE CLEARING. This wasn't something I was notified of in advance, but the next morning when I arrived at *Emma* – and took my little pink fob on its maiden voyage from keychain to sensor – the modest reception area was full of women. They were draped over each other in a way that denoted more than just 'work friends'; there was intimacy in the air, and it smelt like rytuał *We*.

'Marnie,' Coco's voice squeaked from behind me. 'Wait for me!'

I turned to find Coco trotting up the hall. She was wearing a red silk set that could have been pyjamas. It was reminiscent of rytuał's in-store uniforms, and, knowing Coco (albeit for a single day), I felt sure this was intentional.

'Do you know what this "clearing" is?' she said. 'My calendar notification said we're needed in *Britney*.'

'Who set up your calendar?'

'Oh, no one. I just did some research last night. Logged in and had a poke around. You know.'

I was starting to feel as if I hadn't done my homework. Luna appeared from the doors on the left side of reception. 'Good morning, my sweet rytuałists!' she said. 'Let's get clear.'

There was a thrum of activity from the crowd as they collected their bags and laptops and takeaway coffee cups, and walked in the direction of Luna. As Coco and I joined the queue, we found ourselves slotting in behind the identical Lauras. The green-eyed one turned as we approached. 'Good morning, Marnie. Good morning, Coco.'

'Hi,' I said, as Coco, uncharacteristically formally, replied, 'Good morning, Laura.'

'So glad to have you with us this morning. The Clearing is the perfect introduction to life at rytuał,' she said. Our blank expressions prompted her to add, 'You'll see.'

When we were through the doors and down the hall, Coco and I watched as everyone filed into the room called *Britney*. It was much larger than *Billie*, *Jean* or *Amy*, and as was customary, Eva had already arranged a large platter of elaborate pastries on one side of the room. The chairs were laid out in rows, and the women ahead of us were practical and neat as they filled each seat in order. Luna was waiting at the front of the room, deep in conversation with someone whose face I didn't recognise. She leant coolly against an oak side table as they spoke. I took my seat between Laura and Coco in the third row as Luna reached for the hand of the woman she'd been speaking with. I dropped my eyes to the floor, suddenly hyperaware of how desperately they wanted to examine the gentle slope of her waist. The soft silhouette of her perfect hair.

Rytuał

'Good morning, rytuałists,' Luna said, and my eyes obediently returned to her. 'It's Tuesday morning, and that means it's time for The Clearing. Would anyone like to volunteer to go first?'

I heard rush of air against skin as multiple women threw their hands to the ceiling. I was still at a complete loss as to what was happening.

'Ruth?' Luna said, pointing to a woman at the back of the room. Her chair scraped the floor as she stood up. She was tall, maybe six feet, with wild red curls. Her skin was coated in freckles. 'I would like to clear an altercation I had with a man on the tram this morning,' she said, staring straight ahead. 'I must have bumped him by accident, and he pushed me into the woman in front of me.'

Luna clicked her tongue against the back of her teeth disapprovingly.

'Then the tram stopped and I fell, and when I was on the ground he kept shouting at me. I had my headphones on but when I took them off I heard him call me a . . . well, he was saying some really awful things.'

'What did he say?' Luna pressed.

'I'd prefer not to repeat it.'

'Ruth, you cannot let this man win by burying your trauma. What did he say?'

'He called me a . . . carrot-top whore? Which doesn't even make sense, but he was shouting, and it really affected me—'

'Ruth, thank you for clearing this with us. rytuałists, please join me in affirming Ruth.'

Green-eyed Laura took hold of my left hand. When I looked over at Coco, the woman on her right had done the same. I took Coco's free hand and waited for further instruction.

'Together we rise, divided we fall. We are the fallen women and we work as one. Fallen woman, fallen woman, fallen woman,' the crowd chanted, with complete certainty.

Ruth must have returned to her seat, because Luna was quick to move on. 'Who's next?' she said, her eyes scanning the crowd. From the front row, on the left-hand side, an arm I recognised came into view. Luna smiled when she saw who the hand belonged to.

'Rose. One of our longest-tenured rytuałists. Please, share your clearing with us.'

Rose stood. She was dressed in an oversized brown pinstripe blazer and undersized black suede skirt. Her black tights were embossed with small hearts. She opened her body to face as much of the crowd as she could while still addressing Luna. 'I broke up with my boyfriend over the weekend,' she said, and I was suddenly reminded of sitting beside Rose on the bench at Ride On!. Time was elastic and deeply confusing. 'We weren't right for each other, but he was sleeping with someone else. He said he thought we "had an arrangement".'

Luna made a show of rolling her eyes. 'I know the answer to this, but please tell the group, what's this man's name?'

'Tom Tucker,' she replied.

Luna took a deep breath. Those in the crowd were quick to do the same. There was a brief pause before they returned to the same chant: 'Together we rise, divided we fall. We are the fallen women and we work as one. Fallen woman, fallen woman, fallen woman.' Coco was already mouthing along.

'Thank you, Rose,' Luna said. Rose returned to her seat as Luna scanned the crowd again. Her eyes glossed over Coco and me, then returned to us. 'Oh, I nearly forgot! We have two new rytuałists with us today. Marnie, Coco, stand up.'

Audience participation was my worst nightmare, and although this was not a mean-spirited comedy show, it still filled me with dread. Coco was so quick to stand I had no choice but to join her. Applause rippled through the crowd as we stood. Green-eyed Laura smiled encouragingly from beside my hip.

'Marnie and Coco, as this is your first clearing, you're welcome to pass, but do either of you have something you'd like to share?'

Coco's hand flew towards the ceiling.

'Coco?'

'Well, I'm back on the apps at the moment, and the other night I met up with this woman, but she was, like, a completely different person to her profile. I didn't even know people catfished anymore! I had to ask her—'

'Coco, I think you've misunderstood,' Luna said, with a grin.

Coco inhaled sharply and covered her mouth with her hand.

'Would someone else like to provide an example?'

Green-eyed Laura raised a hand, modestly, letting it stop at shoulder height. I could smell the tacky sweetness of her fake tan.

'Darling Laura. What have you got for us?'

She stood up.

'Well, I did clear this last week, but my landlord recently let himself into my apartment. When I got home he said he was there for maintenance, but there was nothing to repair. When I asked him to leave he asked me out for a drink, but then my partner came home and hit him in the jaw. So, that was helpful.'

Giggles echoed through the crowd.

'And what was this man's name?'

'Robert Walsh.'

The crowd chanted again. 'Together we rise, divided we fall. We are the fallen women and we work as one. Fallen woman, fallen woman, fallen woman.'

'Perfect, Laura. Thank you.' Laura took her seat. 'Do you see what I mean, Coco?' Coco shook her head, panicked. A man on the tram, Tom, Laura's landlord. *Billie*, *Jean*, *Amy* and *Britney*. The space between my ears was full of unnecessary facts about cleaning products and celebrities. I couldn't solve the problem. 'Marnie?'

Rose turned her head from the front row, and I watched her lips form the word *'Men'*. Because each of the encounters the women had cleared was with a man. And I was still yet to find any men inside the walls of *Emma*.

'I, uh.' I felt blood rush to my cheeks. 'The other night I went home with a man who asked me to transfer him half the cost of the ride home. But, I paid for the ride home. He didn't even pay for it.'

Someone let out an exasperated sigh.

'What was his name?'

'Justin,' I said. 'Justin, ah, Langton. Langfield!'

Luna grinned. She nodded, and the crowd repeated the chant once more. 'Together we rise, divided we fall. We are the fallen women and we work as one. Fallen woman, fallen woman, fallen woman.'

'Coco, does that make things clearer?' Luna said, and although this could have been cruel, there was a softness to her delivery that felt maternal – as though she really wanted Coco to work it out for herself.

'I think so,' Coco squeaked.

'Well, you've got a week to work it out, my love. Take a seat.'

I snuck a glance around the room, at the excess of rouged cheeks and arched brows – I'd never seen so much beauty in one place. I made a mental note to buy a new mascara. Wash my hair. Look into the cost of a nose job. There was just so much I didn't know.

~

'So, today we'll begin with a bit of product training, followed by some one-on-one shadowing. There's a lot to learn, and we don't expect you to get it all immediately, but the more you put into learning the basics the easier things will become.' Rose collected her ponytail and tossed it over the back of her shoulders. 'If that makes sense?' When women added 'if that makes sense?' to the end of a sentence that made perfect sense, it made me want to riot. I said it all the time.

'Your laptops should be ready by this afternoon, so we'll pivot to e-learning then.'

I looked over at Coco, who always seemed to have drunk one too many shots of espresso. We smiled at each other, nodded, and returned our eyes to Rose.

'Great. Let's get started.'

We were seated at the same long glass table that had separated Luna and me the week before, inside the meeting room called *Jean*. At the centre of the table, a predictably artful pile of figs and smoked almonds was flanked by a white teapot on one side and a French press on the other. As I reached for the French press, Rose deposited a spiral-bound tome on the table beside me. She provided Coco with an identical volume.

'It's the rytuał Employee Resource Guide!' Coco declared, prematurely, reaching a hand across the table towards me. 'The rytuał bible.'

'That's right,' Rose said. 'Thank you, Coco. Let's open to page three.'

I leafed through pages dedicated to each product. Glazed Lip Oil. Bloom Cheek Tint. Sheer Dew Foundation. Brightstar Eyeshadow. Lash Paint Mascara. The Glow Show Bronzer. Three humble skincare offerings: Cleanse, Treat, Hydrate. One fragrance, soon to be two. Ten products to generate more than two hundred million dollars in profit, but of course there were different shades of each vial, pot or palette. A little block of ingredients danced beside each picture: sodium-benzoate-ascorbyl-phospho-limo-copherol.

'We'll begin with the lip oil, because how could we not?' Rose continued. She pulled a tube from her pocket. 'The first time I tried this product, I was sitting on Luna's lounge room floor.' She stared at the back wall, caught in a private screening. 'She told me she was starting a makeup brand, and I thought she was joking. But then she showed me this.'

'How did you two meet?' I asked. Rose paused for a moment, even less than a moment – a split second – as if she was deciding which answer to give.

'I was modelling a lot in my twenties. I met her at a shoot one day. There was something magical about her, even then.' The words felt well-rehearsed. 'The lip oil was the first product Luna wanted to make, because at the time matt lipstick was dominating the market, and she hated the way it dried the lips.'

Rose kept her focus on the facts in front of her. Her voice was soothing. I let myself be held by the idea that things could be as simple as combining the right ingredients; that the right ingredients even existed.

Eleven

For each day of our training, lunch was provided. I would soon learn that there was rarely ever reason to bring lunch from home, or leave the office during lunch hours – between the trainings, manager meetings, external supplier summits and lunch just for the sake of it, most days were catered.

When rytuał did lunch, they went hard, and there was always a tablecloth. As we walked into the kitchen I caught Eva re-arranging squares of golden focaccia as if they were to be a permanent fixture. Only after moving one piece to four different locations did she turn back to the stove and retrieve two giant pots of soup. On the table, three separate clusters of wine bottles were presented at one-metre intervals.

'Shall we take a seat?' Rose asked. The light shining through the kitchen window caught her perfect side profile.

'Sure,' I said. Coco and I sat on either side of Rose. The table was set for at least fifteen, and as we took our seats, people flowed into the kitchen in dribs and drabs.

'Coco, what were you doing before you joined us at rytuał?' Rose asked as she reached for a piece of focaccia.

'I was running my own business. Online. Not like this, much smaller.' She fiddled with a ring on her left middle finger; yellow gold with a jagged pink stone.

'That sounds like the perfect education for a role with us.' She smiled, polite but definitive. There would be no further questions. Rose was comfortable in the silence.

'I'm sorry about Tom,' I said, leaning towards Rose and nearly whispering. Rose turned all the way around to face me.

'It needed to happen.' She exhaled like a full stop. Eva coughed lightly from behind us. I looked around to discover that at least twelve very shiny people had filled out the remaining place settings.

'Lunch is served. Today we have Moroccan lentil stew with fresh-baked focaccia, as well as a rocket and pear salad with apple cider vinegar dressing. Bon appétit.'

'Drink? Pink or bubbles?' Rose asked, already reaching for a bottle of rosé.

'Pink. Thanks.'

'I'm not really a wine person,' Coco interjected from just beyond Rose's shoulder.

~

When we returned to *Jean*, a MacBook had been positioned in front of each of our chairs, unmarred by fingerprints or careless behaviour – they were brand-new, still slick with protective plastic. As we took our seats Rose simply said, 'Take your resource guides home with you and move through them at your own pace. It's not something that needs to be learnt by rote, but it will help.'

My eyes were heavy after a glass and a half of rosé. As I stared at the last page we'd consulted, I tried to discern a product *Feature* from a *Benefit*, to no avail. I shut the book and looked up at Rose.

'Let's move on to the nitty-gritty. If you could both please open your laptops.'

'Are we going to do any more product training?' I asked.

Rose looked back at me, blankly. Coco peered over the top of her already-open computer.

'Do you feel you need more?' Rose said, puzzled. 'The opportunity to digest the information is yours now.'

I swallowed. 'Of course, sorry.'

'I know what I'm doing this weekend!' Coco shimmied her shoulders with delight. It was hard to imagine Coco existing prior to her commencement at rytuał, which is to say it was hard to imagine her having been born more than forty-eight hours prior.

'Let's get started,' Rose said. 'The password is printed on a sticker inside your laptops.'

I pried the smooth metal lips open. A label beside the built-in camera read *HAGAR0305*. I cocked my head to the right. The numbers were my birthday. The word, I didn't recognise.

'What's the matter, Marnie?'

'Are the passwords, like, related to something?'

'They always contain a woman's name and your date of birth. It's like the meeting rooms: we use the names of women we believe deserved a better story.'

'Mine says Hedy!' Coco said. 'Oh! Hedy Lamarr? My dad loved her. Loves her. She's dead, he's not. Oh no! Was I not supposed to tell?'

'It's fine, Coco. I don't think any of us will be hacking into your computer any time soon.'

'Who's Hagar?'

Coco perked up again, relentless in her enthusiasm. 'From the Bible! She was an Egyptian *slave*. She was forced to carry Sarah's child.' I didn't want to ask who Sarah was.

'Thank you, Coco,' Rose said, before pressing on. 'BlissScreen is our customer service software. Through this platform we can communicate with our customers over multiple channels.'

I fed the letters into the password box. My staff portrait filled the circle above my name. Something had happened to the photo that made my face look taut and uncomfortable, although there was a chance that it was just my face.

When I pressed enter, the BlissScreen interface appeared. A selection of folders ran down the left-hand side of the window, with titles such as *Orders*, *Returns* and *Sensitive escalations*. My cold, stretched face stared back at me from the circular profile picture at the top right corner of the screen.

'Here at rytuał, the majority of our customer service work is done by our partners overseas. We keep our sensitive customer escalations for the team on the ground here, just to ensure we can recover as many customers as possible. If that makes sense.'

'What's a sensitive escalation?' Coco asked.

'Anything we receive that requires a'—she searched for the words—'light touch.'

'Like, complaints?'

'Something like that.' Rose smiled, no teeth.

I clicked on *Sensitive escalations*. Hundreds of unanswered emails appeared within the little folder, as if Mary Poppins were purging the contents of her bottomless satchel. The subject line of the first email read YOU FUCKING SLUTS STOLE MY MONEY.

'Isn't this, like . . . a lot?' I said, scrolling through what appeared to be a never-ending list.

'It is, but it's just what happens. In the beginning, you sell fewer products, so you face less criticism. As the size of the consumer base grows, so does the number of detractors. And the number of people who have – how should I put this – an opportunistic nature.' Rose retrieved a white keyboard from a shelving unit at the corner of the room. As she placed it on the table, she clicked a little black remote twice; the lights in the room dimmed, and the *Sensitive escalations* folder was projected onto the wall behind her. With the remote, she opened the first email. 'Always such creative language,' she said, sighing.

> I BOUGHT ONE OF YOUR CREAMS FROM THE WESTVILLE STORE THE DAY BEFORE MY WEDDING AND IT MADE MY FACE SO RED I LOOKED LIKE A RADISH IN ALL THE PHOTOS. TRIED TO RETURN IT BUT THE WOMAN AT THE STORE SAID I'D USED TOO MUCH. I AM REQUESTING A REFUND AND A FREE MASCARA.

'We prefer to contact people by phone when we can. That's why the telephone field is mandatory.'

'Why?' Coco asked.

'People are more amenable on the phone. Shall we give Sandra a call?'

She scrolled to Sandra's contact information, and with another click of her remote a dial tone flooded the room. After four rings, Sandra answered.

'Hello?'

'Hello, Sandra. My name is Rose. I'm calling from rytuał cosmetica. Is now a good time?' She spoke at a slightly lowered pitch. It was soothing, but firm.

'Are you a real person?'

Rose laughed, a Bravo TV kind of laugh. 'As far as I'm aware, I'm a real person.'

'Well, good.' Sandra sounded disappointed. 'The girl at your Westville store said I couldn't return the cream I bought. It ruined all of my wedding photos.'

'Do you remember who it was you spoke with at Westville?'

'She had long hair. Big eyebrows. Eyes like a bug.'

'Thank you, Sandra. That's really helpful. I can see that your initial purchase was made in March, which is outside our returns window—'

'I'm about to walk into the supermarket so I don't have a lot of time.'

'I won't keep you, I promise. I'm just trying to get a clear picture. I want to be able to help you as best I can.'

'Okay.'

'So, you purchased rytuał Hydrate in March, but given it's now June, may I ask if anything else has been going on for you in the interim?'

'What do you mean?'

'Outside of this incident, is there anything going on for you that might be causing you distress? No need to share if you don't feel comfortable, but life does contain a variety of textures. It's helpful for us to get the full picture.'

Sandra was silent.

'Life is really hard, Sandra. Sometimes it all feels like too much. I understand.'

'You don't know me—'

'You're right, Sandra, I don't. But I'd like to.'

Sandra went quiet again. Then, a little whimper made its way into the phone, muffled by a hand or a sleeve. I couldn't believe what I was hearing. Rose stared up at the ceiling, biding her time.

Eventually, Sandra said, 'I'm fine.'

'Okay, my apologies. I must have misread.'

'He left.'

'What was that?'

'My husband. He left. Two months, that's all it took.'

'I'm so sorry to hear that, Sandra.'

'Yeah, well, what can you do.'

Rose paused. She was an athlete of empathy. She made it look so easy. 'Has anyone told you that it wasn't your fault?' she said, eventually.

Suddenly, Sandra was sobbing. 'How do you know that?'

'It's okay, Sandra. I promise. Everything is going to be okay.'

'Thank you. I—'

'We'll send out a small gift to thank you for your considered feedback. Could I ask you to share your postal address with us in the same thread as your original message?'

'Yeah. Okay. Thank you. It's been a hard day, I'm sorry.'

'No need to be sorry, Sandra, I'm glad we could help. I'll get that complimentary gift sent out to you right away. Be gentle with yourself, Sandra, and feel free to call back with any other questions. Thank you.'

'Bye—'

Rose ended the call. She slid the remote into her pocket.

'We want to minimise returns as much as possible. The small gift we send is a sample-size cheek tint and a handwritten note. Much cheaper than a refund. Any questions?' As if she'd flipped a switch, Rose's voice had returned to its regular pitch. I looked at Coco. Her mouth was wide open. For once, she was speechless.

~

At 5.02, Rose dismissed us. As we stepped out into the hallway, the smell of rytuał *She* flooded my nostrils. 'They must be pumping that through the air vents or something,' I said to Coco.

'They have diffusers positioned in the walls throughout the office. It's in the resource guide.' Her dimples punctuated the end of her sentence. We turned towards reception, and as the glass doors parted I saw Luna sitting bolt upright, cross-legged on one of the plush pink couches. A lime-green knit jumper hugged her torso.

'Marnie!' she said, as she sprang up to wrap her arms around me.

'Wow, I love that jumper. So fun. So chic,' Coco said, hovering awkwardly beside us. Luna eventually removed her arms from my waist and turned to Coco. 'Thank you, Coco. It was my grandmother's.'

'Your Polish grandmother?' Coco said, her eyes opportunistically wide.

'That's right.'

Rytuał

'Fajna stylówka!' Coco spluttered, as if she were sneezing. She kept her wide eyes pinned to Luna's face. When I looked over at Luna, she was nodding, but her eyes were void of recognition. 'I'm Polish, too! On my dad's side. Mum's family are from Korea,' Coco added.

'How wonderful!' Luna said, finally. 'Sadly, I never learnt the language, but I hope to one day.'

Coco's smile clung to her face for dear life. Eventually, Eva appeared behind us and said, 'Coco, I'll see you out.'

Red patches bloomed on Coco's neck. She did as she was told. When Coco was gone, Luna turned to me and said, 'Drink?'

~

The sun had begun to set beyond the windows in Luna's office, which cast a warm glow over its contents. Everything was expertly positioned to ensure the room was cosy, but functional. Once inside, Luna peeled off the jumper, revealing a baby-pink T-shirt. 'Please, sit,' she said as I hovered in the doorway. I moved obediently to the velvet couch.

'Espresso martini?' she asked, already pouring from a bottle of vodka.

'Why not?'

'I could give you a list of reasons if you want, but none of them taste as good as coffee and vodka.' She looked childish as she raised the cocktail shaker above her head and jolted it from side to side. Her arms were surprisingly muscular. The T-shirt had exposed seams that crept up the front of her body and wrapped around her shoulders.

'How was your day?' I asked as she lowered the shaker back to bar level and split its juice between two glasses.

'You can do better than that,' she said.

'Sorry, that was a weird thing to ask.' My cheeks sizzled.

'It wasn't weird, Marnie, it was just boring! Ask me something that matters. Ask me something you actually want to know the answer to.'

'I don't know, I don't really have any questions—'

'Okay, I'll go first then.' She scooped up the glasses and made her way over to the couch. 'Do you remember Mr Lloyd?'

'Who?'

'Mr Lloyd. He taught Year Four. Short, balding?' She handed me a martini glass with a look I could tell was pointed, but couldn't work out what it was pointing towards.

'Oh, yeah! I remember that guy. Always wore cargo shorts.'

'That's him.' She nestled into the arm of the couch. When she'd found a comfortable position, she flicked off her loafers and let them drop to the floor. They bounced off the shiny concrete like a set of dice. 'Handsy.'

'Oh, god. Do you mean . . .? I didn't know that. With you?'

She nodded, attempting a slack smile.

'Does he still teach?'

'No, no. He's dead now. I just . . . I didn't know if you knew.'

'I didn't, although my memory is really bad. I have about four memories from the ages of zero to ten.'

'Too much life to remember it all,' she said. 'You did well this morning.'

'At The Clearing?'

She raised her glass to lip level as she nodded.

'It's men, right? That's the secret?'

'It's women,' she said, correcting me. 'But, yes, we clear altercations with men that might detract from our performance at work. Things we're struggling to let go of. The systemic fuckery of it all.' She made a twirling gesture with her hand to indicate *et cetera, et cetera.* 'What else can we do?'

'That's great,' I said. 'I love that.'

'You haven't drunk anything. Is something wrong?'

I scrambled to pick up the glass. The brown liquid was cold and sweet. 'It's delicious,' I said.

'I know.' Luna pulled her phone from her pocket and tapped at it purposefully. Ambient synth music filled the silence. I tried to find the location of the speakers, but after two laps around the room my eyes gave up.

'They're in the walls,' Luna said. 'Everything's hidden in the walls here.'

'Oh,' I said. 'Right.'

'Tell me something else,' she said, leaning over her legs towards me. 'Tell me something I don't know about Marnie Sellick.'

'There isn't much to tell,' I said, while simultaneously tearing through my life's memories for something upbeat and interesting. 'At my old job, I once had to mop up a woman's vomit while she continued to participate in a cycle class, which really made me re-evaluate my own commitment to fitness.'

Luna laughed, then downed the rest of her drink. She stood up from the couch and moved to the window, staring out at the fading light. After a moment, she said, 'I'm a pretty straightforward person. When I let someone in, I let them all the way in. I love fast and I love fiercely. I don't do things by halves.'

'Okay.'

'I want to love all of you, Marnie. But you have to let me in.'

'Okay.' I pressed my thumbnail into my index finger. Something rumbled around in the space below my vocal cords, but I couldn't let it out. Not yet. It was a cockroach and a bad smell. It was a mistake made so many times over. It was the worst thing I'd ever done, and it was just something that happened to me.

~

The prize was for the best unproduced screenplay written by a person under the age of thirty. I thought the age limit was probably counterproductive, but as a person under the age of thirty who really needed a win, it felt appropriate to say I was thrilled that Fifth Act Film was shining a light on emerging creatives. They held a function in honour of the finalists and invited the industry to sniff them out. This, of course, was designed to showcase Fifth Act's great taste, as the scripts they wanted to produce had already been optioned. The winner received a modest cash prize in addition to a year-long mentorship.

Spencer Healey had been an executive producer at Fifth Act for seven years. Before that, he'd been a development producer and a sports journalist. He was a chameleon: equally at home smoking cigars with crusty masculine types and sifting over romantic failures with young women. Everyone loved him. He was so charming that his lazy right eye often went unnoticed. I shaved right down to baby-soft skin every time I saw him.

The function was held upstairs at a pub in South Melbourne. I felt like a glass of rosé, but rosé was apparently not a basic beer, wine or spirit. 'It's the *most* basic wine,' I said to the bartender.

A beefy laugh erupted behind me.

We hadn't been introduced yet, but we'd emailed. We'd spoken on the phone once – when he was sharing the good news – but my brain was coke and mentos as I tried to process what he was saying. I hadn't taken notice of his voice, only what the call meant. 'She has a point,' he said, as he stepped in beside me. He was wearing a white shirt – open collar – under a navy-blue suit jacket. His silver hair, swept ever so gently to the right, had stubborn strands of blond. His shoulders looked as if they'd been shaped by an ice-cream scoop. He was a foot taller than me, and he was wearing a wedding ring, but I was too young to remember which finger a wedding ring was worn on (which is to say I noticed it straight away, and wilfully ignored it). If you'd only seen a still image of him, it wouldn't make sense, but the equation of his confidence, his height and a third, indefinable thing made him an obvious choice. 'I've got it,' he said. 'Pour the woman a rosé.'

'Thanks!' I was out of breath.

'It's nice to finally meet you, Marnie.' He held out his hand and I shook it. It was nice to cosplay professionalism. It made me feel as if I might one day understand it. At the time I was working at a theatre bar with a handful of people I'd gone to uni with. A handshake was exotic.

'Likewise. Thank you so much.' I smiled, then struggled to return my mouth to neutral. It sat somewhere between a full grin and an attentive curve, and it made me look possessed. I know because I checked in the mirror when I got home that night, when I was replaying the night over and over, still catching my breath.

'Are you here alone?' he asked. Mum was on night shift. It was before the first seam had begun to pucker. I'd asked my housemate, Sophie, who also worked at the bar, to come with me but she said she was working. I knew she wasn't working at the bar that night – we all had access to the rosters – but she did have a lot of writing samples and no creative employment on the horizon, and I think that was the real work she was talking about.

'I am,' I said. 'Dani brought her whole family, though, so just pretend a few of them are with me.'

We both looked towards Dani, who had written a young adult feature film, which was fitting given she was still a very young adult. As her mum leant over to fix Dani's shirt collar, her Louis Vuitton bag slid down her arm to the floor. The entire extended family rushed to assist her. He laughed again. It was thrilling. 'Of course you're this funny in person, you're a riot on the page.' He turned his back on Dani. 'You're an incredible talent, Marnie. I'm so glad we'll be working together,' he said, and I felt as though he was holding something that belonged to me.

'Spencer, we're about ready to start.' Lily appeared beside us. I didn't know she was Lily, then. I thought she was another Richmond young professional who could tell I didn't belong. She was wearing an Apple Watch. It flashed incessantly with new email notifications; she was the duck's legs flapping wildly underwater. He placed his hand on my hip as he left – feather-light, peppered with plausible deniability – and said, 'It was so nice to meet you.'

Later, after I'd checked my smile in the mirror, I turned off all the lights and let myself imagine his hand cupping my hip again. Even revisiting it felt dangerous – I had to do it in the dark, under the covers, in porcelain silence. I wanted his hand to do other things. I wanted it to reach inside me and touch the hunger I was yet to fully understand. Maybe his hand could translate it for me. That was the root of it all; I wanted him to make sense of me.

Twelve

'Hello?'

'Hi, good morning.' Coco was already sweating. 'Am I speaking with Francesca?'

'Yeah. Who's calling?'

'My name is Coco, I'm giving you a call from, ah—'

'From where?'

'rytuał cosmetics.' Her eyes widened with panic. 'rytuał cosmetica.' She fiddled with the gold ring that guarded her left middle finger.

'Oh. Okay. Well, yeah, I ordered something from you and when it arrived the foundation had exploded all over the box.'

'Yes. Right. But I was just wondering . . . if that really happened?'

Rose started to sweat, too.

'What? Are you calling me a liar?'

'No, I'm sorry, no. I just wondered if . . .' She looked to Rose for guidance, but received none. 'I was wondering if there was anything else going on?'

'What are you talking about?'

'Did the foundation really explode, or did you just want another one?' Rose turned to face the wall. It was a disaster.

'Is this a prank call? If it's not, I'll call consumer affairs. You sent me a box with a broken foundation. You have to replace it or refund me. What was your name again?'

'Coco,' she replied, without thinking. Rose shook her head. I covered my face. I wanted to turn myself inside out on Coco's behalf.

'If you don't send me a new foundation, Coco, I'm going to make sure you're the one to pay for it. So you better run on down to your shitty little warehouse and—'

Coco ended the call.

'What happened?' Rose turned as if she'd heard strange footsteps approaching behind her.

'I hung up.' Coco was shaking.

'Why? We could have recovered her.'

Rose wasn't wearing any makeup, which I wouldn't have noticed if I hadn't seen her wearing a full face of 'no-makeup makeup' so many times before. The reality of 'no makeup' was nothing like the counterfeit. Which did seem like a tear in the fabric of reality, or perhaps a cruel Ponzi scheme. When my brain returned to the room, Coco was properly crying. Rose was standing at an uncomfortable distance, not really doing anything about it.

'We'll refund her. I'll do it at lunch. Marnie, why don't we try a role-play,' she said. A slug of snot fell from Coco's nose to her lap.

Rose came to sit in the seat beside me, and we swivelled to face each other. I felt exposed, my body soft and vulnerable – like audience participation, I really hated role-play. Plus, I was wearing a pair of jeans that was half a size too small, and as a result my stomach was starting to gurgle in protest. Rose fastened her eyes to mine as my cheeks began to glow. Finally, she closed her eyes and took a deep breath. After a moment, she opened them and said, 'Ring-ring,' in a singsong tone, which was an extremely serious way to make a pretend phone sound.

'Hello,' I said.

She was quick to correct me. 'You're calling me, remember?'

'Right.'

'Ring-ring. Hello?'

'Hi, my name is Marnie, I'm calling from rytuał cosmetica. Is now a good time?'

'I'm about to pick up the kids from school—'

'I won't take up much of your time, I . . .' We hadn't discussed what Rose's fictional frustrations were, and for a moment I considered breaking the fourth wall to ask, but her probing stare gave me the feeling that she really wanted me to just get on with it. 'We received your email regarding your recent order. I'm so sorry that the cheek tint isn't working out for you.'

'It gave me contact dermatitis. My doctor said I should take legal action.'

'I'm so sorry. Were you prescribed any kind of topical treatment for that?'

'A cream. But I want my money back.' Rose was stony-faced. I could feel Coco leaning across the table to get a closer look.

'I completely understand, but can I ask you a couple of questions first?'

'I told you, I'm about to pick up the kids. I just want a refund.'

The fact that this was only a role-play had no effect on how fizzy the whole thing made my insides feel. 'How old are your children?' I said. I had no idea where I was going with this.

Rose's eyebrow twitched, but she kept up the act. 'Nine and four.'

'Right. That must be a lot for you. Are you . . . working as well?'

'No. I want to go back to work, though. I just—'

'Need more time?' For a brief moment, the conversation became a painless dance. These imaginary characters – Rose, a harried suburban mother of two, me, a competent customer service professional – took on a life of their own.

'Yes,' Rose said. 'I want more time to myself.'

'Of course. I understand. If I could get a few details about the treatment you received for your dermatitis, I'd be happy to coordinate a refund for you.'

'It's okay, I really have to go in a second.'

'You're more than a mother,' is what I said next, which was not something I'd ever imagined myself saying to another woman, role-playing or otherwise.

Rose softened. 'Thank you for saying that.'

'So, I'll just need the date of your reaction, as well as the date you received medical care—'

'You know what? It's fine. I'll give it to my sister. Her skin is tougher than mine.'

'Are you sure? I'd be happy to sort this out for you.'

'No, it's fine. Thanks. Have a good day.'

We relaxed into our chairs, as if released by a pulley system.

'That was good, Marnie. Really good.'

From the other side of the table, Coco raised her hand.

'I agree, like, totally, so good. Great recovery. But, feedback-wise, Marnie, remember yesterday Rose said to only ever apologise in a general way, like, "I'm sorry to hear that," because if you say "I'm sorry," you're kind of accepting the product fault as, like, our fault. Isn't that right, Rose?' Coco ran a hand through her hair, smoothing over her bob. I wondered what it would feel like to punch her in the face.

'Well, yes, Coco does have a point, but I don't think it's—'

'We're just, like, rytuał's front line, and I think we have to remain, like, risk-aware. Don't you think, Marnie?'

'Oh, fuck off, Coco,' I said, without thinking. Coco recoiled like a wounded puppy.

'Marnie! We don't speak to other women like that here,' Rose said.

'Sorry. Sorry, Coco.'

Rose exhaled. 'I'll need to call Luna. I'm sure you read in the resource guide that one of the key pillars of our business is respect for and support of all other women. All other rytuał employees.' I had not read this in the resource guide. I hadn't thought about the resource guide since I'd packed it away the day before. 'Coco, why don't you take lunch. There should be a grazing board and some pastries in the kitchen.'

'I'm okay, I can stay here—'

'Go.'

Coco slunk out of her chair and out the glass door.

'I didn't mean it,' I said, half to Coco, half to Rose.

Rose sighed. 'Come on.'

I followed her out the door.

~

When we arrived at Luna's office, an entire burnt Basque cheesecake was awaiting our arrival, which seemed excessive for a meeting that had been called not ten minutes prior. Various jugs of liquid accompanied the cake on the coffee table, and of course there were also figs and smoked almonds. Luna was sitting at her desk, fiddling with a pot of something. She was wearing a dark denim matching set – a tiny crop top and oversized pants. Her shoes were chunky patent leather lace-ups. Everything she wore looked brand-new. It probably was.

'Good morning, Luna,' Rose said, as she pushed the large door open.

'Good morning, two!' A suite of grammatical idiosyncrasies populated the rytuał communications guidelines. Addressing the recipients of an email, or the population of a room, by the number of people involved was one of the most baffling rules. It made perfect sense, but at the same time it made no sense at all. Occasionally I googled it to recall if I'd learnt it before I arrived, or if it actually was specific to rytuał. And then in two months' time I would do it all over again: like beating out a word's syllables until it was empty sound.

Luna jogged out from behind her desk enthusiastically. When she was standing in front of us, I saw her decide who to greet first. She took two steps towards me, but Rose intercepted, pulling her in for an over-the-shoulder hug. When Rose released her, she wrapped her arms around me.

'Shall we sit?' she said, motioning towards the cheesecake and the couch behind it.

Rose took a seat in the middle of the couch. She poured herself a cup of black coffee. Luna brushed a finger over my arm as we moved to opposite ends of the couch. When she was seated, Luna poured from another jug, which revealed a bright-blue slime.

'Blue Majik,' she said. This did not make things any clearer. 'You should try some.' She poured a cup of slime and passed it – via Rose – to me. I expected something reminiscent of blueberry, but the reality was dirty moss.

'Mmmm,' I said, smiling at both of the women. 'Delicious.' I chased it with a huge handful of almonds.

'Now, what happened?' Luna leant into the arm of the couch, angling herself to face us both.

'We had an incident in our training session this morning, and I just think it would be helpful for Marnie to be reminded of the business's foundational pillars.'

'Is that really what you think would be helpful, Rose?' Luna reached for a fig and slid it into her mouth, unhurried.

'Yes, I just think—'

'Marnie, what did you do?'

Still negotiating almond fragments, I replied, 'I told Coco to . . . fuck off. I'm sorry, I don't know what—'

Luna rocked back into the arm of the couch and slapped her thigh. Laughter filled the room. 'You didn't,' she said, between gasps.

'I did.' I ran my tongue all the way around my mouth, digging at the last little bits of almond skin. 'I'm really sorry.'

'Luna, we need to explain to Marnie that this company is a safe space for women.'

'Rose, that's enough. Marnie, don't tell anyone else to fuck off while you're at work, okay?'

'But what about—' Rose stammered.

'I have a solution. Marnie, I know this is only your first week with us, but I'd like to formally invite you to Friday Night Drinks.'

'Luna!' Rose squared her body with Luna's, perched on the very edge of the couch. She was close to critical mass.

'Sure, I'm free on Friday. Which bar?'

Luna laughed. 'It's not that kind of drinks. You'll see.'

'She's not ready.'

'Rose, I think you need to remember that you work in Training. This isn't a Training issue, this is a Human Resources issue.'

'Do I need to speak with HR?' I asked.

'I am HR,' Luna replied. Her eyes were glowing. 'It's not really orthodox, so I send all HR emails from the Cleo Henning account.'

'You're Cleo Henning?'

'Mmm-hmm!' She nodded as if this was routine information, which set a precedent for the way I was supposed to react. The rytuał office was a well-oiled machine. The only HR professionals I knew spoke with persistent vocal fry, mainlined true crime documentaries and referred to cocktails as 'cocky-Ts'. Which is not to say that I was anti-HR, I was just pro-Luna. And I had spent too much time on the internet.

'I don't see how this is going to help,' Rose spluttered. Luna placed a hand on her knee.

'Just trust me,' she said. After a few seconds of silent negotiation, they both turned to face me. 'Friday Night Drinks will be held in the basement from 5.30 p.m. this Friday. Bring a comfortable change of clothes.' She kept her hand on Rose's knee and winked at me, which from anyone else would have seemed misplaced, but from Luna it was thrilling.

~

As Rose and I descended the stairs, her phone buzzed persistently in her pocket. When she glanced at the screen, her face dropped.

'Who's that?' I said, a little too nosy, but spending time with Luna made me bolder.

'It's nothing.' We arrived at the kitchen and turned left. 'Tom won't stop calling me.'

'Begging you to take him back?' I said, with a laugh, but Rose's deeply serious expression confirmed that yes, that was exactly what he was doing. 'Wow, I've never had anyone beg me for anything. The power must be overwhelming.'

'It's really annoying, actually.' She walked a few paces ahead of me. Something had shifted between Rose and me in Luna's office, but I'd missed the catalyst and was struggling to catch up. 'Don't tell anyone about Cleo Henning. Luna shouldn't have said that.'

'I won't,' I said. 'You can count on me.' I did a little salute, but Rose was still preoccupied with her phone. 'Friday Night Drinks sounds fun.'

Before Rose could reply, we rounded the corner to the room called *Jean*, and Coco appeared at the door.

'Welcome back, girlies. What's the latest?'

Rose walked straight past Coco, opening the door with a swift flash of her fob. 'Nothing, Coco. Let's get back to work.'

Thirteen

When I arrived at the office on Friday, Eva was suspiciously excited to see me. She jumped up from reception and ran over to greet me – presenting a mug of black coffee and a miniature blueberry danish. 'Happy graduation,' she said.

'Thanks,' I replied, accepting the bounty. She continued to stare. 'What? What's wrong?'

'Nothing! Nothing is wrong at all, everything is so right.' I took the coffee and pastry with me as I walked the familiar path to *Jean*.

The little grey screen informed me that the room was occupied, but Rose was nowhere to be seen. I was ten minutes early, which was five minutes late on Rose's time. I moved to my usual seat and began to unload my things. As I slid my laptop out of its sleeve, Coco arrived.

'Hey,' I said, fumbling at the bottom of my bag. 'I'm sorry about yesterday—'

'Totally fine, babe. It's water under the bridge.' She threw herself into the seat opposite me. She was even higher-energy than usual.

I pulled the resource guide from my bag. 'Have you been asked for your bank details or anything? I know payday is next week but I haven't filled out any forms.'

I typed *HAGAR0305* into the password window. When I returned to Coco, she stared back at me with a manic smile. 'What? Why is everyone staring at me today?'

'Friday. Night. Drinks.' She was on the verge of a scream.

'What about it?'

'We're only in week one of our training. We're not supposed to be invited until, like, week five. This is *huge*.'

'Oh! I was going to tell you about that. I'm sure you can come, too.' It was a flaccid gesture.

'I know! I am!'

'What?'

'I'm going too.' A frilly squeal finally left her mouth. 'I'm so glad we get to experience this together.'

'How did you know I was going?'

'Um, Luna told me.' She shook her head, as if it were blindingly obvious. My heart beat out of time.

'When?'

'We had a drink last night.'

I laughed. It seemed ridiculous, to think of Coco and Luna sitting across from each other in any private setting – Luna staring off into the distance, bored out of her mind, while Coco rambled on about her favourite rytuał social media campaign.

'What's funny?' she asked.

'Nothing. That's great. So cool.'

Rose arrived at the door. 'Good morning, two. Are we excited for tonight?'

'Literally so excited I can't breathe. Seriously, if I pass out, that's why.' Coco looked at me as if we were announcing our engagement.

'Same,' I added. She squealed again.

'Well, let's hope that doesn't happen. As tonight is the first Friday Night Drinks for both of you, there are a few things to keep in mind.' Coco interlaced her fingers in her lap and sat up like a straight-A student. I sat on my hands. 'What you'll experience this evening is intense. It's an opportunity for the whole team to come together and bond over a shared emotional experience. Everything we do on Friday nights is in the name of personal growth. Just remember that.' She paused to make sure we were keeping up. 'Be respectful, try to listen more than you speak, and be open to anything that comes up. I think that covers it. You'll see. But, I'm getting ahead of myself! First, let's run through some common product complaints, and then share any personal product stories that might be useful when communicating with our customers.'

I hadn't realised I was staring at Coco, my face wrapped in concern. When she caught me, I was quick to return my attention to my computer. Coco did the same. Or, we pretended to return our attention to our computers. Internally, we were circling the same thought: Luna.

~

On Fridays in the hour before lunch, the rytuał cosmetica trade meeting was held in the room called *Britney*. Everyone was required to attend, even those for whom a weekly trade meeting was inconsequential. I was becoming exceedingly familiar with *Jean* and *Britney*, which made me wonder if anyone ever scheduled a meeting in *Billie* or *Amy*, or if something was wrong with them. *Britney*'s configuration shifted with each occasion; when we'd visited for The Clearing, the chairs had been arranged widthwise, so that the front of the room was the far side as you entered. On this day, the stage was set on the right-hand side, with the chairs lined up lengthwise. The room felt bigger this way, which was disorienting. Coco, Rose and I took our seats close to the door.

The red-headed woman from The Clearing, who I recalled was named Ruth, took to the stage, alongside another woman I was yet to meet. There were just so many women. I had to remind myself that I'd only been employed by rytuał for five days. As Ruth pointed a remote at the back of the room, the rytuał logo materialised on the wall beside her. The woman I didn't recognise, who came up to Ruth's chest, had a micro fringe and a huge, nervous smile. She was wearing a pink mohair vest over a white shirt. I watched as she clocked Luna wandering into the room, the corners of her mouth struggling to reach further up her face in response.

'Good afternoon, everyone,' she said, as she wrestled with the collar of her white shirt and the neck of her vest. 'Let's get started.' A respectful silence descended. 'First, a cleansing breath. Let's take a deep inhale.' We inhaled. 'And exhale.' We exhaled.

From behind me, leaning against the window that separated *Britney* from the rest of the building, Luna said, 'Beautiful, everyone,' and the woman I didn't recognise reapplied the same uncomfortable smile.

Ruth took a step closer to centre stage. 'I'm Ruth,' she said, 'head of Finance, for those who are new to our weekly trade meetings.' She looked directly at Coco and me. Coco did a little wave.

'And I'm Noor, head of Retail,' the woman I didn't recognise added.

Ruth changed the slide to reveal a pie chart. The text that explained what each segment represented was pink, which meant it was near impossible to read from a distance. 'This week we've unfortunately fallen short of targets both in store and online, which is disappointing but not a complete surprise.'

'Why isn't it a surprise?' Luna pried.

Ruth swallowed and took a small step closer to the projection. 'The launch of a new competitor.'

'Which competitor?'

'Lumo Beauty.' She went to the next slide. A photo of Emily Lumo – reality TV contestant turned influencer turned comedian and fashion designer, and now creator of a beauty brand – filled the screen. Beside her blinding white teeth and golden tan were three bottles of product. Numbers were presented beside the bottles, but again, they were near impossible to read.

Noor chimed in. 'We did anticipate that skincare would drop throughout Lumo's launch week, but makeup and fragrance dropped with it, which was not in our projections. We chalk this up to the skincare campaign, and upon reflection we believe . . .' Noor's voice wavered, as if she had something stuck in her throat. 'We believe it would have been more successful to push makeup throughout the month of their launch. Because they're skincare only.'

Ruth changed the slide – a bar graph of some variety – but Luna tapped her nails against the glass and we all turned to face her. She groaned. 'I can own that,' she said, edging closer to the audience. 'We doubled down on skincare because of me. Noor suggested focusing on makeup, but I didn't listen. I apologise, Noor. You were right.'

'That's okay,' Noor replied, elated but trying to keep it under wraps. 'It's fine.' I watched as Ruth tried to work out if Noor would continue and, when she realised Noor was instead preoccupied with smiling at Luna, forged ahead.

'Despite this,' Ruth said, 'projections for Q4 are positive as we prepare to pivot to the release of rytuał *We*.' The graph disappeared, replaced by a fragrance bottle – the familiar hazy white glass and chrome cap that housed rytuał *She*. 'We're confident that fragrance will continue to be a great profit driver as we develop our new skincare offerings.'

Ruth looked over at Luna, so we all looked over at Luna. 'Can I tell them?' Luna said, bursting with childlike enthusiasm. Ruth and Noor both nodded, but they weren't nearly as excited by their shared secret as Luna was. Luna flitted to the front of the room and wrapped an arm around Noor. 'After a lot of very tedious conversations surrounding the future of rytuał cosmetica, we've decided that our next offering will be . . .' She looked to Noor, who looked to Ruth, who looked to Luna. 'A night serum. Brand-new formula. A new hero ingredient.'

Immediately, people began to clap. 'Incredible,' someone said from behind me. 'Genius,' said another voice. Coco added, 'It's definitely retinal.'

'But that's not all!' Luna said, above the hubbub. 'I was going to save this for later, but I think we're all in need of a pick-me-up. I'm pleased to announce that the name of this new product will be'—she eyed the crowd, from right to left—'rytuał *Eve*!'

A standing ovation took place before Luna had even finished speaking. I joined Rose and Coco in getting to our feet, smiling like carnival clowns. Luna did a small curtsy. She let the applause continue. As I beat my palms together, I thought to myself, *Finally*. And I really was happy, that afternoon, as we celebrated the serum called *Eve*, in the room called *Britney*.

~

After lunch, I was about to round the last corner back from the bathroom when I heard Coco's signature nasal timbre. She was trying to whisper, but it was a setting they forgot to include in her code. I stopped just before the hall unravelled into the bright light of the kitchen – Coco's black Mary Janes paced behind a large pink pillar underneath the stairs that led to Luna's office.

'I don't have access to my discount yet,' she said. I held my breath, affixed to the wall. 'I only have what they've given me so far.'

My stomach gurgled. Coco paused for a moment, but it was hard to tell if it was a conversational pause or something more reactionary. Eventually, she exhaled, and said, 'This is really stressful for me, Dad. They have this Friday Night Drinks thing tonight and I think we might do, like . . . ayahuasca or something.' She was crying – very softly, it was only just audible. I hadn't even considered ayahuasca as a possibility. I thought it was just a drinks thing.

'Yeah, okay, I'll ask them. I'll do it. We can start selling as soon as the discount clears. Okay. Bye.'

She exhaled. My cheeks began to ache. I didn't know when I'd started smiling. I touched a hand to my face to make sure it was still there. Beneath the skin, my blood simmered with possibility.

Fourteen

At the foot of the stairs to the basement, candlelight sat in waiting. The contents of the ANZ workspace had been cleared to make way for rows of rattan-backed chairs. Luna moved directly to the far end of the room, where two of the chairs faced each other. Beside one, a tall side table housed a collection of crystals, a glass water bottle and two tubes of Glazed Lip Oil. This was Luna's chair.

On the left side of the room, the buffet was host to a predictably artful grazing platter and a selection of drinks. Five carafes held liquids from clear to deep red. Coco pushed past me to take her place on the left side of the front row. Rose hung back, drawn into a conversation with two amazonian women beside the stairwell, their chins at her eye level. They were the only women in the room who looked to be over the age of fifty.

I walked down the aisle and peeled off to the right. As soon as I sat down, my hands searched for something to do. I was hot and itchy, so I stood up and tiptoed past Coco to the table of provisions. I felt her eyes on my back as I passed her.

'Would you like something to drink, Marnie?' Eva asked, as she pre-emptively poured a glass of rosé. 'Take two, I'll pour a second one.' Before I could object, Eva handed me another glass. I was double-parked at the grazing platter when Rose edged in beside me.

'You never forget your first,' she said, collecting a fig and four almonds on a pink napkin. 'Enjoy.' She turned towards the back of the room. I skulked back to my seat, hands full of wine. As I sat down, The Lauras materialised to my right. 'Hi, Marnie,' they said.

'Laura. Laura. Hi, Laura.'

'How are you finding your time at rytuał?' said the blue-eyed one.

'We're so glad you could join us this evening,' said the brown-eyed one.

The green-eyed one said nothing. She took a sip from her Aperol spritz.

'It's great. So great,' I said. I raised my eyebrows and shoulders at the same time. 'The greatest.' I pulled a tube of lip oil from my pocket and coated my lips in it. The Lauras just watched.

Luna's voice from the front of the room rescued me. 'Good evening, sisters. Welcome to Friday Night Drinks.'

People began to clap. Luna paused.

'I'm consistently impressed by this team, and how we've committed to placing people at the centre of everything we do. From the bottom of my heart, thank you.' She placed both hands over her heart, layering them like sheets of pastry. The rest of the crowd mimicked the gesture, nodding in reverence. 'I've been thinking a lot this week about stories. How do the stories we tell impact both our present and future? Our featured rytuałist this week has been influenced quite heavily by the stories the world has told her. I think we can all relate to that.'

The response was a resounding 'Mmmm'. I reached for the first of my wineglasses and drained it. I wanted to fill myself with things, to stop my body from floating away from the rigid chair.

'I should also take this moment to acknowledge that we have two new rytuałists with us this evening. Please, make Marnie and Coco welcome.'

The crowd applauded. It was neat and restrained, but when I caught the faces of the women behind me, their eyes were wild. I turned back to Luna. She was smiling directly at me. I swapped my empty wineglass for the full one.

'As always, I'd like to begin with a grounding practice. Please, take hold of the hands on either side of you.'

Blue-eyed Laura reached for my hand. I wedged the wineglass between my thighs.

'Close your eyes, and come to join me in silence.'

I kept my eyes open until I was sure everyone else had closed theirs.

'We come together after a week of working to change the way the beauty industry operates, in order to change the way that *we* operate. We come here to look inside ourselves, to examine the things we've accepted as truth from society and to challenge these ideals. We come together to push out masculine norms and welcome in the divine feminine. We conspire together to overthrow destructive patriarchal standards, replacing them with the power inside each person present today.' The crowd hummed in agreement. 'Feet flat on the floor, three breaths all together,' Luna commanded. I moved to readjust my legs, but didn't catch my wineglass in time. It shattered against the concrete.

'Fuck,' I whispered. From the corner of my eye, I saw Eva race over to the refreshments table and collect a stack of cloth napkins. I made a feeble attempt to clean up the mess with my bare hands, and by the time Eva arrived with the napkins I could have kissed her.

'It's fine, it's totally fine,' she whispered as she scooped up as much broken glass as the soggy napkins could hold. Luna watched the mess unfold, holding her audience on tenterhooks while Eva cleaned up my act.

'Exhale out any stale air,' Luna continued, at last, as Eva scuttled away with the debris. 'And inhale.' The group did as commanded, with gusto. 'Hold.' My chest crept up towards my chin. 'Exhale, on voice.' The room vibrated with all kinds of battle cries. The Lauras fluttered their lips like horses. We repeated the same thing twice more. 'Wonderful. Let's begin. This week's featured rytuałist comes from our Training team. She's been with me since the very beginning. Please welcome Rose Liu.'

I turned to find Rose hovering at the back of the room. On Luna's instruction, she walked down the aisle to occupy the seat beside her. As she sat down, she shrank into the already-oversized cardigan that cloaked her upper body. *What now?*, I wondered. No one outcome felt plausible, because everything was possible.

'Thank you, Luna.'

'Rose, if you're ready, we will begin the session now.'

Rose nodded.

'You will remain aware of everything we discuss and the events that take place this evening. At any point, you can end the session with the word "Set". Nothing that happens during this session will leave this room. You are safe here. Please confirm with the word "Prime".'

'Prime,' Rose replied.

I often felt as though I was holding a foot in each camp when it came to spirituality. I wanted to believe in something, but couldn't help but find most things disappointing. Despite my desire to be in this specific room, with this specific group of people, I winced at the sincerity of it all.

'Please, close your eyes, Rose.'

Green-eyed Laura's straw gurgled against the last dregs of melted ice and Aperol.

'I'm going to ask you to recall a moment from your past in which you felt unworthy. Can you remind yourself of this feeling?'

'I can,' Rose said immediately. I looked around to discover that a handful of people in the crowd had closed their eyes, too.

'Can you describe any other specific emotions tied to that moment?' Luna leant forwards to bring herself closer to Rose.

'Shame.'

'Extend that.'

'I felt stupid. Childish. Incapable.' Rose's hands were trembling.

'And do you believe these things to be true? About yourself?'

Rose didn't reply straight away. She opened her eyes for a moment. They found mine. She returned to Luna and closed them again. 'No,' she said. 'Not all the time. Only sometimes. Only—' She stopped, but Luna was quick to pick up the slack.

'In relationships?' I wondered how many times Rose had found herself here, in this exact position. 'Do you recognise this as a pattern or cycle in your life?' Luna continued.

'I do.'

'Do you want to break this cycle?'

'I do.'

'Do you consent to allowing me to help you break this cycle this evening, in front of your fellow rytualists?'

'I do.'

'Sisters, rytualists, please agree to assisting Rose in moving through this energetic block, by affirming with the word "Cut".'

'Cut.'

'Rose, please open your eyes.' She followed the instruction. 'Do you feel comfortable sharing the memory you just recalled with the group?'

'It was . . .' She picked at something on the leg of her pants. 'It was the moment I realised my boyfriend was seeing someone else. He was cheating.' She gave the pants a final scratch. 'My ex-boyfriend.'

It was hard to reconcile Tom as someone worthy of Rose's affection, but perhaps that was exactly why we'd gathered in the basement of *Emma* that night.

'Was it the first time?'

She paused. 'No.'

'And how did you find out?'

'I found a hair tie in his bathroom. It wasn't mine.'

Luna pursed her lips and nodded. 'Rose, what kind of woman do you want to be?'

Rose stared above the crowd, collecting her thoughts. As I watched her eyes zigzag tentatively across the ceiling, I had the desire to know her – really know her.

'How do you want to feel?' Luna pressed.

'I want to feel'—her voice wavered, on the edge of tears—'complete.'

'Do you understand that to be able to think something about

ourselves – the fact that we're able to see it as a possibility – means it must already exist?'

Rose nodded.

'So, you are already complete.'

A tear trickled down Rose's face. I watched it fall from her chin to her thigh.

'How would someone who felt complete treat those who've wronged them?'

'I'm not sure,' Rose said, wiping her cheek. Luna stood up from her chair.

'What would it feel like to be sure?'

Rose's eyes narrowed.

'Let's move on to this evening's core activity. Eva?'

Eva jumped up from a seat at the back of the room and skipped to the elevator's metal doors. She tapped at her phone and the engine began to hum. As the metal jaws slid open, a muffled yelp escaped one of the lift's occupants. Whispers moved through the crowd as the two hulking women Rose had been speaking with earlier emerged, lugging a man's body down the aisle. I knew as soon as I saw his scrawny arms, but it wasn't until we were a metre apart that it sank in. Gagged with a rytuał-branded gym towel, shirtless and looking significantly worse for wear, was Tom. He wrestled against the women, but he seemed tired. And I knew from Kahli that he had a moral aversion to load-bearing exercise.

'Thank you, Bibi. Thank you, Liv,' Luna said. I mentally catalogued the names of the Very Tall Women. They forced him into what had been Luna's seat, and tied him down. Tom made another noise, but the towel dulled his best efforts. Bibi and Liv returned to the back of the room.

'Hi, Thomas,' Luna said, walking around the chair to squat in front of him. 'It's been a while.' She removed his gag.

'What the fuck is going on? Rose, help me,' Tom pleaded. The right side of his face was struggling to keep up with the left.

'Rose isn't in charge here, Thomas. It's me you have to answer to,' Luna said. 'And I know how much you love spending time with me.'

'What do you want?'

Tom's eyes moved lazily around the room, eventually landing on mine. 'Marnie? What's going on?'

Luna spun around to face me. As did the rest of the room.

'How do you know her?' Rose stammered, in Tom's direction but also at me.

Luna sprang up to standing. 'Oh, yes, I almost forgot!' she said. 'It's such a small world, isn't it.'

'What?' Rose was panicked. 'Marnie, how do you know Tom?'

'I, uh. I'm sorry.'

'Don't be sorry, Marnie. This isn't your mess.' Luna patted Tom on the shoulder twice, a little too hard. 'Tell Rose how you know Thomas.'

I looked to The Lauras. They made little flapping motions with their hands, as if I was supposed to stand, so I did, but I hated the feeling of everyone's eyes on me. 'I didn't know, until recently. But my housemate Kahli was the woman. That Tom was . . . Thomas . . .'

Luna grinned.

'Did you know that night at Caroline's?' Rose said, struggling to put it together.

'No,' I said. 'No, I only found out after.'

'Marnie, you can sit down now. You've done well.' Luna returned her attention to Tom; she crouched down beside him and stacked her hands on his left thigh. 'Whatever will we do with you.'

'Rose. Please.'

Luna returned the gag to Tom's mouth. He thrashed his head from side to side.

'Rose, I want to ask you again: how would someone who feels complete treat those who've wronged them?' Rose's body was locked in place, her mouth sealed shut. 'We can stop at any time,' Luna added. She gave one final tug on the gag and angled her body back towards Rose. The two women stared at each other – bouncing unspoken objections back and forth, built on memories only they could recall. 'Just say the word.'

'Say the word,' Tom said, his mouth full of cotton. 'Please, Rose, I'll do anything.'

'For those who didn't already know, this isn't the first unworthy man Rose has let into her life.'

Tom started to cry. A circuit broke somewhere in the back of my brain. Was this really happening?

'Earlier in her life, Rose dated a man who was physically abusive to her. She was made to feel as though she didn't deserve love. She has lived most of her life with this as a core belief. Even now.' Luna looked to Rose, who was snotty-nosed and tearstained in a distinctly glamorous way. 'Isn't that right?' she pressed.

Rose nodded.

'And who gave you that scar?'

She held Luna's gaze, suddenly assertive. 'He did.'

'What!?' Tom squawked, followed by what sounded like, 'It wasn't me.'

'Not *him*,' Rose clarified. She glanced at Tom, but only for a moment.

'That's right. So, I'll ask you again, Rose. How does someone who feels complete treat those who've wronged them?' Luna walked over to Rose and ran a finger down the length of the scar on the left side of her face.

'Acceptance,' Rose whispered.

'No,' Luna replied. 'Revenge.'

Someone at the back of the room cheered. The air was sticky.

'Sisters, let's come together to support Rose in breaking this cycle.'

The women began to chant – 'Break, break, break' – and Luna positioned Rose on the left side of Tom. Eva appeared beside her with a gold curling wand. It was plugged into an extension cord, already piping hot. The women continued to chant. Rose accepted the curling wand and returned to Tom.

'I don't understand,' I said, out loud, although the sound of the women shouting made it hard to catch my own voice.

'Tom,' Luna said, as she grasped the back of his head. 'This is for your own good. We just want to make sure you'll never do it again.' He mumbled something I couldn't hear. It was just *break, break, break, break*, in my ears, my chest, in the space between my eyebrows.

'Break the cycle,' Luna said, stepping away from Tom. 'Rose, join with your sisters now in cutting the cord.'

'Break, break, break,' the women cried. I understood in a conceptual sense what she expected Rose to do, but it was all so ridiculous. I wanted to laugh. Rose looked over just as my lips parted, and with her eyes pinned to mine, she raised the hot curling wand over her head and struck Tom in the stomach three times.

Fifteen

I woke the next morning in a cold sweat. The sheets were damp. The light through the blinds said it was mid-morning. I chugged from the stale glass of water on my bedside table. I couldn't remember when I'd left it there. I fished my phone out from beneath the duvet. 10.47.

> **LUNA PETERS**
> Drink later? Come to mine
> at 5. X

I'd crawled directly into bed when I arrived home the night before. It was after two. Kahli had left for a weekend away, so the house was dark and still. I smelt like an animal. I had stared at the women in horror, thinking I was privy to something terrible. But then the room came into focus, as if I'd been given the right prescription. The sounds Rose made each time the metal touched down were primal. 'No blows to the head,' Luna had said. Eventually, she called it quits and we chanted and drank the remaining booze. Tom promised to change his ways, as he wandered in and out of consciousness. Rose stood a little taller. The memory played like a dream. Awe and horror had the same aftertaste.

Sounds great x

She didn't need to give me her address. We all knew where she lived.

~

Luna's treehouse was wedged between two identical grey townhouses, which made the red bricks brighter by contrast. An outdoor staircase coiled its way from the carport to the first floor, arriving at a Juliet balcony. The entrance was hidden behind the carport. I ran a finger over the silver intercom, but didn't push the button. The front door was larger than I expected – I wondered how they found a piece of oak big enough to carve into this hulk of a fixture. I made a mental note to find out how doors were made. It felt important.

My phone buzzed.

ROSE LIU
Hope you had fun last night ♡

I put a heart on the message. I was still staring into the light of my phone when the door sprang open.

'Marnie!' An athleisure-clad Luna appeared. 'I saw someone loitering and hoped it was you, although one of the girls down the street recently discovered that I live here and won't stop asking for work experience.' She stuck her tongue out the right side of her mouth. 'Come in!'

I followed dutifully.

'How did you pull up this morning?' she said, moving swiftly through the hallway. When we emerged into the sunken living room, my eyes were still making sense of the entrance. Like Luna herself, it was so much grander in person.

'I'm fine, not too bad. Just tired.'

'Please, sit.'

I collapsed onto the couch with one ankle crossed under my body, but my hip cracked so loudly Luna winced. 'I think I might be getting old,' I said.

'We'll live forever. Drink?' It was so contrived, but probably true – if anyone could live forever, it would be Luna. She didn't wait for my response before she bounded off to the kitchen.

'Martini?' she said, out of view.

'Sure.' What I really wanted was a glass of water, but the want was vaporous. 'Can I ask you something?' I said. I heard glasses clink against the countertop.

'You can ask,' she said, quickly followed by, 'I'm just kidding. Go on.'

I listened to her fill the cocktail shaker with ice before I said, 'Is Tom . . . okay?'

There was a pause. Eventually, she returned from the kitchen with two frosty glasses. As she slid one across the marble coffee table and deposited herself onto the couch, she said, 'I don't know what you're talking about.'

'After last night.'

She stared at me as if I was stuck on mute. 'I don't know what you're talking about,' she repeated. I must have made a face, because after a moment she sighed and shuffled to sit up on her shins. 'We never really hurt them. They'll recover, eventually. It's just their pride.'

My mind tripped over itself to keep up. 'But how do you get away with it?'

Luna laughed. 'Men are ruled by shame. From all the noise you'd think it were more prominent in women, but men are just ruined by it. They all have something to hide. We choose wisely. Does that answer your question?' I nodded, despite the fact that this answer spawned a thousand other questions. Luna slapped a palm against the couch cushion beside her. As I inched towards her, I noticed she wasn't wearing a fragrance. Or if she was, it was subtle enough to go unnoticed. I wanted to press my face into the side of her neck.

'What's Kahli like?' she said, leaning into the leather upholstery, cupping her chin in her hand.

'Oh, she's self-assured, but kind of blunt. Smart. Tells people what she really thinks. Except with men, which I didn't know about until recently, actually. I just assumed she was always like that. Which is maybe who I wanted her to be.'

Luna rolled her eyes. 'When are we ever going to stop deferring to these feeble excuses for men?'

'Your guess is as good as mine.'

She stared at me as if she was about to say something else, but her lips remained shut. I let out a nervous giggle; her gaze was hot and all-consuming. It felt as though another conversation was in progress, but I couldn't speak the language. 'Would you like a glass of water?' she said, eventually.

'Yes please.' She danced towards the kitchen again. While she was gone, I pinched at my armpits and tried to get as much air between the fabric and my skin as I could. As I glanced down at the coffee table, I noticed a gold ring beside the stack of coffee-table books. At its centre, a jagged pink stone.

'Oh, Coco left that here,' Luna said when she reappeared. 'Would you mind returning it to her on Monday? You'll see her before me.' She handed me the ring and a glass of water.

'Coco was here?' I said, as I pressed the stone into my palm.

'Yes.' She returned to the couch cushion. 'Is that a problem?'

'Coco's on-selling,' I blurted out, without thinking, or perhaps the opposite. 'She's running a business.'

Luna furrowed her brow. She reached for her drink, and once she'd taken another sip, said, 'Are you sure?'

'Pretty sure. I heard her on the phone to someone. Her dad, I think. She's waiting to get her discount so she can start ordering in bulk.' It was an ugly thing to do.

Luna paused for a moment, picking at the space below one of her acrylic talons. Then, she shrugged, suddenly unbothered. 'I know she is. That's why we hired her.'

'What?'

She sighed. 'We can't enter Europe until we meet their compliance stuff. We want her to keep selling, then eventually we'll use her customer base when we launch. We'll move her to Global Strategy. She'll be looked after.' She swatted the conversation away with her right hand. 'Rose is being promoted next week. She's moving into the Global Training team. Would you be interested in her role?'

I started speaking before I fully understood the question. 'Maybe. I'm not entirely sure what Rose does. Aside from running the induction training.'

'Me either,' Luna said. 'I'm kidding,' she added. 'Don't worry.'

'I know,' I said. 'Don't worry.'

'Something more creative for you, I think. Copywriting?'

'Is that a job you can just . . . give to someone?'

'Did Rose not explain the process to you?'

I shook my head. My body was heavy against the clammy black leather.

'We only recruit by referral. We offer promotion incentives for referrals, but the candidate must stay with us beyond their first FND.'

'FND? Oh, Friday Night Drinks,' I said, and I wanted to swallow my tongue. Why couldn't my brain move faster? 'Is that why Rose is being promoted?'

'Of course. Any other questions?'

'When do I need to find someone?'

'When do you want to leave Customer Service?'

In the months before I'd started at rytuał, I had resigned myself to standing still. The thrill I'd found in trawling the city until dawn with fleeting acquaintances and faceless men had become a stand-in for actually living my life. Because the more I took from the night, the more it took from my days – booze-fuelled evenings birthed long, empty waking hours. But meeting Luna, being with Luna, brought me back to believing that I could make something of my life. That I could want things. And that those things would eventually be mine.

~

We'd been working together for months before anything happened. We'd meet for dinner, discuss problems with the script, and he'd tap the company card on his way to the bathroom.

I didn't know this was unusual. I didn't know anything. The restaurants always had three dollar signs or more on their Google Business Profile. The receipts were above board. It was only ever the last half hour of our dinners that could be held against me.

'Tell me about the bozos,' he said one night, at another Broadsheet-approved small-plates cubbyhole. He fiddled with his wedding ring as he said it. His hands were so erotic to me – I could only look at them for a few seconds at a time. It was the size of them, but it was also their texture, the specific way his skin creased, the hair. He was wearing a white T-shirt tucked into navy suit pants. The fact that his T-shirt made it through the meal unsoiled was further evidence of the space between us. An oily turmeric smudge adorned the right leg of my jeans.

'No one says bozos,' I said. 'That makes you sound old.'

He placed a hand over his heart. 'Ouch.'

'I'm your youth consultant, it's my job to share these things with you.'

'What would I do without you?'

'I have no idea.'

His phone buzzed. He flipped it to face down on the table. 'I'm serious, give me an update on the men of tomorrow. How is it on the front line?'

'It's pretty bleak.'

'It's a real shame they can't just get it together. You're the full package.'

He took a final sip from his whisky. The light shifted across his face. Everything looked different when the proverbial elephant was pan-fried and presented to us both on a platter. 'And what exactly is included in the "full package"?' I said.

He put his glass down on the table. 'Come on, Marnie. You know you're an attractive woman.' He said it as if I'd annoyed him.

'I don't know, it's hard to tell.'

'Really?'

I shrugged. I knew there were different tiers of beauty. I knew I wasn't at a complete disadvantage, but I also knew it wasn't my strongest asset. I was too short in the torso, too broad in the shoulders, my face didn't quite add up. I was fine.

'Well, in the interest of quantifiable data, let me just say that I find you very attractive.'

'Thank you, old man.' I tipped an imaginary hat to him, because what was I supposed to say. My heart was racing.

'Don't be childish.' He reached for his phone. 'Let's get you home, it's late.'

He collected his blazer from the back of his chair and went to find a waiter. He didn't look back. I raced to catch him on his way out the door. A group of twenty-somethings was singing 'Happy Birthday' at a table by the entrance. Their words slurred together, draped across each other like their tipsy limbs. The door was surprisingly heavy; I nearly fell as I pried it open.

'Wait. Spencer!'

He was walking towards his car. He turned around, basked in the neon orange light of a sneaker store.

'What happened? I'm just struggling to understand.'

'You're a smart girl, Marnie. Don't play dumb.' He pulled his phone from his pocket and started typing. I waited for him to say something else, but he didn't.

'Are you mad because you . . .' I paused, shaking my head, wondering if I was really about to walk out into this kind of emotional traffic. 'Because you want to have sex with me?'

He didn't say anything. The silence knocked the wind out of me. We both stared at the pavement.

'I should go,' I said, finally, because it was the right thing to do.

'Yeah. That's a good idea.'

'Okay. Bye.' I turned in the direction of the 96 tram – I lived in Brunswick East then, a city-fringe suburb that had once been home to a stone quarry but was now home to more natural wine bars than people. I clenched my jaw and pressed my thumbnail into my index finger for the whole ride home. When I caught sight of my empty, unmade bed, I felt ashamed of everything I was yet to experience. I looked down at my delicate young hands, and watched them unlock my phone. I watched them open a new message and type, *I want you. Come over.* I chose it. When he arrived at my house half an hour later, I chose it. When he followed me down the hall across chipped floorboards to my room, I chose it. When he knelt down at the foot of my bed and begged to taste me, I chose it.

Sixteen

9.42 a.m. An EDM from a fast-fashion brand touting their *Sustainable picks for spring.* A news alert for milk spiked with hallucinogens. An update from an astrology app: *You are the wind and the water; you are the power and the powerless. Be sure to brush your hair today.* An alert from my banking app: *You've received a payment of $1636.62 from rytual cosmetica.* I scrambled to open the app. *Available balance: $1840.* I fell into a fugue state as I sent money in the direction of each of my debts. I barely drew breath. I barely considered the fact that I hadn't provided anyone with my banking details. When I returned to my available balance, it refreshed to display $496. *You will be paid a salary of $49,000 per annum, less applicable taxation.* I rolled over to lie on my stomach. As I took a breath, the numbers were replaced by an incoming call. My phone was ringing.

'Hello?'

'Marnie? Hi. Sorry, it's me again. I just thought—'

The sound of my heart thrashed against my eardrums. 'Lily.'

'I know you probably don't want to speak with me, but . . . I just wanted to try you again. I left Fifth Act.'

'Right.' I'd only spoken with Lily a handful of times. We'd spent so much time in each other's orbit, but rarely did we actually address each other. She was the only person under forty that Fifth Act employed on a permanent basis.

'I was wondering if you might be free for a coffee today? Just the two of us, just to chat. If it's a no, I promise I'll leave you alone.'

We must have been around the same age, although Lily and I were nothing alike. She was cool – she had a feathery mullet and a septum piercing – but, more than that, she was kind. She really cared about film. It made me feel like a fraud. I think that's why I avoided getting to know her.

'Marnie?'

'Um, yeah. I could do that.'

I heard her fumble with something – a pillow, a T-shirt, a piece of paper. 'Amazing, great. When suits?'

'Calooh in an hour?' Calooh was rytuał's favourite cafe in Collingwood. They gave us a 10 per cent discount – although the favour was not reciprocated. rytuał rarely gave discounts to anyone but employees, and their products never went on sale.

'Sure. I'll be there. I'm really excited to see you.'

'Yeah.'

I hung up the phone and made my way to the shower. When I was done, I wrapped myself in a towel and rubbed a hand over the sweaty mirror. I leant towards it, examining my bare, pink skin. I reached for the bottle of rytuał *She* and spritzed it on my wrists, my collarbones, the back of my neck. As the hot steam fogged the mirror again, my outline began to blur at the edges.

And, for a moment, I became someone else. In a cloud of rose, sandalwood and vetiver, I thought to myself, *Finally*.

~

Calooh was packed, which I should have anticipated given the time, but Lily had already secured a booth. I spotted her at the back of the converted warehouse and we made eye contact, which made it impossible to turn and run without consequence. She was wearing a pair of thick-rimmed black glasses and her fingers were covered in rings. She waved, smiling, and I made my way through the crowd towards her.

'Marnie!' she said as I approached. She stood up, and as I weaved through a group of young mums she hovered beside the table, unsure of what to do with her hands. I heard her inner monologue reminding her to just *'Be cool'*, although perhaps it was my own.

'Hi,' I said. I sat down. She followed.

'How are you?'

I tried to remember our last conversation. She'd spotted me at a networking drinks when things were going south and asked if I was okay, but I was a cruel drunk. After that, I'd seen her once at the Fifth Act office.

'I'm good. I just started a new job at rytuał. The makeup brand.'

'I love rytuał! My bathroom is covered in it. Obsessed.' I scanned her eyelids, cheeks, lips: Brightstar Eyeshadow, Bloom Cheek Tint, Glazed Lip Oil. *Joy*, *Clarity* and *Passion*, although there was a chance the dark-pink colour on her lips was also *Lust*. I was always getting the two confused.

'Yeah, mine too!' Although this wasn't strictly true, it would be soon enough.

'I'm really glad you came,' she said. 'I know I said this the other day, but I've been thinking about you a lot.'

'Really? I haven't thought about you at all.' I didn't mean to sound so thorny. 'Sorry, I didn't mean it like that.'

'No, it's totally fine! We barely knew each other.'

A waiter appeared beside us. 'Coffee to start?'

'I'll have a batch brew and an almond croissant,' I said.

'Me too,' Lily added.

He left without further comment. Lily sighed. 'We don't have to talk about anything you're not comfortable with, but I just wanted to apologise. I feel really guilty for how it all played out.'

'It's fine, it wasn't your fault.'

'I did try to tell them, but they weren't interested. Eventually, I got sick of it all and left. Which was why I called. I should have done it sooner, I'm sorry.'

'You really don't have to apologise,' I said. 'For anything.' Luna's voice echoed through me.

Lily fiddled with her rings, and after a moment, she said, 'He was a nightmare to work for. He really knew how to get under your skin.'

'What do you mean?' I'd never seen Spencer break his charismatic veneer at work.

'Are you serious? He called me at all hours, asking me to do the most ridiculous stuff. I wasn't even *his* assistant. He told me he was doing it to help my career, but all he ever did was remind me that someone else would be happy to take my job. I spent so much time in the bathroom doing fucking breathing exercises, I actually thought that job was going to kill me.'

This was news to me. I'd followed Spencer around the Fifth Act offices like a lost puppy; it was easy to believe his version of events when it seemed like the only option.

The waiter returned. The croissants were plain. Our eyes met as we both decided not to say anything. When we were alone again, Lily said, 'He's gone now. Finally. He started his own creative agency. I'm sure you've heard – Two Pines. Or Two Pines Media. Something like that.' She mimed dry-retching, which was kind of her.

'What about the wife?' I said.

She raised her eyebrows collusively. 'Still together. Did you read the book? It's fucking everywhere.'

I shook my head. Spencer's age-appropriate wife was formidable, which is to say she was the exact kind of woman whose husband I wished I'd never met. I'd seen her books in window displays long before I ever shook her husband's hand. I sometimes wondered if my attraction to him was fuelled by a twisted desire to become more like her. The new book had a green spine and a high-brow, academic font, and Lily was right – it was everywhere.

'Sorry. This must be weird.' Lily pulled her croissant apart.

'No, it's fine. It was ages ago.'

'Not really.' Lily popped a piece of the croissant into her mouth. Mine sat on the table beside me, whole and untouched. 'Do you know who the first wife was? I tried to do some digging. Sabrina said she was young, but that's as far as I got.'

'I didn't know there was a first wife.' I'd assumed it was only ever the formidable author. They owned an old Victorian house in South Yarra together, which seemed like a permanent thing.

'Anyway, I have to be honest,' she said, with a burst of energy. 'I also wanted to meet with you for selfish reasons.'

'Oh, okay.' I drank from the thick ceramic mug – it was bitter, too hot.

'I'm starting my own thing. A company. I want you to come and work with me.'

A mouthful of coffee knocked at the door to my lungs. I coughed with my mouth shut. 'Doing what?'

'Development. But we can work on some of your stuff, too.' This information threw me off balance. I'd always assumed Lily thought I was stupid. Or dull. Uninteresting, vapid.

'Why?'

'Are you serious? All I ever did at Fifth Act was talk about how great you were. Are. I *love* your writing. Obsession and desire are, like, all I'm interested in.'

It's not important, but I wrote a film about an ill-fated affair; a fact so loaded with irony I'm ashamed to admit it. I didn't know the first thing about having an affair when I wrote it. And I've always hated that word. 'Affair' has an American accent and a mortgage. My relationship with Spencer had more consonants. I hadn't opened the file in almost two years.

'I still have a quote from your script in my notes app. Wait, I'll get it—' She fumbled for her phone.

'No, Lily, don't. It's fine—'

'Seriously, I've sent it to so many friends—'

'Please don't.'

She looked up. 'Why not?' She was genuinely concerned. She studied my face for clues. 'Because of him?'

'No. Because of . . .' The thought ran out of steam. 'Me.'

Lily watched, disappointed. We sat in silence for a while before I left her at the cafe with a vague, noncommittal answer.

I knew I wouldn't take her up on her offer – I wanted as much distance from my old self as possible, and I couldn't do that with Lily rooting around in my psyche. On the way home, I found another interview with Luna and turned the volume up so high my ears began to ache. 'I am not a woman in business,' she said, and I assumed there were air quotes involved. 'I'm a force to be reckoned with.'

I opened a new browser tab and typed *Two Pines Media* into the search bar. I allowed myself exactly fifteen seconds to scan the website: masculine typeface, an impressive collection of big-budget clients presented like trophies on the landing page. Everything was in the right place. As my attention returned to Luna's voice, she said, 'There's an inherent destruction of tradition when you work to do things differently. We are creating new paths for women in beauty, yes, but we're also mindfully obliterating the old ones.'

~

On Monday morning we were turfed out of *Jean* and shown to the basement. Stepping off the top of the staircase made my stomach drop, although when I considered the room's contents it was hard to reconcile its functional qualities with the esoteric candlelight of its alter ego.

Coco wore a black ribbed top and a pair of brown knit flares that were so tight around the waist they cut into her skin. She picked at the waistband from the second we arrived until the second we left. 'I hate these pants,' she said. 'I feel so bloated. Do you ever get that?' I turned her ring over in my pocket, still unsure as to whether I would give it back to her.

'Marnie! How was your weekend?' Rose descended the stairs as Coco and I were preparing our workstations. The eighteen other desks were all occupied.

'Hey, Rose.' I fumbled with an HDMI cord at the back of my monitor. 'Sorry, one second.' She watched as I tried to press it into place from three different angles. After the third try I gave up, glowing red.

'How did you pull up on Saturday? You didn't reply to my text.' The question didn't match any coherent answer.

'Fine. A bit dusty.'

'I felt incredible,' she said. 'I barely slept, but I woke feeling so . . . energised.' She grinned. I looked around. Everyone was focused on their respective tasks – even Coco was retina-deep in her first email of the day. When I turned back to Rose, she was waiting patiently for my next comment.

The urge to pick at the scab overwhelmed me. 'I'm sorry I didn't mention Kahli. And Tom. I don't know why I kept it to myself.'

'Oh, don't worry about that. It had to be someone.'

I nodded, leant in close and said, 'Have you spoken to Tom?'

Still smiling, Rose wrapped a hand around my right wrist and walked us both to the bathroom. When she slid through the door and flicked on the light, she was quick to make sure I joined her. She locked the door with the same urgency. 'You can't ask that.'

'What?'

'We don't mention what happens on Friday nights outside the session. That's the rule. The consequences are . . . I told you that, didn't I? It's in the contract, anyway.'

'You didn't.'

'He's fine. Luna always has a plan. Tom had a massive tax debt. All part of the ritual.' Rose's expression was matter-of-fact. She didn't catch the pun.

'Is it always like that?' I said.

'Like what?' She didn't offer an answer. 'I'm serious, though. Keep it to yourself.'

She caught her reflection in the mirror and wiped a stray smudge of pink from the corner of her mouth. 'And don't tell Luna we've spoken. It's my first day in the Global team.'

'How's it going?'

'Amazing. I should get back. It's an important day. Europe is on the horizon.' She was beaming.

'Why didn't Luna just make you the head of Global Training to begin with?'

Rose gave me a perplexed stare. 'I wasn't ready,' she said. 'Luna knows best. Just trust the process.' She plucked a piece of fluff from my right shoulder and edged past me. 'I'll see you later?' she said, already halfway out the door.

When I returned to my desk, Coco was chewing absent-mindedly on her right thumbnail. 'The inbox is literally insane today,' she said.

I rolled my chair towards her and spoke directly into her ear. 'Hey, I don't know if anyone told you, but we're not supposed to say anything about what happened on Friday.'

She stared back at me blankly. 'What are you talking about?'

'So you know?'

'Shhh,' she whispered. Little flecks of spit hit the ribbed fabric across her chest.

I pushed myself away from her desk. 'I know about the on-selling.' It tumbled out of my mouth without a strategy.

There was no real threat to Coco's place at rytuał, but I wanted her to believe that there was. 'You left this at Luna's.' I handed her the ring. Coco's face dropped. Before she could say anything, Noor appeared beside us with two cardboard boxes. She was sweating.

'Your complimentary products,' she said as she released the heavy boxes with a thump. 'Well, this is your June allocation. Fifteen more in December. We took a guess with your foundation shades.' She slid them across the desk and left without further discussion. Coco lurched for one of the boxes and ripped it open. As I opened mine, the smell of rytuał *We* wafted out of the box. Fifteen products – one foundation, three lip oils, two cheek tints, a mascara, three eyeshadows, a bronzing palette, cleanser, treatment, moisturiser and a bottle of rytuał *We* – stared back at me from their throne of white textured paper. It was worth at least a thousand dollars, and for a moment I did wonder if it would have been more productive to raise my salary by two thousand dollars per annum, but the thought disintegrated as I began to apply one of the cheek tints in the reflection of my monitor. The shade was called *Simplicity*.

Seventeen

At home that night, I found Kahli wrapped in her duvet again. As I turned on the lights and she turned to face me, something caught in my throat. Her face was red and swollen. I made an 'Oh!' noise, as if I'd just discovered her squatting over a public toilet. 'What's wrong?'

'Nothing,' she said. 'It's fucking dumb.' She muted the TV.

I dumped my backpack and the box of complimentary products on the counter and went to sit beside her. 'What kind of dumb? Stubbed your toe, or clicked a link you shouldn't have?'

She rolled her eyes. 'Tom officially ended it. Don't say anything, I know. I didn't even want to be with him, obviously, I just—'

The memory of Rose throwing her weight behind the curling wand played out behind my eyes. At least this proved he was alive.

Kahli wiped the bottom of her nose with her palm. 'I just hate this feeling. It's pathetic.'

'It's not pathetic at all,' I said. 'If anyone's pathetic, it's Tom. That guy always smelt like a blueberry vape – like, just grow up and smoke a cigarette.'

'Vapes *are* embarrassing,' she said, with a half-sob, half-laugh. 'He said he needs to focus on himself for a while, but that's *all* he does.'

'Did he say anything else?'

She pulled her phone from beneath the blanket and exhaled as she tapped through to the message. '*I need to do some inner work before I can be in a relationship again. Rose helped me to come to this conclusion. I'm deeply sorry for what I did, and I really enjoyed our time together. Keep the vibes high, Kahli. You're a real one.*'

'"You're a real one"?'

'I guess I am,' she said, with a wry smile.

I placed a hand on the outline of her shin. 'How do you want to feel?' I said, with a confidence I often couldn't grasp in Kahli's orbit.

'What?'

'You said you hate this feeling. How do you want to feel?'

She crossed her arms, suddenly wary. 'Have you been listening to those life coaching podcasts again?'

'I'm serious!' I said, with a laugh, although the realisation that Kahli knew about the life coaching podcasts stung – for the record, it was just one, and I only listened to six or seven episodes, and she wasn't a life coach, she was a holistic counsellor. 'How do you want to feel?'

Kahli softened. 'As though I don't have to bend myself out of shape . . . to be loved. Or something.'

'Kahli, to be able to think something about ourselves means that version of us must already exist. Did you know that?'

'What do you mean?'

Luna's influence was in my blood like alcohol. It changed my brain chemistry. Or maybe it was the Bloom Cheek Tint I'd applied that afternoon – transcending the skin's barrier, it surged through my veins. I loved the way it felt, to lean closer to Kahli and squeeze her leg as I said, 'A new life is possible. You just need to break the cycle.'

~

Victoria from Digital Operations came to rytuał by way of a consulting firm. Her previous manager had bullied her relentlessly, which culminated in him locking her in an accessible toilet stall and dropping his pants. He threatened that if she told upper management he'd make her life hell; despite the fact that he'd already done this, Victoria didn't want to find out what else he was capable of. On Tuesday morning, when Luna said, 'Does anyone have anything to clear?' Victoria was first in line.

'What's this man's name?' Luna said, as she weighed his potential; ranking the crimes of those who'd wronged the women in her employ as if it were the waiting list for a new kidney.

'Patrick Fletcher,' Victoria stammered. She was jittery and wide-eyed.

'Together we rise, divided we fall. We are the fallen women and we work as one. Fallen woman, fallen woman, fallen woman.'

Luna paced the length of the room, tilting her head from side to side. Time slowed down as we tried to interpret whether this meant Patrick was the obvious choice – the race to guess who would show up in the basement each Friday night was a high-octane sport. 'Thank you, Victoria,' she said, and my money was on Patrick Fletcher.

~

The next email in the queue had no subject heading, and the body of the message read *refund please*. The all-caps emails were easier, in a way – you clicked the phone icon with the understanding that your conversation would begin at a ten and end at a two (provided you asked the right questions, delivered the right answers). Customer service was choreography; you just had to convince the other party to follow your lead. My stomach still lurched each time the dial tone flooded my headphones, but I'd always hated answering the phone. It made me feel tired and misunderstood.

'Hello?'

'Hi, am I speaking with Susan?' I said.

'Yes.'

'My name is Marnie, I'm calling from rytuał cosmetica. Is now a good time?'

'Oh, hi,' she said, as if my presence was a relief. 'Yes, I wanted to return the lip gloss. It wasn't the texture I was expecting.'

'Lip oil,' I corrected. 'The Glazed Lip Oil?'

'That's the one, I think. Could I post it back to you? I don't know when I'll be in town next.'

'Of course, Susan, I'll just need to ask you a few questions first, if that's okay.'

'That's fine, but I'm in a bit of a rush—'

'I won't take up too much of your time. Just for my own curiosity, what kind of texture were you expecting?'

She paused. 'I suppose something less . . . wet? It's very shiny. I hadn't purchased one of your products before, and I wandered into the store while I was killing time. It's a nice colour, but I think I'm a little bit too . . . mature, maybe.' She laughed. 'I'm a bit older than your usual customer.'

'How old are you?' I asked, following some invisible thread that I hoped would lead me home again. 'If you don't mind my asking. It's good for us to receive this kind of feedback. We are an inclusive brand, after all. We're all about women.' From across the pod of desks, brown-eyed Laura looked up from her monitor.

'I'm sixty-one,' she said, lightly, as if she was surprised to find herself answering the question. 'And what about you, Marnie? How old are you?'

'I'm twenty-nine.'

'That's what I thought. You never think you'll age out of something like makeup, but it's quite the shock,' she said. 'Life doesn't ever really feel cumulative. Until you buy a lip gloss – pardon, lip oil – and realise it's only made for lips that are pulled taut by an excess of collagen.'

'But isn't the real problem that we all want to look the same? That we think there's one specific way to use these products? We should be using them to highlight our differences.'

She paused. 'You're probably right, but I live in the real world, Marnie.'

'Have you tried the lip oil with a liner? It can—'

'I really appreciate your time, Marnie, but I've been around long enough to know when I need to cut my losses. Could you email me a returns label?'

'Of course, but first, let me send you something. I have a, um—'

'I'm going to hang up now,' she said. 'Thanks again, Marnie. It's—'

'Wait, Susan. You feel as though youth is a high vantage point, but youth isn't power,' I said, and I wasn't dissociating per se, but I did hear the words leave my mouth of their own accord. 'Not when you're young, anyway. It smells like power but the consistency is off. I see someone your age, and the time it's taken to form solid opinions, and I just ... we want what you have. If I saw you wearing it, I'd buy it. Not some idiot twenty-four-year-old.' While I was speaking, the other two Lauras appeared above their monitors. But it wasn't just The Lauras; the entire office was staring at me.

On the other end of the line, Susan chuckled. 'That was a lovely speech. A little melodramatic, but I think that was the point.'

'Can I send you something? It's just a small gift, but I think you'll enjoy it. It's one of our Bloom Cheek Tints. The shade is called *Elegance*, which feels fitting.'

'Sure,' she said, exhaling. 'That would be lovely.'

I confirmed her postal address and provided the requisite details. She didn't mention the refund again. By the time we hung up, a standing ovation had formed on the office floor. When I shrugged out of my headset, they began to cheer.

'Incredible,' green-eyed Laura said, from two desks over. 'Incredible recovery.'

'Masterful,' brown-eyed Laura added. 'I've never heard anything like it.'

'We should get drinks,' blue-eyed Laura said, as she looked to her brown- and green-eyed counterparts. 'To celebrate.'

'I'd love that,' I replied.

As the applause died down, I heard Coco say, 'Yeah, great job, girl,' but by that point I was on to the next email; the next contender, the next problem to solve. It was a feeling I'd known once but had since lost sight of. It was all I'd ever wanted – for my best to be good enough.

~

'It changed my life,' brown-eyed Laura said, while nursing an elaborate blood-red cocktail. 'Friday Night Drinks literally changed my life. Before rytuał I was, like, a totally different person.'

We were huddled around a high-top table at Caroline's. The three Lauras stood on one side, as though I was auditioning to complete their share house or feminist string quartet. The other two nodded, fervently, as they sucked on their own bright-coloured drinks. I swirled the dregs of a glass of orange wine, watching as the dark sediment muddied the amber liquid.

'Have you all . . . done it?' I said. I swallowed what was left of the wine and wished I hadn't.

'Uh-huh,' said the blue-eyed Laura.

'Yep,' said the green-eyed one.

'Seriously, though, you wouldn't have recognised me, Marnie. We wouldn't have been friends,' the brown-eyed one continued. Were we friends?, I wondered. But I was happy to accept whatever this was. Their attention was going straight to my head, and the sensation was not unpleasant. 'My brother was, like, ruining my life. Luna really did something to him. Like, now he asks me questions. And I'm not scared to advocate for myself.'

'Really important,' said the blue-eyed Laura. 'You have to advocate for yourself.'

'What about you?' I said, to the green-eyed Laura. 'Who did Luna . . . for you?'

'This guy I used to work with. He was kind of stalking me. It wasn't that bad, but—'

'Laura! Don't minimise your trauma like that. It was really bad. He was scary.' Brown-eyed Laura shook her head.

'Yeah,' green-eyed Laura conceded, the shadow of a memory passing over her expression. 'But Luna totally made it go away for me. She's incredible.'

'Why don't they tell? Surely at least one of them has gone to the police . . . or something?'

The Lauras looked to each other, as if silently negotiating how much they could reveal.

'Well, there was this one time . . .' blue-eyed Laura said.

'But the police didn't believe him, and when he came back to the office, Luna . . .' Brown-eyed Laura trailed off.

'He came back to the office?' I said.

'Luna took care of it. She always has a contingency plan. If you get weird texts or he shows up at your house, you just have to tell her. It's really not a big deal,' said green-eyed Laura. I reached for my glass, forgetting it was empty. Green-eyed Laura noticed. 'Another round?'

'How did it start?' I said. 'Friday Night Drinks.'

They collapsed into knowing giggles. 'It's hard to remember exactly, but—'

'Well, it used to be just talking. We all used to come here on a Friday and vent, but then we started doing it at the office—'

'And then Luna had the idea to start doing The Clearings.' They all nodded. It was hard to keep up with who was saying what, which Laura was Laura, if they actually did all look the same.

Green-eyed Laura had a beauty spot on the left side of her top lip, but that was as far as I'd got in differentiating them further.

'Then the featured rytuałist thing started,' green-eyed, beauty-spotted Laura said. 'And then Luna just thought . . . why not bring them in? The men. Because there's only so much talking can do. And here we are.'

'Right,' I said. 'Just like that.'

'Just like that.'

A moment of silence descended. As I opened my mouth to ask something else, blue-eyed Laura leant across the table. 'Do you have any idea who yours will be?' The others followed, all three of them leaning across the small table as though I was in possession of party drugs or state secrets.

'I'm not sure yet,' I said, and they believed me.

~

Behind the bathroom mirror, my complimentary products sat; lined up on the shelf like Russian dolls, perfectly positioned in order of application. I was taking my time with them, only adding a single product to my routine at a time. But when I arrived home from Caroline's that night I went straight to the bathroom, locked the door and turned on the light. In the mirror, I had the brief thought that I didn't recognise the woman staring back at me. My skin tone had evened, the bags beneath my eyes had faded and my lips had shed the stubborn layer of dry skin that had previously clung to them. It was still me, of course, but as I leant towards the mirror I did wonder who 'me' really was. If the 'me' I remembered ever really existed. As I examined my steely-blue irises, I realised that Luna's face was becoming more familiar to me than my own. Or, was it that my face was beginning to resemble Luna's?

I opened the mirrored cupboard and pulled one of each product from the shelf, ferrying them to the vanity with the utmost precision. Sheer Dew Foundation, in shade P2. Bloom Cheek Tint in *Fortitude*, for something new. The Glow Show Bronzer. Lash Paint Mascara. Glazed Lip Oil – I stuck to *Lust*, given Luna's preference for it. I applied each of the products slowly, lovingly. As I ran the pads of my fingers across my cheeks, I closed my eyes and inhaled the faint, nutty scent of the foundation. There was a drop of Luna's essence in each of the rytuał products. Applying them made me feel closer to her; as if everything I didn't know about her could be found at the bottom of a bottle.

When I'd applied the foundation, cheek tint, bronzer and mascara, I paused. I fingered the lip oil's textured lid; staring into the syrupy pink liquid, rotating it back and forth beneath the light. When I returned my eyes to the mirror, a warm glow spread through my chest. I didn't recognise myself at all. I grazed the applicator wand over my lips as they found the shape of a grin.

~

'*Do it!*' a voice cried from the back of the crowd. I heard myself cheer. Patrick Fletcher wore a pair of faded grey boxer-briefs. He was bulbous and slimy, like a toad. Victoria made her own oat milk; she had kind eyes. She was standing over him, holding a thick black leather belt, with Luna's head perched on her left shoulder. I watched as Luna placed a hand around Victoria's waist, and a jolt of electricity shot through the centre of me.

She whispered something in Victoria's ear, as the toad tried to wriggle out of his gag.

'Sisters, please assist Victoria in moving through this energetic block by affirming with the word "Cut".'

'Cut,' we all cried.

'Right, Victoria. Over to you.'

I could only see the back of her, but Victoria's ponytail was shivering. Luna whispered something else in her ear, and Victoria raised the belt overhead. 'You fucking piece of shit,' she screeched as the leather descended, cutting a red line across the toad's torso. 'You tiny-dicked piece of shit.' She whipped him from the other side. The sounds he made were muffled by the gag, but they were high-pitched and frail, and not at all what I'd expected. After a few repetitions, Luna took hold of the belt and wrapped it around his neck.

'Say it,' she said, to Victoria, whose ponytail had since stopped shivering. The toad's eyes bulged from their sockets as Victoria cracked her neck from side to side.

'I am . . . I'm more than what you did. And you're nothing. *Nothing*,' Victoria said, staring directly into his eyes. Luna dropped the belt and returned to stand beside her. The toad's head lulled forwards, but he was still conscious. Just.

'You'd better not do it again, Patrick. I'll be watching. And you really don't want to mess with me. I'm fucking crazy.'

~

The Friday after that, Natalie from Accounts Payable took the floor. She was smaller than Luna, with a bleached-blonde shag and full, glossy lips. Natalie's ex-boyfriend had stolen thousands of dollars from both her and her close friends. He paid it all back and she agreed not to press charges, before she got a call one night from a twenty-two-year-old woman she'd never met, who revealed that he'd been sleeping with her for an entire year. More than anything else, Natalie couldn't work out how he found the time. Luna helped Natalie carve the word *LIAR* into her ex-boyfriend's chest with a small white device Coco was quick to identify as a cauterising pen. Apparently, they were easy to come by on eBay. When the smell of burning flesh overwhelmed the room, Eva lit two sticks of limited-edition rytuał *We* incense. The man's name was Pete.

A month passed like this. Arriving at *Emma* on a Monday was like boarding a moving train; in the blink of an eye it was Tuesday morning, The Clearing; Wednesday, Thursday, counselling strangers through post-purchase regret; trade meeting Friday; Friday Night Drinks. I was finally starting to understand how one built a career – it was easy to go to a place, perform tasks, leave the place and return again when you had a higher purpose. When I'd watched the hordes of young professionals descend on Richmond salad bars I became preoccupied with death, but within the walls of *Emma*, under Luna's watchful eye, I was the most alive I'd ever felt. My hair was growing at an astonishing rate. My sleep was deep and restorative. But I couldn't stop thinking about her. Around every corner, behind every door. Luna was a powerful drug, and my tolerance was growing.

Eighteen

It was a Monday when I ascended the stairs for lunch to discover Luna waiting just across the threshold. I jumped as our eyes met. The effect she had on my nervous system was immediate and intense.

'Did I startle you?' she said. 'I was just coming to see if you wanted to grab some lunch.' She was wearing an ankle-length black silk dress, with short sleeves that revealed her tattoos. I often found myself sneaking glances at them, as if they were some private part of her. She had the rytuał logo stamped on her right inner biceps. I'd taken a risk on a red velvet miniskirt that morning, but hadn't considered how challenging it would be to actually sit in. I still hadn't mastered the art of The Outfit.

'Sounds good,' I said, as a ringing noise filled my ears. 'I was just heading to the kitchen.'

'Fuck the kitchen,' she said, her eyebrows up to no good. 'Let's go out.'

~

The dining room was below ground. A sliver of natural light poked through the thin rectangular windows at street level. Even in the early afternoon, the light was so low you could only consult the menu by sliding it beneath the mushroom lamp at the centre of the table. When a waiter approached us, Luna was quick to order for two. She was warm and familiar, and as he read the order back to her she placed a hand on his forearm to congratulate him. When he returned with two glasses of wine, she swiped hers and raised it in a toast.

'To Monday!' she said, as she drew the glass to her lips.

'To Monday,' I echoed.

Her phone sounded from the tiny bag she'd slung across the back of her chair, but she ignored it. 'So,' she said, with a wicked smile.

'So,' I echoed, again.

'You were in my dream last night.'

'Oh, was I? What was I doing?'

She reached for my hand across the table and wrapped it in hers. She didn't answer; instead she said, 'I think it's time for you to speak at The Clearing again. I want to know more about you, Marnie. We all do.'

I was approaching the stage of my crush where throwing myself off a small bridge for a piece of her wasn't out of the question. Which did worry me, a little, but not as much as it turned me on. It had been so long since I'd swallowed the taste of longing. 'Okay,' I said. 'I can do that.'

She lit up immediately. 'Wonderful,' she said. 'Just wonderful.' She downed the rest of her wine as the first course arrived. Thinly sliced tuna with a shoyu dipping sauce. A small bowl of pickled vegetables. We ate in silence for a moment, before Luna looked up at me with a mischievous grin. 'Should we go get a burger?'

'What? Why? This is amazing!'

'Yeah, but I actually feel like a burger.' She ruffled a hand through her glossy mane. 'Let's dine and dash.'

I was struggling to catch my breath. 'What?' I looked over at the waiter. He was staring dead-eyed into his phone, leaning up against a wall at the back of the room.

'I mean, we didn't even really dine,' she said. 'I just . . . changed my mind.'

'I don't know—'

'Come on, Marnie, live a little.'

'How, exactly?'

'You tell me.'

I looked at the waiter again. 'I could go outside, I guess. To make a phone call.'

Luna nodded, grinning.

'Then you could sneak out after me?'

'Perfect.'

I shrugged. Tiny fireworks spewed glitter into my guts. I retrieved my polyester blazer from the back of the chair – I'd tried to machine wash it once and it had never really found its shape again – and pulled my phone from my bag. Luna smiled along, pantomiming the supportive friend of a Very Important Woman in Business. The waiter nodded encouragingly as I reached the door, because this was a place for serious people to plan their next moves. To move fast. Break things. When I reached the top of the stairs, I had to throw my head between my knees to avoid another fainting episode. We'd barely eaten anything, anyway. I don't know why I was making such a big deal out of it.

I walked a few metres up the narrow laneway. I still had the phone pressed to my ear, a layer of sweat forming between the screen and my cheek. I kept it there until I heard Luna shout, 'Marnie!' from behind me. We giggled as we dodged idle pedestrians. When we reached the top of the laneway, she took my hand. 'Where did you come from?'

'Coburg,' I said. 'Before it was cool.'

She laughed. 'You're it,' she said. 'You're all of it. You're everything.' It brushed up against the memory of something else, but god it felt good.

'I can't wait to hear what you share with us tomorrow,' she said, but I was lost in the heat of her hand against mine. Her scent. How explicit it felt to slide my fingers between hers.

~

'Good morning, rytuałists,' Luna purred, from the end of the room called *Britney*. I was sat in the front row, beside Ruth, who smelt overwhelmingly of laundry detergent. 'Tuesday morning, yet again.' My pulse was quick and strong. Some weeks there were five or six women with a story to share; other times, the air was dense and still as we awaited a single volunteer. But there was always someone. 'Who would like to go first?' Luna said, in my direction. Her hair was piled into an elaborate bun, with two loose tendrils framing her face. The hem of her black long-sleeved top ended before her skirt began, and the glimpse of her smooth, olive stomach made me feel deranged. I took a breath. Raised my hand. Luna glanced to the back of the room, the right, then found her way back to me. 'Marnie Sellick,' she said. 'What would you like to clear?'

I stood, hesitantly, and brushed some lint from the front of my grey knit jumper. I'd prepared a short paragraph, but when my eyes met Luna's, all that came out was, 'Spencer Healey.'

~

The deadline for the next draft had been extended three times. Whenever I wrote something new, Spencer would find something wrong with the old pages. I'd take the feedback and rewrite the old pages, only for him to find a problem with the rest of it. In the beginning his notes were framed with enthusiasm, but by the third extension they came without complimentary cushioning. I wanted to be everything he'd seen in me, which meant writing what he saw coming out of me, but I could never quite clear the bar.

Even as his enthusiasm for my work waned, he kept me close. We went to Sydney for a film festival. He pushed me in and out of conversations as though I were a tray of finger food. I hadn't written a word in weeks. We booked an Airbnb in the Blue Mountains for the week after the festival. The sex we were having was urgent and fast, as if we needed to get it over with before we remembered that we'd done it before. Before we watched ourselves back and said, 'It's all a bit clichéd, isn't it?'

Mum called just as we'd started to talk half-heartedly about dinner one night. Spencer was splayed across the centre of the bed, one hand in a bag of Doritos and the other propping up his phone as he watched the football. The first time we'd stayed in a hotel together I'd let my phone die on the first day. I didn't charge it again until I got home. When I answered the call, Mum was frazzled.

'Do you have my passport?' she said, straight out of the gate.

'Hi, Mum. I don't, is it in the study? First drawer?'

Spencer looked up from the screen and rolled his eyes. He said we were 'enmeshed'. He thought I needed to create some space. I never introduced them.

'I looked. It's not there.' I heard her slam something shut.

'Why do you need it today?'

'I'm going to Canada. I need it for the airport.'

'Why are you going back to Canada?'

'I just need my passport, Jenny. Do you have it?'

It was the first time anything like this had happened. Jenny was her older sister, but she'd died ten years earlier. Mum had lived in Canada in her early twenties. I stepped through the glass sliding door onto the balcony. The spa bath was empty, coated in a mineral glaze. The air was so cold it cut into my eyeballs.

'Mum, are you okay?'

She was silent for a while. 'I'm fine. I just need my passport,' she said, eventually, before hanging up in an exasperated flurry. I went inside.

'I think something's wrong with my mum.'

'Huh?' His hand was still inside the bag of Doritos.

'Something's wrong.' My hands were shaking. I was two metres away from the bed, but he didn't stand up. He just stared, with his hand in the bag of Doritos. We'd been drinking – not a lot, but enough to make our eyes heavy. Enough to make this all a huge inconvenience.

'I'm sure she's fine. Why don't we just wait until the morning? It'll be a nightmare trying to get a flight now, anyway.' Spencer had platinum status with two separate airlines, so we both knew this was a lie.

'Please. I need you to drive me back to Sydney.' The rental car was in his name. I sat in the armchair opposite the bed and curled my knees up to my chest.

'She probably just wants attention.'

I jumped out of the chair and ran over to him. When I got to the bed all I could think to do was thump his chest with my fists. He tried to sit up as he flicked the bag off his hand, but I straddled him. 'What are you doing?' he said, as I hit him again. He grabbed my wrists. I felt the centre of my chest crack open, followed by a rush of air to fill the vacuum. It was just over a year since he'd knelt at the foot of my lumpy share-house bed, and a year since I'd felt as if I was calling the shots. In the intervening months I'd contracted and tightened into a brittle fraction of myself. I didn't know relationships could make you this sick. He was a dirty habit I couldn't kick – I hated him, but I hated myself more.

'Why are you doing this to me?' I said. It came out with a sob. I let my arms go slack. He released my wrists and stared up at me with an unfamiliar expression.

'Doing what?' He slid himself out from under me, suddenly wary, and moved to the other side of the bed. I sat up on my knees. Exhaled. My face was hot as my eyes spat tears down my cheeks. He laughed as he shook his head. 'No,' he said. 'No, don't do that. You don't get to change the narrative when it suits you—'

'I didn't know what I was doing. I just wanted to feel like I was—'

'What? You wanted to feel like what? Because plenty of women get by in this industry without opening their legs to whoever offers to help them. You're too old for this, Marnie.'

'I'm too old?' I said. 'I'm too old for you now? Is that it? Did you even think I was good?'

He looked down at the sheets. It was a cruel thing to do – I don't know that I believed him, but it gutted me nonetheless.

I looked at his left hand, at the plain gold wedding band he didn't bother to remove. 'Would you take your wife back to Sydney?' I said. It was a subject we generally avoided, but as the weeks wore on and the months became a year, I felt her presence like a heavy suitcase I was dragging around with me.

'Are you drunk? Go have a shower.'

'Maybe I should send your wife a message,' I said. 'Maybe she could pick me up from the airport.' I swiped my phone from the bedside table and searched her name on Instagram.

'Marnie,' he said. 'Marnie, stop.' He got up from the bed and lunged towards me. I clicked the message button beside her name as he reached for the phone, but there was too much force behind him and we both fell. My shoulder hit the carpet at a bad angle. The pain was immediate. I cried out as the phone fell from my hand. When he realised what he'd done, his eyes widened. 'Are you okay?' he said, boyish and panicked. 'I didn't mean it.' He scrambled away from me as if I was venomous. I sat up and surveyed the damage. I felt as though I'd been broken in half. My rage dissolved into disgust, and when I looked over at him I thought, *Who is that old man?*

'I think I need to go to the hospital,' I said. 'Can you please book me an Uber?' And despite the fact that we'd been drinking, he did me one better: he drove me there himself.

When we made it back to the Airbnb early the next morning, we crawled straight into bed and turned off the lights. I had to sleep on my left side with my right arm propped up on a pillow, and as I closed my eyes I felt him shuffle in behind me. 'You have to forgive me,' he whispered as he kissed the back of my neck. 'You have to forgive me, Marnie.' He placed a hand on my right hip and it made my body stiffen. It wandered desperately around the waist of my underwear, and when he wriggled his fingers beneath the elastic I said nothing. His breath was hot against the back of my neck but I said nothing.

Later, as the glow of the codeine wore off, the truth hit harder than the pain: this man could never have made sense of me. He was yet to make sense of himself.

Nineteen

At 2.12 p.m., as I was gearing up to phone a customer who'd left the name *NONEOFYR BUSINESS* on their BlissScreen submission, a text from Luna lit up my phone screen.

LUNA PETERS
Come over later? X

Coco was typing furiously beside me, and as I reached for the phone she threw me a judgemental glare.

In an instant, the afternoon became an inconvenience. I checked the time at three-minute intervals. Luna hadn't specified when she wanted me to come over, just that it would be later. How much later? What was later, really?

I took the tram home and stuffed two pieces of peanut butter toast in my mouth. I watched the time like a magpie. 6. 6.15. 6.30. 7.30 was an appropriate time to arrive. 7.30 was later. But when I arrived at Luna's front door, the windows were dark. I pressed the silver button on the intercom to no avail. As I turned to leave, ego bruised, I heard Rose's voice call out, 'Marnie?'

I turned too quickly. The muscles in my neck did not approve.

'Hi! Rose! Sorry, I was just looking for Luna.'

'Don't apologise.' She was wide-eyed and warm. 'We were getting some work done. Come in.'

I followed Rose down the hallway. Tealight candles flickered at intervals along the floorboards. When we arrived at the living room, the candles reached a crescendo in an altar on the coffee table. It looked as if the table itself was on fire. In the glow of the flames, Luna smiled. She was sitting cross-legged in front of the couch, draped in a baggy white T-shirt. Her hair was pulled taut in a thick ponytail. 'Hi, Marnie,' she said. 'Join us.'

When I perched on the ground beside her, she reached for my hand. Rose sat on the other side of the table and closed her eyes. I closed my eyes, too.

'In the name of the Goddess, the Daughter and the Fallen Woman, we come together to ask for guidance,' Luna said.

'We drink from the well of your spirit,' Rose crooned in response.

I nodded. Then I remembered that no one was looking, so I said, 'Yes.'

'We make physical what you share with us through your blessings, Fallen Woman.'

'We create in your image,' Rose said.

'We ask for your help in removing obstacles. We pray to you for answers on how to keep rytuał alive for many years to come.'

'We ask that you share your wisdom with Luna, to benefit us all.'

'I am here to receive.'

Rose began to chant, 'Show her the way. Show her the way. Show her the way.' The tune was precarious, but after three rounds I found the shape of it. I don't know how long we continued like that for. My pelvis began to ache from sitting cross-legged, but as the words looped around each other the pain came and went. Each individual sound became a focal point, then dissolved into the soup. Right in the centre of it all, when I felt as if my body had begun to belong to the sound, Luna shrieked, *'I see!'*

I flung my eyes open. Luna was standing. She ran to collect a journal from the kitchen table. Rose still had her eyes closed. She placed both hands over her heart and bowed her head towards them. Under her breath I heard her whisper, 'Thank you.' I tried to sit as still as possible, but the ache in my hips returned. I sat up to a kneeling position. The room was silent, aside from the scratch of Luna's pen on paper.

'What just happened?' I asked the room, but mainly Rose.

'Luna got a download,' she said, as if this answered the question.

Luna finished scribbling and shook out her arms. Fluttered her lips. Rose watched with unflinching adoration. Eventually, Luna released her hair from its tower and said, 'Anyone for a cheese board?'

~

'Why him?' Luna said, from the opposite end of the couch. She'd sunk three glasses of skin-contact white and two fingers of whisky, but her consonants were still crisp. The tail end of a cheese board was resting atop the residue of candle wax. I was struggling to finish words. On the other couch, Rose had her eyes closed.

'Who? Spencer?'

Luna nodded. 'It's the thing I still struggle to understand.'

'It's hard to explain,' I said. I rubbed my eyes and sat up straighter, hoping this would be sufficient, but Luna's eyes were laser focused.

'Try,' she said.

'He's, like, violently charming. I thought that if I could be the one he wanted, I could be . . . I can't make the words match the feeling. You know those people that kind of—'

'Light up the room?'

'Well, yeah—'

'You have that,' she said. 'You do know that, right?'

I blushed aggressively in response.

'You don't think so?'

'No,' I said, laughing. 'Definitely not.'

'Interesting,' was all she said.

'Is it my week? Is that why you're asking me this?'

'Your week for what?'

'Friday Night Drinks. Is it . . . Spencer?'

Luna shook her head. 'Not yet.'

'Why did you ask me to speak at The Clearing? I thought it meant—'

'I told you. I want to know more about you, Marnie. I want to know everything.' She plucked a grape from the debris of the cheese board and slid it into her mouth.

Something compelled me to say, 'I get caught up in people. It happens all the time.'

She swallowed the grape and rolled her shoulders back. 'Who was the last person you got caught up in?'

The truth was impossible, so instead I offered, 'Kahli. She seemed so shiny at first. It felt as if her life was full.' Rose rolled over to lie on her side, opening her eyes again. 'It's not, though.'

'What's her story?' Luna said. 'What happened to her?'

'What?'

'Does she have a core wound?' Luna teetered on the edge of a laugh. I didn't understand if I was supposed to follow her in earnest.

Rose sat up. 'Can we at least stick to one phase of the induction protocol, please?'

'This is as good a time as any,' Luna said.

'I'm lost.' It felt as though Rose and Luna's audio was out of sync with their movements.

'Marnie, there's a part of the recruitment process that I didn't explain to you. We look for a certain kind of person.' Luna placed a hand on my ankle. 'We are a business that operates with a specific person in mind. Statistically, yes, but also ideologically. Surely you've realised that?'

'Yeah, you . . . You only hire women.'

'That's not strictly true.' Her stare was litigious.

'It's not that we only hire women,' Rose interjected. 'We just don't hire men.'

'In order to fuel the kind of personal growth we ask our employees to undergo throughout their time here, we look for people who've experienced life in a certain way.'

'Experienced *men* in a certain way,' Rose said, beating her to the punchline.

'I don't understand.'

Luna chewed on her bottom lip, considering her next move. 'A culture fit is the most important thing for us, does that make sense?'

I nodded.

'We stand for specific things. One of those is that we want to help people heal.' She stared at me, expectantly.

'So, you only want to hire people who . . .' My sentence ran out of steam. 'What, hate men?' I laughed.

Rose said, 'Yes,' but Luna said, 'Not quite.' The answer was somewhere between yes and not quite.

'But why? What does it do for the company?'

'It gives us purpose. A North Star.'

'Is this a joke?'

Luna began to walk her hands up the sides of my legs. She crawled over me until I could smell the whisky on the tip of her tongue. 'Nothing about this is a joke.' She lowered her face all the way down to mine, and paused as if she was going to either bite me or kiss me. I held my breath. Instead of either of those options, the thing that materialised was raucous, uncontrollable laughter. Luna toppled over the edge of the couch onto the floor, narrowly – expertly – missing the coffee table. I was frozen in place.

'Your face!' she spluttered. 'Oh, that was good. That was so good.'

I shimmied to rest my back against the arm of the couch. It was about as comfortable as a hipbone. 'Yeah,' I said, trying my best to laugh. Where did the joke begin and end? Luna shook her head and crawled back onto the couch. When I looked over at Rose, she was staring at the floor.

When she'd composed herself, Luna said, 'We'd really like you to recruit someone, Marnie. It's time to leave Customer Service.'

I looked around the room. The books that were normally stacked on the coffee table had been relegated to a timber stool beside Rose's couch. On top of the pile sat a familiar title, and the sight of it reminded me of Lily. It had a green spine and a high-brow, academic font, and its author was formidable.

'Kahli could be a great option,' Luna continued, but I wasn't listening.

As I stared at the book, it morphed into the memory of Lily chasing dutifully after Spencer, her Apple Watch flashing incessantly.

'Marnie?'

I met Luna's gaze. 'I have a better idea,' I said.

~

The Fifth Act office only had one meeting room. It was positioned beside reception, wrapped in floor-to-ceiling glass. When I arrived, a sad plate of mini quiches was already positioned at the centre of the table. I watched a fly bounce across the surface of the table before landing on a particularly inedible-looking quiche.

Lily appeared at the door with a polite but pained expression. I watched her type my coffee order into her notes app. Her eyes lingered on the screen as she said, 'They won't be long.'

First came Marie, the human resources director. Then Sabrina, the managing director. Then Spencer. They entered in a cloud of small talk and took turns acknowledging me. Spencer sat to the right, Sabrina in the middle and Marie beside her.

'Did you catch the tram here?' Marie asked, and when I said, 'Yes,' she nodded.

'Terrible weather we're having,' Sabrina added, and when I said, 'Yes,' she nodded.

Spencer didn't say anything. Lily never returned with my coffee.

I didn't need to hear what they said to know exactly what they were saying. Due to a failure to deliver the materials as promised, my mentorship would be terminated. I could take the script elsewhere, but Fifth Act would need to be compensated for development costs should anyone decide to produce it. They were 'greatly disappointed', but hoped this would help me to 'refocus.'

Spencer nodded along but contributed nothing beyond, 'Yes, I really enjoyed working together but ultimately we are running a business, and in this instance we need to act in the business's best interests.' They wished me well, chasing the bad news with flowery platitudes about my talent and potential, but kept a firm hand on the door as it closed behind me. No one ate any of the quiches.

Lily walked me to the elevator. As she pressed the down arrow, I heard her whisper, 'I'm sorry.'

When I was alone, I sent a text:

Are we done?

A reply came back with uncharacteristic speed:

> I wanted things to end
> differently as well, Marnie, but I
> think this is best for all parties.
> If you have any questions
> for me please let me know,
> otherwise I wish you well in
> your future endeavours.

I found his name in my contacts. When it went to voicemail, I spat *'Fuck you'* into the phone and hung up. It felt good to finally be so childish. The elevator doors opened at ground level and I was absorbed by the flow of pinstripes bustling down Collins Street. It was the last time I'd seen him. Or Lily.

~

When I got home from Luna's house that night, I sat on the edge of my bed and typed out a new message.

~

That Friday evening, as I watched Noor, head of Retail, and Luna tear clumps of hair from a man's skin with dangerously hot wax, my phone burnt a hole in my back pocket. I was yet to receive a reply. Over the space of three days I'd realised how outlandish the whole idea was, and I was starting to regret ever sending it.

'Are you okay, Marnie?' Rose whispered when she caught me staring into space.

'I'm fine. Just, you know. Considering my approach.'

'For what? Recruitment?'

I nodded as Noor taunted, 'It's more hygienic, Shaun. And I just like it better this way.'

Rose shuffled her chair closer to mine. 'Listen to them,' she said. 'All anyone ever wants is to be heard. Listen, and they'll do just about anything.'

I nodded again.

'It's all in the resource guide,' she added, as she returned her attention to Noor.

On the tram home, my phone gave one sustained buzz.

> Hi Marnie!! So sorry for the delay –
> just got home from a shoot in New
> Zealand. I can do tomorrow?? Or
> Sunday at 2? Xx Lily

Twenty

Sitting in the same corner booth at Calooh, I toggled anxiously between apps as the waitstaff came and went. I checked my internet banking app three times before ordering a long black. My life was playing out in cafes and bars, over wine and cheese and shots of espresso. I suppose it always had done, but rytuał's emphasis on dining, entertaining, the art of the *spread* had turned the dial up to eleven. Despite this, when I was alone I often found myself subsisting on tinned chickpeas and rice. I went to bed hungry and counted the loose change I found around the house. A divide was forming between the life I was afforded inside the walls of *Emma* and the life I could afford on my own.

My phone shook with a new message.

> **LUNA PETERS**
> Let me know how it goes. X

As I went to type a reply, I heard boots clacking across the concrete floor. I stuffed the phone in my small leather bag and repositioned my bra straps on my shoulders. When I looked up, Lily was beaming. 'I'm so glad you reached out,' she said, and I had to press my thumbnail into my index finger to steady myself.

That morning, I'd retrieved the Employee Resource Guide from its hiding place beneath my bed and scanned the chapter titled RECRUITMENT STRATEGIES. In it, a series of worksheets encouraged different tactics depending on whether the potential hire was a 'warm' or 'cold' lead. I had classified Lily as warm, given her interest in me, but wasn't sure if this was the correct metric. As I continued to press my thumbnail into my index finger, I mentally repeated the worksheet's first directive: *Provide a sincere compliment (it must be sincere)*. Lily was wearing a pair of pearl earrings with an abstract silver shape attached to the bottom of each sphere. 'I love your earrings,' I said. I meant it.

'Thanks! My friend Sashi made them for me for my birthday.' She ran her fingers over the pearls, smiling. 'I love your jacket.'

The black bomber jacket I'd pulled from my wardrobe that morning had a hole in the right pocket and needed to be dry-cleaned. It was unremarkable, which made me wonder if Lily's compliment was sincere. When my coffee arrived, she ordered her own, and I remembered the worksheet's second bullet point: *Conduct your meeting under duress*.

'I don't have very long,' I said. 'Things are . . . crazy at the moment.'

'Of course,' Lily replied, with a smile, as she rearranged herself against the vinyl booth. 'I'll get right to it—'

'Oh. No. I . . . Sorry.'

'What?' Her face fell.

I leant over the table. 'I've been thinking a lot about you. About how Spencer, and Fifth Act, treated you. You didn't deserve that.'

A bemused expression drew her eyebrows towards each other.

'I'd like to help you start a new chapter.'

'What do you mean?'

'Lily, have you ever wanted to work for a company that values your unique life experience?'

As I reached for the white ceramic handle of the coffee cup, my fingers shook. I returned my hand to the table's wooden grain and looked over at Lily, who was not reacting in the way I had read a warm lead would. I took a breath. 'Sometimes we creatives assume that the only job we'll be satisfied with is a role within the arts. But the soft skills we possess are so transferrable. And valuable! It's just about believing that you're worth more.'

'Worth more?'

'Freedom and stability are possible,' I said. 'You don't have to choose.'

Lily ran her hands through her hair. 'I'm confused. Are you asking if I . . . want to work at rytuał?'

I reached for my coffee again, this time with a steady hand. After I'd taken a sip, I replied, 'I'm asking if you're ready for a new chapter.'

Lily let out a soft laugh. 'I'm a film producer,' she said. 'I thought you wanted to work for *me*.'

'I was hesitant at first as well.' I edged a hand across the table, but she pulled away. I was starting to sweat. 'Just come and meet Luna.'

'The founder?' Lily looked around the cafe uncomfortably.

'Yes. Luna's incredible. Just come and meet with her—'

'I think you've misunderstood. I don't want to work for rytuał, I . . . want to make things. I thought you did, too.'

My heart sank. Lily's coffee arrived and we both stared at it for a moment. I was at a loss: the worksheet had only accounted for a positive response.

'Are you okay, Marnie?'

'I'm fine.'

Lily opened her mouth to say something else, but hesitated.

'What?'

'There was someone else, after you,' she said. The words made me want to peel off all of my skin and leave it as a tip. 'A production assistant. Not for as long as you, I don't think—'

'It was a year. For me.'

Lily nodded. She let silence fall, but only for a moment. 'If we do this properly, we can change things. This isn't a pity offer, Marnie. I'm serious.'

She waited for me to respond, but it was too late. I felt as if I was falling backwards. It was a feeling I knew well.

~

I didn't cry when it ended. I waited for tears, but instead I developed a kind of vertigo that made me feel as though I was always in retrograde. After a week of struggling to get out of bed, I went to the doctor and they wrote me a script for antidepressants. I never filled it. Instead, I lay in my mum's bed and watched spiders cast their webs across the ceiling. Mum had moved into full-time care, and I was supposed to sell the apartment, but I couldn't stand up for longer than a few minutes at a time. I wasn't really awake, but I never slept.

Rytuał

One night, I watched myself reach for Mum's keys and stumble down the stairs to the car park. I watched myself turn the keys in the ignition and back out of her car space, narrowly missing a cement pillar and an unassuming Honda Jazz. I left my phone on the kitchen table, but I knew where I was going. I drove south. The roads whispered, 'Left, right, left,' and before long I was parked outside a house in South Yarra. I keyed the four-digit code at the gate and crept through the garden, down the path that hugged the side of the house. When I got to the kitchen window, my eyes focused on his broad shoulders, draped in a black knit jumper, as he leant over the kitchen counter and unlocked his phone. I watched him type something, smiling, and I wondered how young she was, how tall she was, how much of him she could hold in her mouth.

He glanced towards the window. My heart fell to my guts and, for a moment, I thought we were looking at each other. I opened my mouth to say something – what, and to whom? – before I heard footsteps further down the path. I swore I heard my name, and when I saw the outline of his wife's face in the dark, I ran. It wasn't until I was safely cocooned inside the dark car, inside the smell of my mother, that I lay my arms over the steering wheel and howled until my grey T-shirt was soaked with tears.

The falling feeling subsided, although that face had haunted me for weeks. It was only a split second, but I knew it was her. I hated her violently, but I hated myself more.

~

I left the cafe in a hurry. Shame surged through my veins. As I exited the cavernous warehouse, the cold air was a relief. I turned right towards Smith Street and the tram home, but as I went to pull my phone from my bag I collided with another body. I recognised the scent of her before anything else.

'Luna,' I said. 'What are you doing here?'

In an all-black workout set – buttery-soft, bobble-free leggings with a matching long-sleeved top – Luna stared back at me as though I'd asked her why she was drinking a glass of water. 'In desperate need of caffeine,' she said, nodding in the direction of Calooh. 'Oh! How'd it go?'

'Can we go to your place? I feel like I'm . . . struggling to breathe,' I said.

She nodded solemnly and threaded an arm through mine. As we walked towards her house, she checked the footpath behind us obsessively. When I looked for myself, the only person for hundreds of metres was a teenage girl walking a white Pomeranian.

~

Luna was quick to suggest that I lie down in her bedroom. I'd never been upstairs before – the suggestion made my hands clumsy. As we climbed the stairs, Luna moved slowly, and I wondered if she intended to swing her hips in my face or if it was just how she moved. I worried it was the latter.

'Here we are,' she said, when we reached the first door on the right of the landing. It didn't feature in her house tour, which only dawned on me as I took it in for the first time. There was a distinct lack of pink, which surprised me, but the room was so precisely decorated it looked like one of the many fantasy bedrooms I'd saved from my Instagram discover page. I didn't know people could actually live like this. There were two beige rugs, dark wooden side tables, four or five different lamps – already glowing in warm tones from cream to orange. Above her bed, a huge white canvas stamped with the rytuał logo – two sets of lips, interlocked like a chain – in deep red. Her bed was low to the ground, adorned with cream linen sheets. Unlike her wardrobe, everything in Luna's bedroom was the perfect degree of old. On the left side of the room, a huge window sloped at an angle towards the ceiling

'Take a seat,' she said, moving towards the bed. I removed my leather bag and stepped out of my loafers. Luna took hold of my bomber jacket and slid it down the length of my arms. 'Tea?' she said, as she revealed a built-in wardrobe beside the door. She hung my jacket without discussion. I nodded, and she disappeared.

I lay back on Luna's bed and stared at the ceiling. The scent of her was thick in the sheets. I'd struggled to pinpoint exactly what Luna smelt like until I pressed my face into her pillow: her skin smelt like sweet almond oil, or nougat, and something earthy. It was this, mixed with rytuał *We*, that had me roaming the halls of *Emma* in search of my next high. With my face pressed to the pillow, I had the strange desire to know what her sweat smelt like – and not her sweat beneath a layer of deodorant, either. I wanted to bury myself in one of her armpits.

'This all looks a bit *Single White Female*,' she said when she appeared in the doorway. I jumped, scuttling up to sit against the wall.

'Sorry,' I said. 'These sheets are so soft.'

'I'm sure they are,' she said, as she set a cup of tea on the bedside table. 'Lavender, chamomile, and—'

'Rose. Great for the skin.'

'Exactly.' She kicked off her sneakers and came to sit beside me on the bed. 'So. What happened?'

'It was stupid. I don't know what I was thinking, she's not—'

'One of us,' Luna said, like it was a full stop. I reached for the mug. When I took a sip, the scalding hot tea burnt my mouth. Luna watched as I returned it to the bedside table. 'Well, there's always Kahli. It's normal, don't worry. It took Eva four attempts, and even then I had to coach her through it.'

I ran my tongue over my top teeth. The analgesic effect of the burn was soothing. 'I forgot about that feeling,' I said. 'Feeling locked out. Does that make any sense?'

'It makes perfect sense,' she said. 'It's why I started all of this in the first place.'

'rytuał?'

She smiled. 'Well, the lip oil came first. I can't say I knew exactly what I was doing at the beginning. Although, it did come off the back of a nasty break-up. Always a great motivator . . .' She drank from her mug. 'Once I had something valuable – once *I* had value – I realised I could decide what I did with it. So, I created a place where I would never feel that way again. And when all these remarkable women shared the same story with me, I wanted to give them that dignity, too.'

'How did you just "decide" not to feel something, though? I can barely decide on a coffee order.'

She put her mug down on the bedside table and sat up on her knees. As she spoke, she placed a hand on my cheek. 'When you've been hurt like I have, your only two options are to repeat your past mistakes or devote your life to making sure you don't.'

'Who was it?' I said. 'That teacher?' Our faces were so close that the almond oil–nougat smell overwhelmed me.

She nodded. 'I'll tell you about it one day.' She didn't remove her hand from my cheek. 'I promise.'

I leant towards her and, as if it were happening in both slow motion and fast forward, we kissed. Her lips were devastatingly soft. I reached for the back of her head, but she pulled away. My heart sank as she crawled off the bed.

'Sorry—'

'You should move fast with Kahli,' she said. 'Tonight. You should ask her tonight.'

'Okay.' My vision blurred as she paced at the foot of the bed.

'I need an assistant, Marnie. You're the only one I trust. I need you to recruit someone so that I can promote you. It's very important.'

'Okay.' Her clipped consonants stung. 'I'll do it tonight.'

She stared into the distance as a sour feeling spread from my stomach through my entire body.

I said, 'I'm sorry for—', but Luna didn't hear me.

'Take a bottle of wine with you,' she said. 'I'll grab one.' She ran out of the room and down the stairs.

I reached for my leather bag, my hands shaking, and opened my text thread with Kahli.

Free tonight?

~

In the red glow of the club's pulsing lights, Kahli grinned. She threw her arms around her body like an inflatable man at a car dealership. We'd finished Luna's bottle of white wine, moved on to shots, and eventually I followed Kahli into the back of an Uber bound for Fitzroy. When I'd sent the text that afternoon, she replied straight away, and her enthusiasm softened the blow of Luna's rejection.

'I'm getting an espresso martini,' she shouted, over the din of bad house music.

I nodded and she disappeared towards the bar. I was biding my time, but I didn't have long – I needed her to actually remember the conversation tomorrow. I closed my eyes and raised my arms over my head, swaying my hips from side to side. When I opened them again, a familiar face flashed past my eyes. 'Luna,' I said, hurling myself towards sweaty bodies, but as quickly as her face appeared, it was gone. The lights began to strobe, and all around me all I could see was the faces of men. Boys, really; tall and gangly, with harsh, pained expressions. Or were they smiling? It was hard to tell. I felt someone grab my shoulder, and as I turned towards them I threw my arms out, pushing a body away from mine. Kahli's espresso martini leapt from the plastic cup, drenching the front of her grey one-shoulder top.

'What the fuck?' she yelled. 'Marnie, what the fuck.'

'Sorry!' I said. 'I'm sorry.' She rolled her eyes and dropped the empty cup to the floor. Her outrage was short-lived. 'Bathroom?'

I followed her through the mess of damp backs and loose limbs to the heaving women's bathroom. At the sink, she pulled sheets of paper towel from the dispenser and ran them under the tap. 'So, you kind of ditched me,' she said, her eyes glued to the stain.

'What? When?' A woman pushed past me to the sink beside Kahli's. I was standing just behind her right shoulder, watching her in the mirror.

'I've barely seen you since you started at rytuał.' Kahli dabbed ferociously at the brown spatter.

'I didn't think you'd notice,' I said, and she whipped her head around more quickly than I expected. 'Because you're so busy. You've got so many other friends.'

She shrugged. 'Well, I did.'

''Scuse me.' Another woman brushed past me to the sink.

Kahli dropped the wet paper towel in the bin. 'Do you need to piss?'

I followed her into one of the stalls. I needed to pull myself together. 'How's work?' I said, as Kahli rolled her black tights down to her knees. She sat down with a thump, and I leant against the stall door.

'Fucking terrible,' she said. 'I'm this close to quitting.' She didn't actually display how close 'this' was. 'Sometimes I just wonder if there's more to life than Microsoft Excel.'

I slid down the length of the door, to squat at Kahli's eye line. 'Me too. I think that all the time.' My heart was racing.

'Do you want some ket?' Kahli said, before she'd even reached for the toilet paper.

I shook my head. I needed to focus. 'Tell me about your dad. What was he like?'

'Huh?'

'Your dad. You said he died. What happened?'

'Why do you want to know that?'

'I just . . . I want to know more about you, that's all.'

She made a gun with her fingers and pointed it directly at my chest. 'You're under arrest for listening to that sad life-coaching podcast without your headphones.' She laughed, wild and twitchy. 'Police. He died at work.'

'I'm so sorry, Kahli.'

'It's fine. My mum's way happier now. She met a guy called Craig at a salsa class and now they live in an off-grid tiny house together.'

'Right.'

Kahli reached for the toilet paper. 'Why are you looking at me like that?'

'Come work at rytuał,' I blurted out, skipping over all of the recruitment worksheet's eight bullet points. 'We're always looking for like-minded individuals to join the team.'

Kahli perked up. 'Really? Doing what?'

'Well, everyone starts in Customer Service, but—'

'Fuck no,' she said, as she threaded a toilet-papered hand beneath her. 'Sorry, no offence.'

'People move quickly. Luna's really passionate about upwards mobility.' Kahli flushed the toilet. 'She just offered me a new job. As her assistant. Executive assistant. And I think it's just the beginning of—'

'Are you gonna go or what?' Kahli stood up, towering over me.

I pushed myself away from the floor to join her. 'Kahli, I'm serious. Just come and meet Luna.' I paused, trying to settle on a unique selling proposition that would pique Kahli's interest. 'She'll . . . change your life.'

Kahli stared back at me with an expression I couldn't quite place – the needle teetered between disgust and delight. After a moment, she readjusted her one-shoulder top and said, 'Okay.'

As we tumbled out of the stall, I opened a new text to Luna.

I got her. X

Twenty-one

On Monday morning, Coco and I were met with an alert that the BlissScreen inbox had reached capacity. The barrage of complaints we faced each day had led me to believe that the inbox could expand and contract in relation to the number of customers who'd been prescribed hydrocortisone ointment that week, but evidently this was not the case.

'Whoa,' Coco said, tucking one foot under herself on her chair. 'What the hell.'

The first submission I opened read:

> When are you going to acknowledge the allegations??
> Tick tock, rytual, your customers deserve accountability.

My stomach dropped. The next message read:

> Disappointing but not surprising.

Hundreds of variations on the same theme spilt out of the inbox. When I looked over at Coco's screen, she was already googling *rytual cosmetica cancelled*. I rolled my chair over to her desk and watched as she clicked through the search results, eventually landing on a post at the top of the r/rytualcosmetica subreddit. It had thousands of comments. The username was 'badrytuals'. The account was only twenty-four hours old. By the time Coco and I had found it, the rest of the office had cottoned on, too. All twenty monitors in *Emma*'s basement displayed the same five paragraphs:

> I was employed by rytuał cosmetica as an in-store adviser for just four weeks. I had always admired the brand, and was particularly drawn to its founder, Luna Peters. When I began my training, however, I was horrified to discover that the work environment at rytuał is plagued by a culture of fear and intimidation.
>
> Luna Peters has created a business structure in which she is able to manipulate her employees for personal gain. During my time at rytuał I discovered that the 'HR lead' is a fictional character – a moniker for the founder herself to manage complaints as she sees fit.
>
> I came across this information after a troubling altercation with Luna Peters. One afternoon, as I was closing the flagship Fitzroy store, Luna arrived and asked if she could search the back of house for a product sample she had mistakenly left there the day before. I obliged.

> When we were alone in the back of house area, Luna made a joke about the size of my breasts, and asked if she could compare them with hers. When I declined, she told me that the company was focused on breaking taboos, and that if I didn't do as she said I would be upholding destructive patriarchal norms.
>
> I submitted a complaint to HR, which was when Luna revealed that she was indeed the only person with access to this inbox. When I threatened to take this information public, she physically harassed me and said she would ensure I didn't find another job in the beauty industry. She is a predator and a bully, and she must be stopped. Sharing here in case anyone else has had the same experience.

My face flushed. I remembered Luna's solemn expression as she'd clambered off the bed – away from my awkward, wanting lips – and abruptly changed the subject. This story didn't make any sense; Luna was unpredictable, but she wasn't stupid.

We looked up from our screens at the same time. Nervous eyes darted around the room in an attempt to intuit allegiances, but no one said anything. As the silence wrapped itself around our necks, the door at the top of the staircase flew open. 'Good morning, rytuałists,' Luna said, smiling as she padded down the stairs. Coco frantically closed the browser window.

'Luna—' one of The Lauras said, as she stood from her desk. 'Um, there's something we need to talk to you about.'

'Can it wait? I need to speak with Marnie first.' She traipsed over to my desk and tapped her ombre orange-and-pink nails on the wood.

'Sure,' Laura said. 'Okay. Yeah. No worries.'

Luna nodded and finally turned to face me. 'My office?' she said, expectantly. As I followed her up the stairs, I felt the heat of nineteen sets of eyes watching us leave.

~

'What do you think?' she said as she presented me with two small glass bottles. Both had dropper heads affixed to the top, but one was made from emerald-tinted glass and the other was a deep red. The labels on both bottles read *rytuał Eve – packaging sample v. 6*. 'Which is better? Green is giving garden of Eden, red is giving . . . I don't know, womb?' She laughed and flopped onto the couch. 'Come on, Marnie, help me.'

'It's hard to say.' I stared at each of the bottles, but Luna's hands were distracting. I couldn't help but imagine them splayed out across her breasts; measuring their circumference against her palm.

After a moment, she said, 'Go on, ask me.'

'Ask you what?'

She raised her eyebrows as she placed the bottles on the coffee table. 'Ask me if it's true. I know you've seen it.'

I took a step towards the couch. 'Well, is it?'

She gave a performative huff. 'No. I did go to the store that day, but she came onto me. When I turned her down she threatened to tell HR I'd sexually harassed her, so I said . . . I am HR. *That* was my big mistake. We have the CCTV footage from the back room, it's on my computer. I can show you—'

'But what about Friday Night Drinks?'

'We knew Isabel wasn't the right fit from the beginning—'

'Isabel?' The scene came into focus: Isabel's pixie cut attached itself to her blood-red uniform as she spoke to Kahli at the rytuał store.

'Do you know her?'

'I met her once, at the store. With Kahli – she's friends with Isabel's sister. I hadn't realised.'

'Strange girl,' she said. 'I got the feeling she might cut off all my hair and try to sell it on eBay or something.'

'So she never came? To Friday Night Drinks?'

'No,' Luna said, cool as a cucumber. 'She was on probation.'

'Right.' I looked out the window. Two women, mummified by layers of merino, were drinking espresso in the courtyard. As if it were just another Monday morning. Maybe it was.

'Should we chat about the other night?' Luna said, as she signalled for me to join her on the couch. The urge to hit my head against the edge of the coffee table was overwhelming.

'I'm sorry,' I said. 'It was inappropriate—'

Luna cut me off. 'I'm thinking ninety k to start, with a bonus structure we'll nut out later.'

'What?'

'For your new role. Executive Assistant to the CEO.' She grinned. 'This is the swiftest we've ever seen someone progress.'

'I thought Kahli had to make it past her first Friday Night Drinks—'

'I know, but I'm desperate for an assistant. I'm sure we can make an exception just this once. Plus, I have a good feeling about her. You and I have similar tastes.'

I watched as she collected the two bottles from the table and held them up to the light.

'Ninety thousand is nearly double what I make now,' I said. 'That would change—'

'Everything?'

'Yes.'

~

When I opened the front door, Kahli was quick to pipe up from the kitchen. 'Hi!' she called out. 'I'm ordering food, do you want some?'

'Maybe,' I said, as I wriggled out of my sneakers. 'Are you paying?'

'Sure.' Her voice was uncharacteristically peppy. When I got to the kitchen, she jumped up from her stool and handed me her phone, delivery app at the ready.

'What's the catch?'

'No catch,' she said. 'Today at work I just thought, fuck it, you know? Wallenheimer is so crusty; everyone's ancient or, like, obsessed with crypto. I got the calendar invite from Luna and I thought . . . Marnie's right. This is a great opportunity.'

'Totally,' I said. 'Did you . . . see the post?'

'What post?'

I pressed my thumbnail into my index finger. 'Nothing. When's your interview?'

'Tomorrow. Go on, order something.'

I scrolled through the menu and picked a noodle dish at random. Isabel's name had been rattling around the space between my ears all afternoon. As I handed the phone back to Kahli, I said, 'Hey, what's the deal with Isabel?'

'Clea's sister?' she asked, as she pressed *Place order* and discarded the phone on the bench. 'I don't know her that well, but she's fun. A bit intense.'

'What does that mean?'

'When we were in Mykonos there was this thing. It's not a big deal, we were super drunk. And it was ages ago.'

'What happened?'

Kahli returned to one of the stools and wrapped her right leg over her left. 'I mean, the caveat is that she ended up going to rehab, so I can't really judge her for, you know . . .' She pursed her lips and moved them from side to side. 'One night the two of us came home early, and we were out on the balcony and she kind of tried to kiss me? But then when I pulled away she joked that she was going to push me over the edge. She didn't, obviously, and she apologised. She's been sober for, like, years now.'

'Right.'

'Why do you ask?'

I debated whether sharing this information with Kahli worked in my best interests or against them, but she was bound to find out anyway. It was a miracle she hadn't seen it already. I pulled my phone from my pocket and opened the post from badrytuals. Her eyes widened as I slid it across the counter. 'Luna says it was the other way around. She has the CCTV recording.' An inscrutable expression came over Kahli's face as she thumbed through the post.

'Is this true?' she said, pausing on the paragraph that mentioned Luna's approach to HR. Kahli's bubbly demeanour had dissolved – she was stony-faced now.

The full story would take all night, and there was no way to provide Kahli with the relevant context and omit any mention of Friday Night Drinks. Those who had made it past probation at rytuał seemed perfectly content – by the time I'd arrived, *Emma* was a well-oiled machine. Which is why I returned Kahli's grave expression and said, 'No.'

~

'Good morning, rytuałists,' Luna said the next day, in the room called *Britney*. 'I know we're here for The Clearing, but I thought it might be appropriate to address the elephant in the room.' A nervous titter spread through the crowd. Luna was wearing a blue ankle-length dress that was covered in small bows. At the centre of her chest, the fabric made a V-shape that was held together – loosely – by one of them. 'Do you want to ask questions? Or should I speak first?'

Coco's hand shot up to the ceiling. 'I guess it's not so much a question, but more, like . . . I just wanted to say that I stand with you, Luna. I support you.' A few people muttered in agreement.

'Thank you, Coco. That's sweet.' From the left side of the room, I saw another hand. 'Noor?' Luna said.

Noor stood up from her chair, her eyes on the floor as she said, 'I think it's important to clarify . . . um, we in the Retail team want to know. Is Cleo Henning . . . real? I understand she's external, but . . .' She trailed off.

Luna stared at Noor for a moment, her face suspended between a smile and a scowl. Eventually, she clapped her hands together and began to laugh. 'Oh, Noor! Sweet Noor. It's a great question.'

'Thank you,' Noor said, quietly.

But Luna didn't provide an answer. 'An external HR lead is no longer an appropriate solution for our growing business.

I'd like to find a suitable replacement among our ranks. If you wish to apply, please send me an email after The Clearing. This will not be a position that requires you to recruit a new rytuałist in order to progress.'

'Okay,' Noor said, as she shrank back into her seat.

Luna scanned the crowd, and when she saw that there were no further questions, she said, 'I know this is a difficult time for many of us, but I want to assure you that I'm creating space for you all – your concerns, your anxiety – and I can promise you'—she placed a hand on her heart—'I will take care of this.'

After a moment of silence, someone began to clap. It was slow to build at first, but gradually everyone joined in. The sound grew from polite applause to a thunderous roar. Luna took a small bow, and when she stood she said, 'That's enough. Now, who has something they'd like to clear?'

From beside me, a hand. Priya from IT stood before Luna had even acknowledged her. 'I do,' Priya said, and it was back to business as usual.

Twenty-two

On my way out the door, Luna tugged at my hand. 'I need you,' she said, as the flow of traffic continued around us. 'Help me with Kahli.'

Rose's stern face appeared beside us as she said, 'Are you sure that's a good idea?'

'Oh, god, Rose, you're obsessed with rules. Live a little, my love.'

Luna jostled through the crowd, dragging me with her. As we emerged into the hallway, I caught Rose's eyes through the glass. She shook her head disapprovingly and looked away.

~

'Kahli, it's such a pleasure to finally meet you.' Luna reached across the table for Kahli's hand. Her orange-and-pink nails wrapped around Kahli's fingers with the grip of a boa constrictor. Seeing the two of them in the same room felt like trying to watch two movies at the same time.

'Likewise,' Kahli said. I watched the space between her spinal vertebrae inflate. Corporate peacocking was natural to Kahli. 'Nice nails,' she added, as she ran her eyes across Luna's talons. 'SNS?'

'Gel-X,' Luna said as we all sat down. 'Although it's still decimating my nails.' Despite the banal subject matter, Luna stared at Kahli quizzically. They were perfect sparring partners, and she could smell it straight away. 'Please,' she added, extending a hand towards the platter at the centre of the table.

Kahli plucked an almond from the pile and brought it to her nose. 'Are these smoked almonds?'

'Is that a problem?'

'Smoked nuts taste like burnt mulch. No offence.' She returned it to the platter.

Luna grinned. 'None taken. I like your candour.'

Kahli didn't say anything. The equation wasn't adding up. Luna's heat hardened Kahli, like boiling water hardens an egg but melts butter – and of course, I was butter. 'Kahli was a consultant at Wallenheimer,' I said, desperately hoping to revive the conversation.

It wasn't until Luna looked over at me and said, 'That's not relevant, Marnie,' that I realised things were going well.

'So, Kahli. What do you know about rytuał?'

Kahli leant forwards. 'You have to move faster to stay ahead. You'll need a new hero product soon. The lip oil was a game changer, but it's at the end of its life cycle. I'm thinking skincare. It'll be skincare. Brand perception is luxury, high-end, aspirational. I think—'

'That's enough,' Luna said. My stomach flipped, but she was still grinning. It didn't affect Kahli at all. 'Do you like our products?'

'The foundation is a little hard to use. I like the mascara, but I think you should invest in tubing. People want tubing mascara—'

'Do they?'

'Absolutely.'

'What else?' Luna was enjoying this. She bounced in her chair like a toddler. 'What about me?'

'What about you?'

'What do you think about me? Be honest.'

'Well, everyone wants to be you.'

'Not everyone,' she mused. 'Some people want to fuck me, too.' She made a face that reminded me of the purple devil emoji Kahli frequently sent me when she wanted me to join her in making bad decisions. Kahli raised her eyebrows, but this didn't deter Luna. 'So, which one are you?' Luna said, stacking her forearms on the table. I searched for her eyes, but she was consumed by Kahli. Fascinated by her.

'I don't think that's an appropriate question,' Kahli said, although she didn't recoil. It was a power grab, nothing more.

'Of course,' Luna said, nodding. 'Just kidding.' And this was all it took for Luna to offer Kahli a job.

~

When we'd ushered Kahli out of *Emma*, Luna turned to me and said, 'Grab your things from downstairs and move up to my office. I have a supplier meeting this afternoon, but I want you to make me a spreadsheet of our competitors' night serums – go through the reviews and highlight keywords, complaints, any common features. Can you do that?'

'Sure,' I said. 'Of course.' It seemed like something The Lauras would have done months ago, but I was in no position to turn down a task.

Luna winked as Eva appeared with a camel trench coat and Luna's red-tinted sunglasses. 'Thank you, Eva,' she said, as she slid her arms into the coat. 'I'll see you later.' She leant towards my cheek and kissed the air just beside it. And then she was gone.

I returned to the basement, where Coco was at the tail end of a call to someone who'd dropped their bottle of rytuał *She* and thought we should be the ones to replace it. 'I completely understand that, Yolanda,' she said. 'I just wonder if . . . Of course, yeah, it's so awful that your dog died. Really sorry to hear that.'

I took a cursory scroll through the inbox. The messages regarding the allegations had miraculously disappeared. When Coco hung up the phone, she rolled her chair towards my desk and said, 'Do you have your Career Conversation with Rose this afternoon as well?'

'What's that?'

'Planning for who we'll recruit. And what we'll be promoted to. Who are you recruiting?'

'I've already recruited someone. I'm working as Luna's assistant now. Executive assistant.'

'What?! That's crazy, who did you recruit?'

'My housemate. Kahli.'

'Ohhh.' She nodded. 'The one who . . . with Tom. Thomas.'

'Yeah. That's her.' I fumbled to unplug my laptop from the monitor.

'Well, hope you do some great executive assisting up there, girl!' She returned her eyes to the screen.

I slung my backpack over one shoulder and collected my laptop, keyboard and mouse. When I'd wound my way up to Luna's office, it was dark – in the afternoons, the sun dipped below the nearby apartment buildings, and Luna's elaborate lighting scheme came in handy. As I pushed the weighty glass door open, the room lit up, because a life at rytuał was a frictionless one.

It was the first time I'd visited Luna's office without her, and I couldn't shake the feeling that I was doing something wrong. I walked over to her desk and nestled my laptop in front of her hulking silver computer, but as I sat down I must have nudged the mouse – the giant screen illuminated itself, presenting me with Luna's staff portrait and a prompt to enter her password. I stared at the box, wondering how many secrets were hidden behind its plain grey shape, but the thought of Luna discovering my betrayal was enough to return my gaze to my own screen. I also didn't know the password. On the desk beside the keyboard, Luna had left a tube of lip oil. It was *Lust*, the dark-pink shade I was becoming increasingly familiar with, and it was half empty. I looked around the silent office. As quickly as I could, I plucked the tube from the desk and rubbed the thick pink liquid over my lips. I was disappointed to discover that it felt exactly the same as the one I had at home – some desperate part of me had hoped that Luna's would be different.

I opened a new spreadsheet and five browser tabs. I did as I was told, retrieving product *Features* and *Benefits* (which I could now differentiate: the former being a fact about the product, the latter something it could offer to customers) from our competitors and compiling them in consecutive white boxes. When I looked up, three hours had passed. The sky was inky blue.

Rytuał

As I closed my laptop, Luna's computer lit up again. Notifications were flashing in quick succession at the top right corner of the screen. There must have been hundreds. Without the password, all I could see was the apps they were coming from. When I pulled my phone from my bag, a text from Kahli presented itself on screen:

Have you seen this??

She sent a link. It directed me to r/rytualcosmetica. It was badrytuals. Another post:

> After sharing my experience of working for rytuał cosmetica, I was contacted by hundreds of individuals who offered support and resources, and I want to begin by thanking everyone who rallied behind me. I now feel that it's important to provide context on my time at rytuał – context I did not initially offer out of fear that it would dilute my message. During my employment at rytuał I was caught up in a very private, all-consuming battle with alcoholism, which resulted in my drinking at work. rytuał were able to provide me with the CCTV footage from the day Luna visited the store, and as a result I have decided to retract my allegations. I was also contacted by rytuał's HR lead, who confirmed to me that the business is committed to fostering a culture of mutual respect and emotional safety. I sincerely apologise for any harm I've caused. I will delete my posts in seven days.

I scrolled through the comments. The first one read:

Babe no one asked for your life story

It had 215 upvotes.

I locked the screen and slid my laptop into my backpack. And that was that.

~

The man's name was Mason. He had been married to Priya for seven years. They had separated eighteen months before he found himself tied to a chair in the basement of *Emma* – a decision that was all Priya's. Mason didn't want to be divorced, so when the time came he made the dissolution of their marriage as difficult as possible. He wound up with the majority of their shared assets, but even that wasn't enough. When Priya started dating again, he found her new partners on social media and contacted them obsessively. He just wouldn't leave her alone.

Luna pranced around the chair as Mason struggled to keep her in his line of sight. His head flopped from right to left as Luna continued to circle him. Priya stood to the right, awaiting instruction, but Eva didn't hand her a weapon. There were no weapons in the basement that night.

Until this particular Friday night, I'd assumed that the men would always be punished according to their crimes. Rose had found Kahli's hair tie, so she hit Tom with a curling wand. The Toad dropped his pants for Victoria, so she whipped him with a belt. No one had explained it to me, but it seemed kind of obvious. As Luna came to stand in front of Mason, I gripped the edge of my chair. I wondered how she would punish a man whose crimes were mostly paperwork.

'Mason, Mason, Mason,' she said. 'Whatever will we do with you?'

'I'm sorry,' he said, although the gag made pronouncing consonants near impossible. 'I'm sorry, please—'

'A little too late for that,' Luna said. 'Don't you think?' Mason started crying. Sobbing, really. 'Oh, don't you dare fucking cry.' She crossed her arms at her chest, considering her options. 'Priya, come here.' Priya did as she was told. 'What do you have to say to this man?'

'I, um, I want to say . . . You need to stop, Mason. It's over.'

Luna nodded. His sobs intensified. 'Mason, what did I say about crying?' She moved to stand directly in front of him. As he looked up at her, she sighed, and before he could say anything she threw her right fist into his cheek. It was so fast, so precise.

'Luna!' Rose said as she stood up on the other side of the room.

'It's fine.' Luna walked away from the chair as she shook out her fist. Mason's gag turned red and he made a sad wailing noise. He didn't call Priya a bitch, or Luna a whore. He wasn't angry, he was scared. Fear smelt like burnt hair and vinegar, when you took the time to notice it. Rose returned to her seat.

'You heard her,' Bibi said, monitoring the proceedings from the back of the room. 'Stop crying.' I realised I'd never heard her voice before. It was rich and gravelly in a way that brought to mind childbirth and social smoking. Liv nodded in agreement.

'Priya, I want you to hit this man once for every time he disappointed you.'

'I don't know if I can—'

'Just trust me.'

Priya walked to Mason's chair and stood tentatively in front of him. I let my eyes close just enough to blur his features. In low resolution he could have been anyone, or specifically someone else. I kept staring through lazy eyelids until Priya raised an open palm and said, 'You never made me come! Not even once!' Her hand smacked the side of his face. As his cries filled the room, they flew over our heads as if they were intended for someone else.

Twenty-three

'So, Kahli. Cleo Henning mentioned that you had some questions regarding your contract. We're in the middle of an HR reshuffle, so I thought it would be best if you and I spoke directly.'

Luna used the name Cleo Henning so casually that it was easy to forget she wasn't a real person. I was sat to Luna's left, in the room called *Jean*, as Kahli leafed through the contract she'd been sent the week before. My presence was unnecessary and potentially inappropriate, but neither party seemed to care.

'Yes,' Kahli said, crossing her legs beneath the table. 'I just want to clarify a few things before I sign.'

I had signed my rytuał contract hours after receiving it. I hadn't even considered a negotiation.

'Go on,' Luna said. 'I'm all ears.'

I was running my thumb across the skin of my right hand when Kahli looked over at me. Luna had gifted me a ziplock wallet with three samples of a potential body balm. I didn't know my skin could feel so soft. I gave an encouraging smile.

'Well, for starters, this salary doesn't reflect my experience,' Kahli said. 'I understand that this is an entry-level position, but I have a wealth of customer-facing experience, and—'

'How much do you want?' Luna said. She was unbothered.

'Eighty k,' Kahli said. 'I was on ninety-eight at Wallenheimer, but I'm willing to compromise.'

'Okay,' Luna said, as if it was the easiest decision she'd make all day. I was shocked by the directness of it all.

'Great,' Kahli said. 'Now, on to hours of work . . .' She shuffled through the pages.

'Not so fast,' Luna said. 'Now it's my turn.'

'What do you mean?'

'Well, we've done one for you, now we do one for me. That's just good business.'

I thought that the more time I spent with Luna, the easier she would be to predict, but this was not the case. I had absolutely no idea where she was going with this.

'Okay,' Kahli said. 'Shoot.'

'Tell me something about you.'

Kahli laughed, but she maintained eye contact with Luna as though they were dance partners – deciphering if she was serious, how serious she was, and what it would cost her. It was an elaborate routine.

'What do you want to know?'

'I'm not sure,' Luna mused. 'Something worth eighty k.'

'What is this, collateral?' Kahli scoffed.

I watched Luna change tack in an instant. Her mind was whirring, taking the raw data from Kahli's disgruntled expression and translating it into a way she could get her onside. This was the heart of Luna's genius: she made herself the most powerful person in any room. There are many people for whom this would have been a red flag, but watching her control the room's climate only made her more alluring.

'No,' Luna cooed. 'No, Kahli. I just want to get to know you.' She reached her hand across the table. 'I can see how that might have sounded manipulative, but I just want to know who you are. Show me a part of you no one else sees.'

'Why?' Kahli looked over at me again, but I kept my eyes on my lap.

'Because I want to look after you,' Luna said. 'But first you need to let me in.'

Kahli's lips remained clamped shut, but Luna loved a challenge. 'What was your father like?' she said, and as I watched Kahli's shoulders soften just slightly, I knew Luna had won. Maybe Kahli was butter, after all.

~

'Does anyone have anything to clear?'

For the first time since my arrival at rytuał, no one raised their hand. The silence was overwhelming. Luna glared at the crowd, but still no one raised their hand. 'Anyone?' she said, as people sank into their chairs. I wasn't sure if you could clear the same person twice. The last man I'd had more than a passing conversation with was keto-breath Justin.

'Wow,' she said. 'This is a first.' It was hard to discern if Luna was surprised-intrigued, or surprised-mad. A few nervous giggles surfaced as a result. 'Seriously? No one?' She looked at me, but I had nothing to offer.

'Okay, then,' she said. 'I guess I'm going rogue.' She laughed, but it had the sharp edge of surprised-mad.

As we stood up from our chairs, Luna made a beeline for me. 'I need your assistance, assistant.'

'Okay,' I said, as two out of three Lauras brushed past me to the door. 'What did you have in mind?'

~

'Can you drive?' Luna said on the footpath outside *Emma*. The keys were already midair – I threw my left hand out just in time to catch them.

'Of course.'

'Great,' she said. 'This is us.'

A black Audi had been parked outside *Emma* for as long as I could remember, but it was somehow always spotless.

'Can you . . . *not* drive?'

She opened the passenger-side door and shook her head. 'Why would I?'

The car was electric, or hybrid, or it was just expensive. When we were sealed in the cabin I wrapped myself in the seatbelt and sat, stunned, trying to work out what happened next. 'What's wrong?' she said. Impatient, she leant over my lap and pressed a button. The engine hummed.

'I've never driven a car like this,' I said.

'Welcome to the future.' She plugged in her phone and tapped at a map on the touchscreen console.

We drove east. After the tramlines ended there were art-deco apartments, and then there were cream bricks, and then there was grass. The speed limit edged higher as the number of cars on the road decreased. We pulled into a cul-de-sac tucked behind the freeway. The houses were photocopies of each other, their differences eerily small. 'The destination is on your left,' the GPS announced, and the map disappeared.

'Where are we?' I said.

'Guess,' she replied with a playful grin.

'Is this where you . . . grew up?' I looked out at the rest of the street. It was entirely unremarkable. She shook her head. On her side of the road, the door to a house opened. Luna saw my eyes shift to the right. She spun her head around to the window, and when she caught sight of the person in the doorway, she shrugged down to the bottom of her seat.

'Get down,' she said.

I slid to the floor and held my breath, waiting for Luna's instruction. Eventually, a diesel engine roared to a start somewhere down the street. 'We need to follow him,' she said. 'Can you do that?'

~

It was a suburban pub, built in the early 2000s and marked by novelty architecture. A glass dome covered the dining room, and the children's playground snaked around the building like the outer modules of a space station. Places like this orbited a different sun to Smith Street and its chic vegan ramen bars.

At the entrance to the public bar, Luna pulled me behind a wall. 'Follow my lead,' she said. 'We need to get him to the car.'

'Who is he?' I stammered, but she was already gone. She crossed the sour-smelling carpet with long strides. The man was seated at the bar, slumped over a yellow pint. He must have been in his mid-fifties, dressed in worn denim and a blue flannel shirt. Luna took the two seats next to him hostage.

'Hi,' she said, looking all the way down the bar. 'Excuse me?'

The bartender – freshly eighteen, face like a pizza – stumbled towards us. 'We'll have two pints of VB,' Luna said as she placed her black Amex on the bar. The sight of the card made the bartender clumsy. Luna hit an open palm against the seat closest to the man. I sat, gingerly, catching a whiff of his pharmacy cologne. The nervous bartender deposited two foamy pints in front of us.

'VB?' the man said, right on cue. 'I'm impressed.' His voice was thick and hoarse. He had a faint Eastern European accent.

'Why?' Luna said. 'You're drinking it.'

I swivelled on the stool to face him. His skin hung off his skull like a basset hound's.

'Good point,' he said. As he made eye contact with Luna, recognition flickered in his eyes. 'Don't I know you from somewhere?'

'I don't think so,' she said.

'Are you an actress? You look like someone—'

'My cousin,' she said, with complete certainty. 'I have a cousin. She's on *Home and Away*. That's who you're thinking of.' I had no idea if this was true. The man kept staring at her.

'We just moved here from Sydney,' Luna said. 'We're staying at my uncle's house while he's away.'

'Welcome,' the man conceded. He was already tipsy. 'Not the most exciting corner of the globe, but the beer's cheap.'

A laugh shot out of Luna's mouth. I watched the man clock this, conclude that the noise was genuine and smile to himself. 'I'm Laura,' Luna continued. 'This is Maggie.'

'Hi,' was all I could add.

'Antoni,' he said.

'So, why are you drinking alone on a Tuesday?'

He swilled the last of his pint. Before he could answer, Luna added, 'Let us buy you another one,' and although he was shaking his head, she'd already waved down the bartender with her frightening black Amex. She pointed to the empty glass. Eventually, Antoni shrugged.

'I'll let you in on a secret, girls: there's no reward in life for doing the right thing. You'll be punished either way, so you might as well enjoy yourselves.'

'Bleak,' Luna said. 'But I like it.'

Antoni grinned. His smile was yellow, like the beer. The bartender handed a fresh pint to Luna, who ferried it across to Antoni.

'Let's drink to that!' She raised her glass. I followed, and when we both looked to Antoni he did the same.

'Scull.' Luna said. 'Do it!' She began to chug. The beer was acidic and flat as it flew down my throat. Luna kept her eyes on me as we swallowed – *gulp, gulp, gulp*. From the corner of my eye, I saw Antoni do the same.

'Another round!' Luna cried as she dumped the empty glass on the bar. 'Three more!'

'I need a leak,' Antoni said, wobbling on his stool. We watched him stagger to the bathroom.

Without moving her mouth, Luna whispered, 'I'm going to hand you something, and I need you to drop it in his drink.'

When I turned to face her, she just smiled. Beneath the bar, she placed a hand on my thigh. I slid my fingers to meet hers, and she handed me a small, chalky pill. Holding it made my palms sweat. The bartender arrived with three more beers, and

Luna gave a curt smile in his direction. He left us alone as quickly as possible.

'We need to get him to the car,' she said, when the bartender was out of earshot.

'This is insane,' I said, trying to whisper but spraying Luna with spit instead. 'Who is he?'

'I'll tell you everything in the car,' she said. 'I promise.'

I looked up at the bartender, who was staring intently at the back of a bottle of Aperol. I reached for Antoni's drink, raised it to my lips, and dropped the white disc inside. I kept my lips firmly closed as I mimed a sip. Then, I placed it back on the bar.

'Good,' Luna purred. When Antoni returned, he drank enthusiastically from the new glass. Luna's eyes glowed. 'We actually had to get out of the house today because . . .' Luna trailed off, looking at the floor. 'Okay, don't laugh at us.'

Antoni shook his head, bemused.

'The heating broke, and we can't afford to get it repaired. We watched a YouTube video, but it said you needed three people to fix it.'

I raised my eyebrows in Luna's direction.

'You sound like my daughter.'

'You have a daughter?' I said.

Luna pressed on. 'We just need someone to help us with the pilot light. Or whatever it is.'

'Can't you just call your uncle?'

'He'll be furious, it's only been two days. I really don't want to bother him.'

Antoni tilted his head from side to side. 'What's in it for me?'

'We'll buy you another drink,' I said, surprising myself. 'We love drinking with new friends.'

Twenty-four

My hands were slippery on the wheel. I knew a pint was somewhere between one and two standard drinks, but my eyes struggled to make sense of the road as if it were more. Maybe it was because I was circling suburbia, waiting for a middle-aged man I'd just roofied to collapse in the back seat of someone else's car. Maybe it was Luna's grip on my left thigh. Maybe it was the eye test I'd never got around to booking.

'It's just around the corner,' she said, and when we turned the corner and he was still conscious she added, 'Sorry, I'm getting confused. I think we took a wrong turn.'

I laughed at a pitch I hoped was convincing and lurched the car across the road, doubling back to find another street that looked exactly the same.

'It's fine,' he said. 'You can plug your phone in, you know.'

'This car is way too high-tech for me,' Luna said.

'I can do it,' he said, as he unbuckled his seatbelt. He leant forwards and Luna pulled her hand from my thigh. 'Give me your phone.'

'It won't connect,' she said, starting to sweat. I took a right at the milk bar where we'd previously gone left. Maybe it wasn't enough. Maybe it didn't dissolve properly.

'Give it to me,' he said. He was too close: the acrid smell of his cologne made my stomach churn.

'No, it's okay,' Luna said. I kept my eyes on the road.

He swiped at her lap, reaching for her phone, but it was wedged under her thigh. She swatted his hand away.

'Get off me,' she said.

'Uh, I think it's just up here,' I said, taking another right turn.

'I'm just trying to help.' He leant between the front seats and plunged his hand under her thigh. When Luna grabbed his wrist, he tried again with his free hand and she grabbed that too.

'Let it go, old man.'

'We're nearly there, guys, let's just—'

'Where are you taking me?' he said, suddenly rigid.

'My uncle's house,' Luna said, through gritted teeth, but her grip wavered.

His hands flew away from hers, and before I could understand what was happening, he collected her neck in the crook of his elbow. From behind her seat, he growled, 'Stop the car.' And it took three seconds too long for me to realise he was speaking to me.

'Don't do it,' Luna said, and he tightened his grip. She struggled against him, but she didn't scream. I turned another corner. 'Keep driving,' she spluttered, and he must have doubled down, because her gasps became more frantic.

'Pull over.'

'Okay,' I said. 'Okay, I'm stopping.'

As I compressed the brake, I waited for an idea, any idea, but nothing arrived. When the car came to a stop I kept my eyes directly in front of me. It was over. He unhooked his hairy arm and Luna threw her torso forwards, struggling for breath. Antoni fumbled with the locked door.

'Stop playing tricks,' he said, fighting with the handle.

'I'm not doing anything.'

After three clicks of the lock, the door sprang open. Antoni toppled into the street.

'Crazy bitches,' he said, as he slammed the door and staggered off. In the rear-view, I saw him jog away from us, getting smaller with each laboured step.

Luna was still breathing heavily. Her hands traced burgeoning bruises around her neck.

'I'm so sorry,' I said. 'I must have done it wrong. Are you okay?'

'I'm fine.' She sat all the way up. Her face was streaked with tears.

I placed a hand over hers on her neck. She rolled her eyes. I watched them settle on the mirror. Something caught her attention.

'What?'

I turned in my seat, but Luna was already out of the car. There was a shape lying on the nature strip at the end of the street. It wasn't moving. It was the size of a man.

'Get the zip ties,' she said, as she ran towards him.

~

'It's surprisingly spacious,' Luna said, as we stared at Antoni, unconscious and flabby, folded like a wilted flower in the boot of the car.

My hands were trembling. We'd carried him there in three bursts: each time we stopped, we lowered him to the grass and I shook out my hands for as long as I could, before panicking that someone might turn the corner and discover two women standing over a large, dead-looking man. But Luna was calm. She pressed a button, and the car's boot clicked shut.

'Who do you do this with? Normally?'

'Rose. Well, except for Tom. Eva helped with him. Highlight of her year,' she said. 'Are you okay?' Her bruises were starting to ripen. As I stared at the marks on her neck, she seemed to shrink. 'Hey,' she said, as my eyes filled with wiggly tears. 'It's fine. I'm fine.'

'Sorry,' I said. She looped her arms around my waist and pulled me towards her. I nestled the right side of my face into her hair as her open palm circled my lower back.

'Come on,' she said as she released me and trotted back to the passenger-side door. The sudden distance between us made me furious.

I walked to the driver's side and lowered myself into the car. When both the doors were shut, we sat in silence. I could hear her breathing, slow and measured, beneath the sound of my own heartbeat, which was pulverising my eardrums.

'Well?' she said, and she was looking at me, but she didn't reach over to start the car. She didn't push me in any direction. She just sat, her hands in her lap, waiting. 'What now?'

I tried to start the ignition but my eyes couldn't find the right button. Or they didn't want to. 'That's not what I meant,' she said, watching me try to make sense of the car's many functions. When I looked at her, she was grinning. She ran her eyes over me, as if she was giving me some kind of final appraisal, then leant across the centre console. My lips leapt at the opportunity to meet hers, and then we were kissing. The thrill of her tongue against mine dissolved the brittle layer that had formed around my longing, and I was overcome by the feeling that I wanted to be so sweet to her – because I'd been so unhappy when I was hard. She ran her fingers through my hair and it set me on fire. Very gently, she brushed a thumb over my nipple, and it was nearly enough to send me into cardiac arrest.

I reached for the waist of her jeans and fumbled to open her fly, but she stopped me in my tracks. 'Not yet,' she said, but in the same breath she reached over and unbuttoned mine. Her hand crept beneath the scratchy lace of my underwear, and without instruction she found the centre of me. I moaned a pathetic little moan, but it was only pathetic because it was real. 'I will have you,' she said. 'But not yet.' She withdrew her hand and dipped her index and middle fingers into her mouth. I pressed my upper back against the door and bent my knees up to my chest to hide my shallow breathing. She did the same, and when faced with our mirror image we both burst into laughter.

'Maybe spacious was the wrong word,' she said.

I buttoned my fly. 'After that time at your house . . . I thought it was just me.'

'I was just'—she looked down at her nails—'taking my time.'

I nodded.

'Who's the man in the boot?' I said.

'Oh, didn't I tell you?'

I shook my head.

'He's Coco's dad.'

~

When we returned to *Emma*, Rose was waiting. It was after 6.30, and a harsh wind blew down the dark street as we clambered out of the car. 'You can go now, Marnie,' Luna said. 'Rose will take it from here.'

'What?' I looked over at Rose as I pushed the door shut. 'No, I want to help.'

Luna walked around the front of the car, to my side. 'You've done enough, my love,' she said as she ran a hand through my hair again. I felt Rose's hot, jealous eyes from the pavement.

'Did I do something wrong?'

'Can you pop the boot?' Rose said.

Luna reached for my hand, slid the car key from my grip and pressed the button with the icon of an open trunk.

As Rose busied herself with Antoni, Luna returned her attention to me. 'No,' she said. 'You haven't done anything. Rose just knows—'

A harsh thud came from the back of the car. 'Ow,' Rose yelped.

Luna sprang into action and I followed her to the boot. Rose had tried to remove Antoni, but he was triple her size. At least. One of his legs hung over the edge of the numberplate at an angle that didn't make sense. His mouth was wide open. We stared at him in silence, trying to remember how we'd got him there in the first place. 'I'll take his legs,' I said, eventually.

As Rose and I lugged Antoni up the sloped entryway, Luna ran ahead. When she'd disappeared into the reception area, Rose said, 'You were gone a while.' She was shuffling backwards, holding Antoni's shoulders, which meant we were forced to look right at each other.

'It took longer than we thought.'

'Did you stop anywhere on the way back?'

'Why?'

'It's clear,' Luna shouted. She returned a moment later with a wheeled metal stretcher.

Where did she find a wheeled stretcher? Against the frivolous pink backdrop of reception it looked like a punchline, although the joke's set-up had escaped me. A drop of sweat rolled from my upper lip into my mouth.

'Take him to the Lab,' Luna said.

~

Luna flashed her pink fob over the sensor and the silver door slid open. As she crossed the threshold, light filled the room. But it was soft and warm-tinted, like that in Luna's office. We wheeled Antoni inside, and Rose immediately went to collect something from a drawer. Luna played with Antoni's greasy hair as I tried to take it all in. The Lab had existed in my mind as *Emma*'s final frontier – no one was ever seen going in or coming out of it – and yet, in reality it was a disappointment. It looked like a cosmetics lab. There were three rows of workbenches, each covered with scientific equipment, and a long desk on the left side of the room that housed three computers. I don't know what I was expecting.

'Why here?' I said, as Rose returned with a sealed plastic packet and something else wrapped in her hand.

'It's the most secure place to keep them,' Luna said. 'It's like a fortress.'

'Surely you don't just let them . . . run around in here?'

'No, no,' she said, as she glanced over to the right side of the room. Another large metal door, concealing a further chamber. 'But it's time for you to head home, Marnie.'

'What?' I looked at Rose, whose hands were now concealed behind her back. 'No, I want to see how it all works.'

Luna walked the length of the stretcher and came to stand behind me. 'All in good time,' she said, as she wrapped her hands around my waist. 'Go home, get some rest.' She kissed the skin just behind my ear, and whispered, 'And don't you dare tell a single soul about this.'

Twenty-five

At the trade meeting, spirits were low. Ruth fumbled awkwardly with the remote as she revealed another disappointing graph. On the other side of the projector screen, Noor had her gaze fixed on the floor.

'We can't say for sure, given we don't have their figures, but it seems Lumo Beauty continues to outperform in the skincare category, which would be fine if . . .' Ruth's voice wavered. From my place in the front row, beside Luna – whose hand was wrapped around mine, resting on my left thigh – I watched as Ruth slid her hands into her pockets. 'It would be fine if makeup was still performing well, but given the recent . . .'

'Allegations,' Luna piped up. She was wearing a pair of perfectly faded Levis over a sleek brown bodysuit. A black blazer was draped across her shoulders – it matched her Adidas sneakers. 'Call a spade a spade, Ruth.'

'Right,' Ruth said, looking anxiously at Noor, who was no help at all. 'The post has since been deleted, but we think it'll take a while for things to get back to normal. It's not a problem, it's just . . .'

'A bump in the road,' Luna said as she released my hand and stood up. 'It's actually a wonderful opportunity for us.'

'It is?' Noor said, with a hopeful expression that begged for further explanation. Luna, of course, was happy to provide one.

'I'm pleased to announce that the Research and Development team are nearly ready to share the final formula for rytuał *Eve*.' It was the first time I'd considered that the Lab must have employees – where were they? No one in the room called *Britney* had a LinkedIn profile with a role in R&D attached to it. 'It's been a long road, but we want it to be perfect. This product has the potential to revolutionise not only our sales, but the beauty industry at large,' Luna said. 'It's all very exciting.'

'We can't wait to try it,' Ruth said, red patches blossoming beneath her full-coverage foundation.

'I want everyone to save the second weekend of December,' Luna continued. 'I'm planning a very special company-wide retreat for us to celebrate the launch of rytuał *Eve*. It's important that we gather together before we move into this new chapter.' People rushed to retrieve their phones, tablets, physical diaries from bags and pockets and beneath their chairs. I opened a new event in my Google calendar and blacked out the entire weekend. *RETREAT*, the event read. Luna looked over at me as she said, 'It's time for all of us to heal.'

~

On my way back to Luna's office, I rounded a corner and collided with Coco. 'Hey,' I said, too peppy. 'How are you?'

She looked terrible. Or, was I projecting that onto her round face, given what I knew? It was hard to tell. 'Hi,' she replied, her eyes shifting between mine and the floor. 'I'm okay.'

'Okay.'

Silence fell, but neither of us turned to leave. We eventually spoke at the same time:

'I'm sorry for being MIA—'

'It's my week.'

Her full stop sliced through my sentence. 'Oh,' I said, fumbling for a normal response. 'How do you . . . how do you feel about it?' She looked at me, and then it was clear that she actually did look like shit. My imagination had only amplified what was already there.

'I just got the email. I don't want it,' she said. 'I didn't clear anyone, but I know who she'll choose.'

I took hold of Coco's hand and led her towards the kitchen. We hid in the alcove beneath the stairs, the place where I'd first heard her on the phone to her dad. Tears welled in her eyes. 'It's okay,' I said, although I had no evidence to support this claim.

'She doesn't know what he's like.'

'Luna has a plan,' I said. 'She always has a plan.'

Coco nodded. 'I haven't heard from him in days.'

'It'll be totally fine,' I said, and the image of Antoni's limp body folded in the boot of the car flashed behind my eyes. I squeezed Coco's upper arm three times and left her alone in the alcove, returning dutifully to Luna's office.

~

On Friday night, I sat next to Rose in the second row. Luna had lent me her blue dress with the bows, and although it was one-and-a-half sizes too small, I wore it with pride. The bow at the centre of my chest strained against the width of my ribcage and the size of my breasts. Rose noticed straight away, and I caught her eyes bouncing between my sternum and my face.

'How are you going?' I said, smiling like a used-car salesman.

'Good. Fine. Busy with the rytuał *Eve* training plan. Everyone will need to learn about the new ingredients.'

'Oh, yeah, it's retinal, right?' Retinal was one of those words I'd heard often enough to decide I knew what it meant, without actually knowing anything about it – beyond that it was used in skincare and everyone wanted it.

'Sure,' Rose said, with a cool laugh. 'It's retinal.'

I suddenly felt as if I'd flubbed my lines. Before I could ask any further questions, Luna descended the stairs behind us. Her black platform boots were heavy, but she could've been wearing ballet slippers – we were all attuned to the exact rhythm of her footsteps. Coco followed behind her, her gait flighty and uneven. This was when it dawned on me that Luna was normally present from the beginning at Friday Night Drinks. Something was off.

'Close your eyes,' Luna said as she made her way down the aisle. Coco paused at the foot of the stairs. I watched Luna grab her hand and pull her towards the front. Little patches of sweat had begun to form at the pits of her lavender boiler suit.

'We come together today to clear out all the shit society has stuffed into our heads and told us is the truth. Because it's not the truth, is it? It's lies. It's all lies, and it's up to us to deliver justice. And that's why we're here. Am I right, ladies?' She was veering wildly off script.

Regardless, the crowd said, 'Yes.'

'This week's featured rytuałist is a newer addition to the team. She's currently working in our Customer Service team, but who knows where she'll go! Let's put our hands together for Coco Minarik.'

Rose was sitting bolt upright. She clapped politely, a look of concern passing over her expression. Luna took her seat, but Coco was still hovering beside hers.

'Sit down, Coco. We won't bite.' Luna gave the crowd a televangelist wink.

Coco moved reluctantly to the chair. I remembered watching Lily move in the same way towards Spencer one night. It was deep in the belly of a fundraiser – she'd put two and two together and confronted me about what was happening with Spencer the week before, but I was unkind. Spencer was worse. When he called for her, she winced. I was hanging off his arm; the late night haze made us careless, although I don't know we were ever all that secretive.

'Coco,' Luna said. 'You will remain aware of everything we discuss and the events that take place this evening. At any point, you can end the session with the word "Set". Nothing that happens during this session will leave this room. You are safe here. Please confirm with the word "Prime".'

Coco paused. I watched her chew on the inside of her lip. *Just say it*, I thought.

'Prime,' Coco said, but it was so quiet it could have been a creaking chair, a distant gust of wind.

'Bring him in!' Luna roared.

Eva walked to the elevator and tapped at her phone. A motor whirred and the doors opened to reveal Antoni, flanked by Bibi and Liv, and looking worse than he had when he was curled up in the boot. Three days had passed. He was still wearing the same worn blue flannel shirt, but his shoes were missing. He wasn't gagged. 'Coco?' he said, as he laid eyes on his daughter. She was sweating, her eyes wide and skin pale. As they brought him down the aisle, I felt Rose's eyes dart between father and daughter.

When the filthy smell of his body odour passed us, Rose stood up. 'Luna, this isn't how we do things—'

'Oh, leave it alone,' Luna said, as she crossed one leg over the other, entirely unfazed.

'If she doesn't want it, it isn't healing,' Rose said. 'It's . . . abuse.'

Someone at the back of the room gasped.

Antoni looked back at Rose, then moved his groggy eyes across to mine. 'Hey,' he said. 'It's you!'

Luna sighed, ignoring Antoni. She stood up and allowed the women to restrain him in her place. When they were done, Bibi and Liv – tall, and menacing, and probably full of human growth hormone – stood behind the chair, their arms crossed at their chests. As Luna moved towards Rose, Antoni continued to stare me down.

'Darling Rose,' Luna said, placing a hand on her cheek – which, admittedly, sent a sting of jealousy through me. 'I know you're feeling left out, but you have to trust the process.'

'It's not about that. I care about what we do here.'

'You drugged me!' Antoni bellowed from behind Luna, his eyes still affixed to me.

'What?' Coco said, looking from her father to me, then back to her father.

'And I don't?' Luna said, as she leant towards Rose's ear. She whispered something only Rose could hear, and it was enough to make Rose concede. Jealousy had me in a chokehold.

'I'm sure you can all guess that this is Coco's father. Isn't that right?' Luna said, resuming her position at the front of the room.

'Coco, please help me,' he said, but Coco didn't rush to remove his zip ties.

'I'll start,' Luna said. 'This man told Coco she would never amount to anything. He hurt her mother. When Coco grew older, she became his new target. Then, after she'd finally built a life for herself, he lured her back into his web, where they were on-selling cosmetic products to Eastern Europe at a huge mark-up. This in itself is fine, perhaps admirable in an entrepreneurial sense, but any success they had was quickly undercut by shady deals, and gambling debts that had to be paid. And yet, after all this, she still protects him. Why? Coco, can you tell me why?'

Coco was shaking her head. Luna pressed on. 'It was all fun and games at first. I thought it was cute. We were going to enter Europe anyway, why not whet our prospective customers' appetites? But then, he – or his people – started stealing from our warehouse. And do you know what they said when we caught them? They told us it wasn't *Antoni's* business, it was his daughter's. And, lo and behold, he'd made sure to cover his tracks with Coco's name. So, why in the non-secular god's name do you still care about this pathetic sack of shit, Coco? Why can't you see that he's nothing but a parasite?' Luna was shouting; her voice had run away from her. 'Anything to add?'

Coco's eyes crawled up the length of her father's body, coming to rest on his side profile. 'He . . . loves me,' she said, sounding not entirely convinced herself.

Luna moved to kneel at Coco's feet. 'Do you really believe that?' she asked. 'After everything he's done?'

'I don't . . . I don't know—'

'What do you think about the nature of love, Coco?'

'It's complicated, he cares—'

'But does he love you?'

'You're crazy bitches,' Antoni shouted, but his words slurred together. He was drowsier than the other men. Had they all been sedated?

Coco was vibrating like an anxious shih tzu. Eventually, she said, 'No.'

Women in the crowd began to clap. I felt my hands come together in percussive union, too. Rose was sitting up even straighter, on the very edge of her seat. Luna placed a sustained, maternal kiss on Coco's lips, then released her. 'The choice is yours, Coco. Would you like to fight back this time?'

Before she could answer, Eva emerged from the back of the room holding a pink storage crate. Inside, it looked as if there were two bottles and a pink Stanley cup. Luna emptied the crate, placing the two bottles beside Antoni's chair. She held the Stanley cup in her right hand.

'What's that?' Coco said as Eva disappeared again.

Luna wrapped her tongue around the straw and drank from the cup. 'Water. Would you like some?'

Coco shook her head.

'Okay.' Luna shrugged. 'Bibi and Liv, I want you to make sure this man's legs are tied down.' They nodded and wrapped an extra zip tie around each of his swollen legs. His pants were already rolled to mid-calf – as if, perhaps, this was planned in advance. When the women retreated, Luna handed Coco the Stanley cup and said, 'Coco, could I get you to pour this on your father's feet?'

'Why?' she said.

Luna reached for one of the bottles. It was full of a white, chalky substance – somewhere between talcum powder and salt flakes. 'Have you seen *Fight Club*?' she said, flippantly, and I couldn't help but laugh. But that was before I realised why she was asking.

When Coco didn't answer, Luna turned to Antoni. 'What about you?'

He looked up, narrowed his eyes and spat a generous mouthful of saliva in her direction.

'That's a shame,' she said, 'I thought all men had.' On the side of the bottle, in a plain and clinical font, were the words *Lye flakes*. Luna looked over at Coco. 'Go on,' she said, as Coco popped the lid of the Stanley cup away from its base. She sloshed the water over Antoni's feet. He thrashed his head from side to side.

'What's happening? What are you doing?' Antoni bellowed.

'We thought it might be fun to try something new,' Luna said as Coco emptied the cup and took a step back. 'We're going to give you something to remember us by.'

'What?' he said, but it was too late. Luna knelt down in front of him and upended the bottle of lye flakes. Without the gag, his screams were corrosive – much like the lye.

'Just a little chemical burn,' she said. 'I've paid good money for worse.' Luna watched as his skin sizzled beneath the heat of the reaction.

We all craned our necks over the seats in front of us to catch a glimpse. When Luna had seen enough, she reached for the second bottle.

'Someone told me it was an urban legend,' she said. 'That it wouldn't neutralise the burn at all. Quite the opposite, apparently.'

Antoni fell silent.

'Shall we find out for ourselves?'

Still, he said nothing. He hadn't seen *Fight Club*.

Luna tipped the second bottle on its head, and when the liquid met Antoni's blistered skin he let out a miserable cry.

Vinegar. It wasn't the smell of fear this time, it was real vinegar.

Twenty-six

'I thought about the blue jumpsuit, but it's too casual. Don't you think? Would it be too casual? I went with black because it's timeless. Elegant.'

I was staring out the tram window while Kahli prattled on about what she was supposed to wear for her first day at rytuał. She was surprisingly nervous. 'It's fine, I think.'

'Yeah, maybe I'll wear it tomorrow. It's so nice working for a company where people actually care about what they look like, beyond, like, corporate jewel tones. Do you get that? I guess you've never worked in corporate-corporate.'

The sky was grey. I was finding it increasingly hard to keep track of the date. Was it September yet? When Kahli moved on to appropriate work accessories, I closed my eyes. The memory of Antoni's red, pustuled feet shocked them open again. My phone buzzed.

Rytuał

LUNA PETERS
I'm taking over from Rose this morning. Meet me in Jean. X

~

Luna deposited the rytuał Employee Resource Guide on the table beside Kahli's laptop, then proceeded to ignore it for the rest of the morning. 'We try, where possible, to minimise cash flow back to our customers. It's better for business if we can recover rather than refund,' she said as the BlissScreen inbox appeared on the wall behind her. Kahli slid a pair of bottle-green-rimmed glasses over the bridge of her nose, nodding attentively. It was rare to see her focused on anything other than *The Real Housewives*, but I'd never been privy to her personality between the hours of nine and five on weekdays.

Kahli scrolled through the plethora of sensitive escalations that filled the inbox. 'All of these are complaints?' she said.

'Yes,' Luna and I replied, in sync. I moved to stand behind Kahli's right shoulder, peering over the screen.

'Isn't this, like'—she clicked on the first message in the queue. The subject read *I WILL TAKE YOU TO CONSUMER AFFAIRS YOU CUNTS*—'a lot?'

'We're valued at two hundred million dollars, Kahli. This is nothing,' Luna said.

Kahli looked over her shoulder at me, her expression dubious.

'You'll get used to it,' I said. 'It's a great feeling when you can turn things around.'

'Exactly,' Luna added. 'Our Customer Service team really is the heart of our business. Should we give it a go?'

'What do you mean?' Kahli's voice snapped off at the end of the sentence. She cleared her throat as I slid into the seat beside her.

'Let's give them a call. No time like the present. Just remember, de-escalate and delight.'

'That's new,' I said. 'I haven't heard that before.'

Luna tilted her chin just a few degrees to the right. 'Didn't Rose teach you that?'

Maybe she had, but I said, 'No.'

'Kahli, are you ready? Let's do this first one,' Luna said, returning to the task at hand.

'Uh, I—'

But Luna had already dialled the number. From her little black remote, she sent the call to the room's speakers. I still didn't know where the microphone was. 'Just stay calm,' Luna said.

'Hello?' a disembodied voice croaked.

'Hi.' Kahli's body was trembling, but she kept her hands in tight fists underneath the table. 'My name is Kahli, I'm calling from rytuał cosmetica. We received an email from you regarding—'

'I told you not to call me,' the voice said. It was frayed with acid reflux. 'I said email only.'

'Well, you gave us your phone number—'

'Why are you attacking me? You're the one with the product that burnt my face off.'

Luna shot Kahli a glare. I thought back to my own experience in this room, weeks ago. Was there anyone who got it right the first time around? Were they the Technical Leads and Category Managers and Front-End Developers now? I still didn't know what any of the jobs were.

'I'm sorry, let's start over,' Kahli said. 'My name is Kahli, what's your name?' It was wooden and not particularly inviting, but it was something.

'I'm not giving you my details.'

'But you already have.' Kahli couldn't help herself. Being argumentative was coded in her DNA. She'd never worked in the service industry, and she wasn't the kind of person who could just 'let things go'. Which was worrying, and definitely something I should have considered before this moment.

'Are you being smart?' the voice said. 'Are you trying to be smart?'

'No, I—'

'How about this: you give me a refund, or I . . . expose you on social media.'

'Go for it.' Kahli let out a self-righteous laugh. Luna turned to face the wall behind her.

'I'm recording this call,' the voice said. 'I'll release the recording unless you refund me.'

'We don't do refunds,' Kahli said, and Luna whipped around to face her. With one swift movement, she raised the remote to the ceiling and ended the call. Silence fell on the room, aside from the sound of air rattling in and out through a blocked nose. It took a minute for me to realise that the blocked nose was my own. I parted my lips like a fish.

'Go,' Luna said. 'Get out.'

'What?' Kahli pushed herself away from the desk. 'That's what you said.'

'I said "de-escalate and delight".' Spit flew from her mouth. 'We can't say we don't do refunds, it's illegal. We don't do anything illegal here, Kahli.'

I placed a hand on Kahli's shoulder. 'Take a break. There's cold brew in the kitchen.'

'No,' Kahli said. 'You didn't tell me that. You barely gave me any instruction. This isn't my fault—'

'Just get out.' I'd never seen Luna so mad. Kahli considered a reply, but instead opted for a pointed sigh and slow exit. She tried to slam the door behind her, but its soft-close mechanism got in the way.

'Luna, you have to give her time. It's too much—'

'I don't have time,' she said. 'We need quick learners. You told me she was smart.'

'She is, but no one could get that right the first time around.'

'It's not rocket science, it's just talking. It's an entry-level job, for fuck's sake. We'll have to process the refund. And send a gift. We need to recover her.'

'I'll tell Coco.'

'No,' she said. 'I need you to do it.'

'But I don't work in Customer Service anymore.'

'I only trust you.' Her eyes darted around the room, restless.

'Okay,' I said. 'I'll do it this afternoon.'

'I need a moment,' she said. 'Come up to my office?'

'Okay.'

~

When we arrived at Luna's office she was quick to reach for a bottle of Japanese gin. 'Martini?' she offered.

I shook my head. 'Luna, is something wrong?' I perched myself on the edge of the couch while she fussed with the gin and a bottle of vermouth. From the fridge she pulled a jar of fat green olives floating in brine. It was 10.45.

'No,' she said. 'Does it look like something's wrong?' She opened her arms, gesturing to the room, the building at large: her empire. When she'd poured the liquid into a martini glass, she added, 'Compliance is driving me insane.'

'For *Eve*?'

She nodded as she came to sit next to me. 'I just want to get it right. I want it to be perfect.'

'It will be.' We sat in silence. I watched her sip her drink. 'Friday night was different,' I said, eventually. 'With Antoni. It was intense.'

'Uh-uh-uh,' she tutted. 'We don't talk about Friday nights, Marnie.'

I chewed on the inside of my cheek.

'Do you want to try it?'

'What?'

'rytuał *Eve*.'

When I looked at Luna, one arm draped over the back of the couch, two feelings yoked themselves together in the pit of my stomach. The first, dread. It felt as if the tide was rising, and I had so many questions; so many loose ends to tie. The second, and the one I was ashamed to admit, was desire. I was struck dumb by my hunger for her. 'Okay,' I said.

She leapt from the couch and moved to the door at the corner of the room. Behind it was her ensuite, which I'd only let myself use once – it felt too intimate. 'We need to cleanse the skin first,' she said, as I followed her to the pink-and-red tiled room. It was small, but warm. Tiles blanketed the floor and walls. A small shower with a rainfall head on the left, a toilet on the right. In the centre, a brass sink set on a pink marble vanity, with an oversized mirror directly above it.

From one of the vanity drawers Luna produced a white terry-cloth headband and handed it to me. I slipped it on. 'Perfect,' she said. 'May I?' She reached for a bottle of facial cleanser from the row of rytuał products beside the sink. I nodded, and she pumped the golden gel into the palm of her left hand. With her right, she turned the tap so slightly that only a delicate flow of water hit the basin. She placed her left hand under the faucet and let about a tablespoon of water pool alongside the cleanser. Then, she turned off the tap and rubbed her palms together. Notes of honey and cinnamon leapt off her hands into the air. 'Turn around,' she said. 'And close your eyes.' I obeyed.

She rubbed the foam across my cheeks, my forehead, the bridge of my nose. Her hands were gentle, but they moved in clearly defined circles. Cleansing was a precise art form. When she'd completed the requisite number of rotations, I heard her rinse her hands beneath the tap.

'No peeking,' she said.

'Why do I feel as though you're about to shave off my eyebrows?'

Luna laughed as she swabbed away the cleanser with soft, wet cotton. When she'd removed it all, I waited for the serum, but instead a light mist arrived. The clean scent of chamomile.

'What's this?' I said, my eyes still firmly shut.

'Just something we're playing with. A toning mist.'

'It's nice.'

'I know.'

I heard the bottle return to the countertop.

'And now, the moment of truth,' she said, rapping her fingers against the marble in a drumroll. 'I present to you'—the drumming stopped—'rytuał *Eve*.'

The gel was cool against my skin. The aroma was dizzying – rich frankincense, and something floral but not powdery. It was subtle. Refined. There was an earthy note I couldn't place, much like Luna's own scent. Her hands met my skin with assured pressure. She drew circles at my temples, then dragged two fingers up the length of my jaw. My skin tingled but didn't flush. The attention her fingers paid my cheeks was spiritual. When she was done, she withdrew her hands and placed them on my shoulders.

'You can open your eyes now.'

I let the light in as slowly as I could and turned to face the mirror again. 'Oh my god,' I said. 'How did you do that?'

My skin was glowing. It was the kind of glow that usually preceded questions on fertility, but Luna had dispensed it straight from the bottle. I'd subscribed to so many miracle cures over the years, but never once were their claims substantiated. I looked younger, healthier – which is to say, actually healthy. Staring at myself with that glow made the rest of my body firmer. I was stronger. I looked to Luna, who was smiling at me as if she saw all of my potential.

'You like it?' she said.

'I love it.' Before I could say anything else, Luna planted her lips on mine.

The first few kisses were sweet. We moved in and out of each other's orbits with a chaste politeness. I didn't know what to do with my hands. As she slid her tongue inside my mouth, I decided to let them rest on her waist. This was enough of a green light for her to press her pelvis into me, guiding me back towards the vanity. I pushed my pubic bone towards her and our tongues moved deeper; our pace quickened. She slid a hand under my blouse, all the way up to my ragged lace bralette. Her thumb and index finger found my right nipple, and as she leant even further into me, she squeezed it just enough to send a jolt through my entire body.

'Take off your underwear,' she whispered. It was a utilitarian directive; the vowels in the word underwear were so unsexy. Why hadn't someone come up with another word, aside from the mortifying 'panties'? I shook the thought from my head as I shimmied the mess of bunched fabric to the floor, stepped out of the loops and kicked them away. Luna smiled as she pulled the hem of my skirt all the way up to my waist. The fresh air made me shy.

'Get on the vanity,' she said.

I perched myself on the cold marble. I was careful to arch my back over the row of products that claimed the space behind me. Luna spread my legs and lowered her face to the same level as the vanity. I moaned before she'd even touched me. 'Easy,' she said, with a playful laugh.

I gripped the lip of the marble. I had to close my eyes to steady myself. I felt her head edge closer. I held my breath until I felt her tongue make contact; the gentle stroke of it was overwhelming. She moved rhythmically, slowly, coated in saliva. Her tongue was listening to me. Before I could ask for it she took her right index and middle fingers in her mouth, coated them in spit and slowly pressed them inside me. It was this – the not having to ask – that thrilled me most. She curled the tips of her fingers in and up as she returned her tongue to the sweet spot. I let my head rest against the mirror as she pushed and licked and sucked at any resistance I had left. I let out another moan, opening my legs even wider as she moved faster. I wanted to watch her – to cement this moment in my mind in case it didn't happen again. But when I opened my eyes, I caught something moving past the entrance to Luna's office. Someone was in the hallway. Before I could say anything, Kahli's voice said, 'Luna?'

I pushed Luna's head away but it was too late. Kahli opened the door to Luna's office and turned her head towards the ensuite. We made eye contact just as I snapped my legs shut. I watched her look at my knobbly knees, then Luna's flushed cheeks – she was still kneeling on the floor.

'Oh,' Kahli said, stumbling backwards. 'Sorry—'

She lurched from the room, flying down the corridor and out of view.

'Fuck,' I said, scrambling to lower my skirt. Luna said nothing. She just wiped a hand across her glossy upper lip and walked back into the office.

Twenty-seven

Kahli was hiding in her bedroom when I got home. I dumped my keys on the kitchen bench as loudly as I could, and the lack of footsteps that followed confirmed my suspicions. I pulled my phone from my back pocket and typed a message to Luna.

> **Kahli is giving me the silent treatment lol**

I watched the ellipsis appear on her side, then disappear. I closed the thread and reopened it, but there was nothing. I decided to make pasta, and put water on to boil. I stared at my message again until the sound of the pot boiling over threw me back to the present. Finally, a reply.

> **Ha!**

That was it. *Ha!* I wanted to kill myself. I pulled a fork from the top drawer and stirred the pasta.

'Hey,' Kahli said from behind me. I spun around to face her, flicking boiling water out across the tiles like a crop circle.

'I thought maybe you were asleep. Sorry if I woke you.'

'I was awake.'

We both nodded.

'I'm sorry about today. About what you saw,' I said. 'I'm sorry' didn't quite encapsulate the feeling, but it was the easiest way out.

'Totally fine,' she said. 'I actually wanted to talk to you . . .'

She came to sit opposite me at the kitchen bench. The stool groaned as she put her entire weight in the seat – we had found them on the side of the road just after I moved in, and they were my only real contribution to the apartment. Kahli assured me they went for 'three hundred each on Facebook Marketplace, minimum'.

'I don't think rytuał is really the right'—she looked at the floor—'place. For me.'

'What?' My heart began to race. 'What do you mean?'

'Yeah. I just get bad vibes. No offence, it's just a bit . . .' I looked up at her too fast. 'Much.' I felt my face flush. The impact of this information was twofold. First, a dull ache that Kahli hadn't felt the same pull to rytuał's embrace as I had. Second, rising panic that it was imperative Kahli remain at rytuał long enough to participate in her first Friday Night Drinks. The thought of disappointing Luna now, after all she'd given me, was a dark one.

'Come on, Marnie. Luna is like a hot Jim Jones in designer clothes.'

'No, she's not.' I fumbled for a stronger defence, but I was running out of air.

'Clea texted me today. She said she hasn't heard from Isabel in a while.'

'What?' I could hear my heart in my ears again.

'Do you really think that badrytuals account was her?'

'I— Yeah, but it's . . .' The dread overwhelmed me, but I was in too deep. 'I'm sure she's just embarrassed.'

Kahli raised her eyebrows. 'I'm not judging, but today was . . . I didn't know you were . . . *with* her. Did you want that?' She was uncharacteristically prudish.

'Of course I did. I do. You weren't supposed to see that.'

'In the office, though? Very *Mad Men*.' She scoffed, but realised it was unkind and tried to swallow it halfway through.

'Just give it time,' I said, rifling through the cupboard for a colander. 'It takes a few weeks to get used to things.'

Kahli shrugged. 'I'm not really a "get used to things" kind of person.'

Kahli's brief moments of self-awareness were dazzling. I put the colander in the sink and dumped the pasta into it a little too enthusiastically. Hot, starchy water bit at my forearms.

'You just need to wait,' I said. 'Wait until your first Friday Night Drinks. It's worth it, I promise.'

'What's Friday Night Drinks?'

I was starting to feel like a hopeless frog – at some point, the dread would boil me alive. I wondered if this situation was the exception to the rule. I wondered if any of the rules really mattered, at this point.

'Just think about it for a bit longer. You don't know what this means to me—'

'Why are you so upset? It's not like we actually work together.'

'I'm not upset.'

Rytuał

'Are you crying?'

Was I? I raised a hand to my face, and sure enough a trail of salty tears had carved a line down my cheeks. When I looked down at my hand wrapped around the fork, my knuckles were white.

'No, it's just from the onions. In the sauce.'

She glanced at the stove, then back to the sink. 'You didn't make a sauce.'

I let go of the fork and leant over the bench towards her. 'If I tell you something, will you promise not to tell anyone?'

She thought about her response for longer than I would have. 'Okay,' she said, eventually.

'Friday Night Drinks is . . .' I paused, and let out a sigh. 'It's not like a corporate work drinks. It's about healing. It's a celebration.'

'What does that mean?'

'We work together to . . . Like, Tom, for instance. You know how he sent you that text?'

'Yeah.'

'That Friday night it was Rose's turn to be featured, and we—'

'What do you mean by "featured"?'

'Like, it was her turn to receive the healing.'

'Okay.' Her voice wavered. Her face was frozen, and I couldn't decipher her expression.

'So, it was Rose's turn, and Tom was there—'

'Why was he there?'

'Because he was Rose's boyfriend. And he cheated on her. With you.'

'She knew about it?'

'Yeah. She knew. Well, she didn't know it was you. But I did.'

'What?'

'It doesn't matter. The point is, Luna brought Tom to Friday Night Drinks, and for Rose's healing we . . . we kind of beat the shit out of him.' I grinned from the bottom of my spine to the space between my eyebrows. Kahli didn't move. Her face was still frozen. 'It's cool, right?'

I speared two pieces of penne with my fork, and just as I'd wrapped my mouth around the prongs she said, 'Yeah. Cool.'

'So, you just have to stay until—'

'I'm really tired. I might go to bed,' she said.

It knocked the wind out of me, but I smiled. 'Of course. Sleep well.'

She got up from the stool and walked straight to her room. I shovelled the rest of the plain pasta into my mouth as fast as I could. I barely drew breath as I stuffed the soggy mush down my throat. I waited for Kahli to reappear en route to the bathroom, but she didn't emerge from her room until the next morning. I stood at the kitchen bench for another hour, staring at her very expensive furniture, realising I had just made a huge mistake.

~

Luna cancelled The Clearing. On the tram to work, my phone vibrated with the warning of a new email. It plucked me from the depths of Instagram, where I was once again mainlining videos of my favourite middle-aged actress. I don't know why it mattered that she was middle-aged. I don't know why that was the first descriptor that came to mind. She was a number of other things: dark haired, petite, unreasonably beautiful. She looked, I realised, a lot like Luna, if Luna were ten to fifteen years older.

Rytual

From: luna.peters@rytual.co
Subject: CANCELLED | The Clearing

I received a valuable download in my meditation this morning: to clear is to relive, and we want to move forwards, not backwards. Please spend your first hour of work in quiet contemplation – big changes are on the way. X

    I pulled a pot of cheek tint from my bag and toggled to the camera app. As I applied the pink putty in the light of my phone, I focused on its crisp, floral scent. I closed my eyes, repeating the thought, *She has a plan.*

~

When I arrived at the office, Luna was nowhere to be found. No one really knew what 'quiet contemplation' was, so while Eva offered to run a yoga class in the room called *Britney,* a number of us just milled around the kitchen. I was standing by the coffee machine, waiting as it spat out a shot of espresso, when I pulled my phone from my pocket and opened a new browser window. I typed *Isabel Mackie* into the search bar. There was an Instagram profile impressively near the top of the results. I opened it. The last post was three weeks old. I went back to the search results. A few articles about art exhibitions – Isabel was, apparently, a mixed media sculptor – but that was it. I returned to the search bar and typed *badrytuals.* As promised, the posts had been deleted, and all that remained was a handful of news articles echoing the allegations. However, the comment sections on each of the articles were quiet. The internet moved fast.

I opened my last message to Kahli.

> Hey girl, want to grab a drink tonight?

No reply. I was staring down the question mark when I felt someone's presence in my periphery.

'Hi!' Coco said as she breezed past me to the fridge.

I looked up from my screen. She was grinning. 'Hi!' I said. 'How are you? I didn't see you yesterday.'

'I'm great,' she said. She took the jug of cold brew from the fridge and poured herself a glass. 'Really great, actually.' I flipped my phone face down on the bench beside the coffee machine.

'Aren't you going to drink that?' she said, in the direction of my espresso. I fumbled to collect it from the plastic podium.

'Is your dad okay?' I asked. It tumbled out of my mouth before I could remember to whisper.

'Dunno.' Coco shrugged. She opened a draw and retrieved a rytuał-branded paper straw.

'Right. How's Customer Service going?'

'I'm actually finding it really rewarding. It's a privilege to be able to connect with our customers on such a personal level.'

She must have clocked the scepticism that rolled across my forehead, because a second later she took a step towards me and placed a hand over mine. 'Don't worry, Marnie. It'll all make sense soon.'

'What do you mean?'

Rytuał

Her right eyelid twitched. I could smell rytuał *We*, and something chemically sweet – a raspberry deodorant, plucked from a supermarket aisle, I imagined. 'Friday Night Drinks changes you. You'll see.'

~

That afternoon, Luna asked me to proofread the website copy for rytuał *Eve*, despite the fact that there were three full-time copywriters downstairs who had undoubtedly already completed this task. I sat on the couch, with my laptop on my thighs, as Luna worked from her desk. She was wearing a bright-blue wrap top with large, orb-shaped sleeves. A stick of limited edition rytuał *We* incense burnt from the windowsill, its smoke dancing slowly in the fading light.

> **Eve bit the apple, and what did she find? A hydration-boosting, antioxidant-rich serum that promotes cell renewal and fights inflammation, formulated with a suite of supremely nourishing ingredients. The garden was a drag, anyway.**

'Never, in our five years of operating, has a claim been filed against us with Consumer Affairs,' Rose said, as she burst through the door.

Luna stood up. 'Rose, slow down.'

'I can't believe you would let this happen.' Luna made a face as she stepped out from behind the desk and walked towards me. 'This is serious. Eva nearly had a heart attack when she got the call.' Rose held her ground, towering over us.

'Eva will be fine.' Luna let the couch take the weight of her body. She crossed her arms and legs; she seemed to have changed her opinion on the severity of the incident in the time since Kahli's training session.

'Why aren't you bothered by this?' Rose pressed.

'Rose, darling, I understand where you're coming from, but—'

'Where I'm coming from? I'm coming from the same place as you. You built this. It was your idea.'

Luna sighed. 'Come here,' she said, reaching for Rose, but Rose took a step back. They remained two metres apart.

'Why aren't you taking this seriously?'

'Marnie forgot to call them back, so what? We all make mistakes—'

'If they make a fuss about the refunds, people will come looking for more.'

'More what? We have nothing to hide.'

We both looked at Luna. Her delivery was chillingly convincing, but this was an insane thing to say. My heart rattled against my ribs.

'You're getting sloppy,' Rose said. 'This'—she gestured to the two of us with her left hand—'Whatever this is, it's making you sloppy.'

'Rose, I know you're unhappy about Marnie's swift upwards progression, but there's no need for jealousy.'

'I'm not jealous,' Rose said as she crossed her arms. When she realised how it looked, she released them to hang beside her. Despite her emotional state, Rose's hair hung in sleek, scrupulous waves. 'There are rules,' she said. 'Everyone else has to play by the rules. We need to protect the business.'

'But you said it yourself, Rose: I built this business. These are my rules,' Luna said. 'Once Kahli makes it past her first Friday Night Drinks, everything will be in order. Think of it like a loan.'

'*If* she makes it past her first Friday Night Drinks.'

The collar of my shirt threatened to strangle me. I dug my hand inside it and pulled it away from the skin.

'She will be joining us, won't she, Marnie?' Luna looked over at me with steely certainty.

'Luna, I—'

'Won't she?' Luna was nodding slowly.

Rose caught the panic in my eyes, and it was enough to quell her hunger for justice. When we made eye contact, she crossed her arms again. And kept them there.

'Yes,' I said.

'Good,' Luna said. 'That's that. Speaking of, Rose, shouldn't you be getting back to Kahli? Lots to learn.'

Rose glowered in my direction before turning to leave. We watched her descend the stairs in silence – until her glistening hair had disappeared altogether.

'Wow,' Luna said. 'She loves the drama.'

I forced a smile. As Luna returned to her desk, I stood up. 'Have you heard anything from Isabel?'

'Hmm?' She fixed her eyes to the screen; her nails hit the keyboard with a metallic clacking sound as she entered her password.

'Isabel. Kahli said her sister hasn't heard from her.'

Luna shrugged. 'Rehab?'

I pressed my thumbnail into my index finger. 'Can I see it?'

'See what? I'm very busy this afternoon—'

'The CCTV. From the store.'

She finally looked up from the computer. Her eyes were cold. She walked over to the window, her heeled boots making a heartbeat rhythm against the polished concrete. 'I think it's time I told you the full story.'

My stomach dropped. 'About Isabel?'

She shook her head. 'First it was extra homework. He told my parents I needed private tutoring, to make sure I reached my "full potential". They were busy, always working, so it didn't bother them. I think that's why he picked me – he knew my parents wouldn't pry. They were both lawyers. Very achievement oriented.' She stared out at the courtyard, her body angled away from me. 'Then, you know, it became something else. Hands up my skirt, down my pants, just hands, hands everywhere, all the time.'

'I'm so sorry.'

'Then, I finally get over it. I think I'm doing pretty well. I'm twenty-one, and I meet this guy. He's thirty-six, which is funny to me now because I'm thirty-six and I just can't make it make sense. We had nothing in common, but because I'm twenty-one and he's thirty-six I just keep telling myself that he'll know how things are supposed to go. It's exciting, right? I'm eating two-minute noodles in my first share house and I've got a thirty-six-year-old boyfriend.'

I walked towards her, but she pulled away, hiding her eyes in the corner of the window – looking down at the courtyard, where two birds were dancing on the wrought-iron table, bathing in what was left of golden hour.

'Things are good, and then things are bad, and then they're very bad. He doesn't want me to see my family, my friends.

Rytuał

I move into his apartment and he proposes, but we don't have any friends so I just sit around and wait for him to get home from work. It goes on like that for another two years, and in the end I'm this waifish shadow of a person with no friends, no interests, no nothing. But at least I have a husband, right? Lucky me. Then, I find out he's been fucking other women – or should I say girls, because really they were girls – the whole time. One morning I wake up to myself and I realise I've just sought out the same relationship, the same pattern. And I vow never to let it happen again. I will never feel that ever again.' When she finally did turn to face me, her eyes were full of tears. She was trembling.

'Luna—'

She threw a hand in my direction. 'Don't feel sorry for me,' she said. 'Don't you dare feel sorry for me.'

'Of course I feel sorry for you!'

'I don't want your pity, Marnie,' she said, wiping her eyes. 'I just want your trust.'

'I trust you,' I said. 'Of course I trust you.' I closed the space between us, wrapping my arms around her. But her hair smelt different, as if she'd left it a day longer between washes – the earthy smell overpowered anything else.

When I left Luna's office, I made quick strides down the stairs, around the corner and into the bathroom. I didn't have time to lock the stall – I barely made it to the bowl before yellow bile erupted from my mouth. Thank god most of the office was huddled inside *Britney*, listening to The Lauras present their proposed Digital Marketing Calendar for the next year. There was a questions box, if anyone wanted to ask questions, which was not compulsory but highly recommended.

Twenty-eight

Kahli still hadn't responded to my text. Evidently, she did not want to grab a drink tonight. On the tram, I gripped the pole beside my seat so hard my hand began to cramp. Two stops from home, my phone vibrated. One sustained buzz.

    From: hale.kahli@gmail.com
    Subject: Resignation

When I walked through the front door, the house was dark. I'd called Kahli seven times since the email appeared, but she wasn't interested in a discussion. I sent a slew of texts that made less and less sense as they stacked up in our message thread. I stood in the dark kitchen and listened to the trams roll down High Street. I was losing my ability to put things into perspective. My life had quickly shifted from holding a lot of nothing to holding a lot of rytuał, and when I stepped outside *Emma* nothing made sense. My phone buzzed against the marble countertop.

LUNA PETERS
Your turn for FND this week, but we'll do it tomorrow. Our first ever Wednesday Night Drinks. X

~

'Good morning, everyone,' Luna said from the front of the room called *Britney*. She'd sent an impromptu invite for a Company Update. 'Please, be seated.'

I moved to perch myself on a seat in the back row. A sour taste coated my mouth. All night, Luna's voice had zigzagged through my mind: *I don't want your pity, Marnie, I just want your trust.* The dread had reached boiling point, but still I'd showered, boarded the tram, waved to The Lauras as I turned down Emma Street.

'First cab off the rank: I know our hiring process has been a core pillar of the business since we opened our doors, but today I come bearing changes.' Luna smiled as she ran a hand through the ends of her silky locks. 'The key tenets of the process will remain the same, but career progression will now be based on performance instead of recruitment.'

'But how will recruitment be incentivised without it being required for promotion?' Rose's voice asked. The room fell silent as the crowd reckoned with the same thought.

'Why does there need to be an external incentive? Aren't we all working for the common good? We do have the same goals, don't we?' Her tongue was sharp. The silence lingered. Luna held her gaze on Rose, and there were no further questions.

'I think that just about covers it,' Luna said, before finding my eyes in the crowd. 'Oh! And how could I forget. Tonight, a very special event. Our first ever Wednesday Night Drinks.'

A few rows in front of me, someone whispered, 'But I have Pilates on Wednesdays.'

'Tonight, our featured rytuałist is Marnie Sellick.'

~

The afternoon passed with sticky resistance. I waited for Luna to join me in her office, but she'd disappeared after the meeting and didn't return until the sky was dark. I couldn't stop thinking about Spencer – trying to remember the architecture of his face. I wanted to know where they'd found him, what he was wearing. I wanted to know if they'd found him at all. I descended the stairs sometime between three and four, and morbid curiosity propelled me towards the Lab. As I swiped my pink fob over the sensor, I heard footsteps behind me. The sensor turned red. Access denied.

'Marnie? What are you doing?' Coco was wearing a purple gingham dress. Her black bob looked an inch shorter.

'Luna asked me to get something, but my fob doesn't work.'

She took a few steps towards me. A concerned expression drew her eyebrows together. 'Are you okay?'

'I'm fine. Totally fine. Just . . . you know.'

'You know?'

'Preparing myself.'

'You'll be great,' she said. Without warning, she bundled her arms around me. I could still smell her raspberry deodorant, but there was a nostalgic comfort to its pedestrian aroma.

'Just wait,' she whispered, with her head pressed up against my chest.

I took a step back. 'For what?'

'Luna has a plan.'

~

When I arrived, most people were already seated. I hovered at the bottom of the spiral stairs.

'Good evening, everyone,' Luna said, from her throne. 'Please take hold of the hands on either side of you for a grounding practice.'

I tried to picture what he'd be wearing, as if it was some kind of perverted Christmas present.

'We come together after a week of working to change the way the beauty industry operates, in order to change the way that we each operate. We come here to look inside ourselves, to examine the things we've accepted as truth from society and challenge these ideals. We come together to push out masculine norms and welcome in the divine feminine. We conspire together to overthrow destructive patriarchal standards, replacing them with the power inside each person present today.'

I nodded. Would he even recognise me? It was a crazy thought, but I often worried my face alone wasn't enough to remind people of the part I'd played in their lives. I wished I came with my own museum plaque.

'Three breaths all together,' Luna intoned. 'In, out. In, out. In, out.'

I couldn't seem to breathe out properly. I pressed a fist to my stomach. It didn't help.

'I'd like to invite Marnie Sellick to join me.' Luna extended her arm down the aisle. I kept my eyes on the floor as I walked towards the front of the room. The crowd applauded. I sat in the chair beside her.

'You will remain aware of everything we discuss and the events that take place this evening. At any point, you can end the session with the word "Set". Nothing that happens during this session will leave this room. You are safe here. Please confirm with the word "Prime".'

'Prime,' I mumbled.

'Fabulous,' she said. 'Let's dive right in.' I tried to smile, but the corners of my mouth refused to cooperate. 'Why do you think you gravitate towards men who treat you like a doormat?'

The crowd laughed as if they were in on the joke. As though it was, 'Oh, Marnie. There she goes again!' But so many of these people didn't actually know me. Not really. Only Luna could say that about me, and I wasn't sure I wanted her to.

'You can be honest,' she said. 'It's okay.' She leant over and took hold of my right hand. 'You're safe here.'

I looked at the floor, my scuffed loafers, Coco's face in the front row. She was still smiling, but her bright expression was infected with concern. She nodded when our eyes met.

'I struggle to believe I'm worth more,' I said. It was exactly what every other woman had said every Friday night since I'd arrived at rytuał. In as many words, we all struggled with this same problem. The homogeny of our self-harm was depressing.

'And when you call in that kind of energy, what happens?'

'People hurt me,' I replied.

She nodded. 'It's simple, isn't it? In order to change the way our life plays out in the physical realm, we have to change our mindset. I hope the healing we enact tonight can do that for you, Marnie. I hope it can kickstart the new you.'

My knee bobbed up and down as if it was keeping time. 'Thanks,' I said, because nothing else felt right.

'Shall we bring him in?' she said, facing the audience rather than me.

I looked out at their hungry eyes. 'Yes,' they said.

'Right. Let's do it.'

I tried to steady my breath, but it was too late for that. I hadn't made a plan for how I would hurt him. What were my limits? The option to pre-purchase that decision had expired hours ago. I closed my eyes as I heard the elevator doors open. Bibi and Liv's footsteps. I prepared myself to face him.

'Marnie?' he said, but his voice was wrong. Higher in pitch. He sounded younger. I opened my eyes, but instead of Spencer's chiselled grey features, the face in front of me was twenty years his junior.

'Justin?'

~

Curly brown ringlets. A slate-grey North Face vest. Ad guy. Keto breath. So much time had stuffed itself into the space between then and now. His face was only faintly familiar. I looked to Luna. She was grinning.

'Why him?'

'Marnie?' Justin said again, blinking slowly.

'Why not?' Luna stood up, making space for the poor, confused man. Bibi and Liv bound his legs and arms to the chair with zip ties and took two steps to the side. Where had Luna found these women? What did they do for the rest of the week? My whole body was vibrating.

'This isn't funny, Luna. It was just an Uber.'

Eva appeared, holding a Dyson Airwrap and nothing else. Luna was quick to accept it.

'Why an Airwrap?' I said.

'We're nothing if not resourceful.'

'Stop,' I said, fumbling for the thing I was actually supposed to say. 'I mean, set. Set.'

'I don't know what's going on here, but let's just chat it out. We can chat. I love to chat,' Justin said.

'Shut up, Justin,' Luna said. 'You will speak when spoken to.'

He nodded imprecisely.

'Marnie, this is for your own good.' Luna gripped the Airwrap like it was a baton.

'But – he didn't do anything.'

Luna turned to address the audience, unimpressed with my participation. She had a plan. 'This man stole from Marnie,' was all she said.

'He didn't. I never transferred him the money.'

I lurched towards Justin and picked at the plastic ties, but Bibi scooped me up by the underarms and carried me to the left side of the room.

'That was just a symptom of the disease. We're here for all the other women Justin has stolen from. Maybe it's not money; maybe it's time. Their youth. Patience. We create in their image. We do it for them.'

'Do what?' Justin said, his voice high and thin.

I shook my head.

'Fine. If you won't, I will.'

Luna took a step towards him and raised the Airwrap over her head – she cast the same shape Rose had made when she finally decided to give Tom his medicine.

'We're not here for your entertainment,' she said to a cowering Justin, as he pre-emptively winced.

'Wait!' I wriggled in Bibi's arms but her grip was ironclad. I'd heard whispers that both she and Liv were Olympic weightlifters in another life. 'Luna—'

The Airwrap descended, but just as she moved to strike his crotch, Justin bowed his head forwards – bracing for impact – and the baton instead made contact with the back of his skull.

I heard a crack. Luna had put her full weight behind it. Blood trickled from his head, down his cheeks. He didn't move. He didn't draw another breath.

'Is he dead?' a voice squealed from the back of the crowd.

Luna dropped the Airwrap. This was not part of the plan.

Twenty-nine

'We need to move him upstairs,' Luna said. She said it so matter-of-factly that people immediately stood from their chairs and moved to help untie him. Rose led the charge.

'No,' I said. Bibi squeezed my arms a little tighter. 'No, we need to call the police.'

'Marnie, stop,' Luna said, quiet at first.

When I replied with, 'This is serious,' she repeated herself, this time as loud as she could.

'Rose, move this man to the Lab. I want everyone else upstairs in the kitchen. Eva, make a pot of coffee and heat up whatever we have in the fridge. No one leaves *Emma* tonight, understood?'

The room nodded fervently.

'You can let her go,' Luna said as she turned to face Bibi. She released my arms, and I fell forwards, narrowly avoiding a concrete slab to the face. Relinquished of one responsibility, Bibi was quick to join Rose in hoisting Justin's body out of the chair. 'Marnie, stay here,' Luna said.

Rytuał

They carried his body up the stairs. The rest of the crowd followed in a slow procession. I stood up and paced a two-foot square until Luna said, 'Stop that.'

'I didn't send him the money—'

'Something happened. When we went to collect him.'

I didn't want to give her my eyes. I was too angry. I didn't want another story. She walked back to her chair and slumped into the seat. 'We went to this club. I lost Rose in the crowd. It was dark – I mean, obviously, it was dark. I was just going to dance with him for a bit, then I was going to buy him a drink. It seemed simple.'

I let myself scan her features, trying to see past her bravado, but she'd closed the blinds.

'It took me ages to find him. The club had three levels. When I finally spotted him, he was on the edge of the dance floor with this girl. She was young, maybe eighteen. She had her eyes closed. She was really drunk – like, struggling to stand.' Tears began to stream down her face, one by one at first, but then in packs. I watched them with scientific curiosity: they seemed sincere. I sat down.

'He had her pressed up against the wall, Marnie. He was grinding against her, but her eyes were completely shut. She was barely even conscious.'

'I didn't know he was like that—'

'They're never like that, until they are.' She pressed the heels of her hands against her cheekbones and took a breath in. 'I went over and told the girl her friends were waiting for her outside. He jumped off her as soon as he saw me. He made some comment about promising her a ride home, but she just stumbled off.'

There was a spot of blood on the back of Luna's chair.

'I created this for women like her,' Luna said. 'For women like us.' Her chest heaved. 'And when I went to hit him, I lost control. I'm so angry. Why am I still so angry?' She looked up at me with wide eyes.

'We need to call the police,' I said. 'Tell them it was an accident. He broke into the office and attacked us.'

She shook her head. 'We can't afford the attention—'

'Luna. This is serious. We need to act fast.'

'I've got it under control.'

'If you don't go to the police, I will. This is too far. They'll find out. People will come looking for him.'

'The universe has mysterious ways of protecting those who need it.'

'Stop talking like an astrology app! You just killed someone. What's wrong with you?'

She stood up and walked down the aisle, grazing a hand over the backs of the chairs as she passed them. 'If you were going to leave, don't you think you would have done it by now?' I swallowed, forcing saliva down my chalky throat. She turned to face me again. 'No one's keeping you here. You're not tied to that chair, as far as I'm aware.' On noticing my wavering brow, she softened. 'Haven't you ever thought about it? Just once?'

'What?'

'What it would feel like to watch the light leave his eyes?'

'No,' I said, shaking the image out of my head. 'No.'

'Liar.'

She circled the room's perimeter and returned to me. 'I want my life to mean something, Marnie. I want to turn something ugly into something beautiful. They'll never stop. The least we can do is try to level the score.' She positioned her chair in front of mine and leant towards me. 'And what about you? What will your legacy be?' She tucked a strand of hair behind my ear. Her skin smelt sweet again.

'Why wasn't it him?'

'Spencer?'

I nodded.

'I needed to know you were all in first.' She set her palms down on my thighs. Her eyes were bloodshot, but I couldn't stop staring at her lips. *Lust.* The name of the shade was Lust. 'Are you all in?'

~

We climbed the stairs, and drank black coffee and ate leftover caramelised shallot pasta with the rest of the group. When Rose and Bibi returned from the Lab, they nodded, and Luna nodded back. We were all in it together. And that was that.

~

The next morning, in the room called *Britney*, I opened my eyes and wiggled my toes, watching as the tiny bones and ligaments worked together to execute such a pointless movement. I smelt like ham. We inhaled and exhaled as a group three times. Someone else's breath tickled the nape of my neck, and it made me irrationally angry. No one had slept.

'Thank you for being here, my dear rytuałists,' Luna said. 'I sincerely appreciate your support.'

No one applauded. We were all too tired for that. Concrete was unforgiving on the spine.

'I was up all night thinking about a new era,' she said. 'I think we can all agree that the business is at a crossroads, and we're going to need to level up in order to remain relevant. To fully immerse ourselves in the launch of rytuał *Eve*, we'll be extending our office hours.'

Luna's mascara had bled out into the craters that sat below her bottom eyelids. She was sweating. Her eyes darted around the room as if she was waiting for opposition. 'Between now and our company retreat in December, I need everyone here, at *Emma*, at all hours. To facilitate this, we will be installing seventy-five sleep pods in the space next to the office gym. Some of you might remember that this was our original R&D lab, but since moving the Lab upstairs the space has been vacant.'

I didn't know there was an office gym. Someone began to cheer. Good morale was regenerative: it charged itself like a battery when enough people believed. Luna rolled her shoulders away from her ears.

'So,' she said. 'Eva will coordinate amenity kits and new clothes for each of you. The fridge will be stocked, of course. And Friday Night Drinks will be suspended until further notice. Any questions? Good!'

She turned before a hand at the back of the room could shoot to the sky, before one of The Lauras could ask, 'Are we not going to talk about what happened?'

And another Laura could remind her, 'We don't talk about Friday Night Drinks.'

~

By Monday night, Luna had coordinated the arrival and installation of seventy-five capsule-shaped bunk beds. They were dusty pink, with crisp white linen and an adjustable lamp: this could be dimmed for meditation, brightened for reading or switched off entirely for rest, she explained. When she'd led me down the stairs, to the door that now said *Sleep Centre – Available*, I'd expected a glorified hostel, but the reality was much closer to a group suite at the Four Seasons.

'How did you do this?' I said, my jaw slack.

'I've had it in the works for a while. I was just waiting for the right moment.'

Little grey tablets – like the ones that guarded each of the meeting rooms – were affixed to the bunk beds, with their allocated rytuałist displayed.

'Which is mine?' I said, running a hand over the screen that said *Rose Liu – Global Training*. Monogrammed silk pyjamas were folded at the foot of each bed.

'This isn't for us,' she said, laughing as if I'd forgotten something. 'We'll sleep in my office.'

'Oh,' I said. The back of my neck prickled. 'Of course.'

I followed Luna back up the stairs to her office where, sure enough, a queen-sized replica of the sleep pods was wedged between the wall and the back of the couch. She wrapped her fingers in mine and led me towards it, and when we lay down next to each other she whispered, 'I love you, Marnie.'

~

Without the tram ride home, or Friday Night Drinks to mark the end of a working week, time became increasingly irrelevant. A week could contain as many days as you needed it to.

A few days after the sleep pods arrived, blue-eyed Laura stood up from the kitchen's communal table and moved in the direction of the front door. 'I'm going to Calooh,' she said.

'Why? We have plenty of coffee here,' Luna replied from the other end of the table.

Laura froze. 'I feel like a walk.'

'We have a treadmill downstairs.'

The colour drained from Laura's face. 'I need some air.'

Luna shrugged and returned to her gluten-free pancakes, but when Laura got to the front door, it refused to open.

'We're all in this together,' Luna said when Laura returned, ashen-faced and full of regret.

~

A text arrived from Kahli one night, and the sight of her name sent a jolt through my stomach.

> Hey, I went to stay with Clea for
> a bit but I came back last week
> and haven't seen u. Are u ok?

I deleted it straight away.

~

At the beginning of October, we lost an hour to daylight saving. I could see the weeks passing on my phone screen, but the physical change of waking an hour later was what made the word 'October' make sense.

Luna had slipped out of bed before me. I found her in the kitchen, staring into a bowl of oats. 'How long have you been up?'

'A while.'

The sound of her teeth grinding against each other was making its way into my dreams.

I sat opposite her at the table. 'Is there anything I can do for you?' I said.

She was quick to stand. 'I'm fine. I just need more coffee.'

She hobbled to the French press and poured another cup. I was grasping for something helpful to say when Eva appeared at the entrance to the kitchen.

'The police are here,' she said, out of breath. 'They're asking for you.'

She didn't mean Luna.

~

I waved Luna's pink fob beside the cast-iron door, and watched it disappear into the wall. The sun was blinding. I squinted into the light as two burly police officers came into focus. One had a thick grey moustache, and the other had either gone bald or done it himself as a preventative measure. Behind them, Emma Street was unchanged.

'Good morning – Ms Sellick?' the moustache said, holding his hands at his belt buckle.

'Yes, that's me.' They looked me up and down. I was wearing a pink silk nightie I'd inherited from Luna, a pair of loafers and a trench coat. The cool breeze turned my thighs to chicken skin.

'Oh,' Moustache said. 'We didn't expect—'

'We received a missing persons inquiry. We wanted to check your workplace before we searched any further, but . . . here you are.' The bald man kept his eyes just above mine.

'A missing persons report?' I said. 'Is this a joke?'

'It's not, no.'

'We are obliged to ask you if you believe your wellbeing is at risk?' Moustache looked beyond me to the dark wooden hallway.

'You tell me.'

'A simple yes or no will suffice.'

I closed the trench coat over my chest. 'No. My wellbeing is not at risk.'

'Great,' said the bald one. 'We'll be on our way, then. Thank you, Ms Sellick.'

'Who filed the report?' I said as they turned to leave.

'Your housemate was quite concerned about you.' He referred to his phone. 'Hale. Ms K. Hale.'

'Right,' I said.

'Happy Sunday!' said Moustache as they trundled down the street.

I nodded, watching their hips swagger away. I thought about running, but I wasn't wearing a bra. The cast-iron door slid closed before I could consider it further. I pressed my thumb into my index finger as hard as I could.

~

At nine-thirty that night, Luna left for the gym. I counted to fifty after I watched her ponytail disappear down the stairs – holding my breath as I counted. I swiped Luna's spare fob from the top drawer of her desk and dug through the bottom of my backpack to find my house keys. I walked straight past the Product team comparing screens in the kitchen. I walked past Rose listening intently to her navy-blue headphones. When I reached reception, Eva snapped to attention from behind her desk. 'Where are you going?' she said.

'Luna needs some things from the supermarket.' I pulled the fob from my pocket and presented it as evidence. Eva was torn, but I knew she wouldn't want to interrupt Luna mid-workout.

'Be quick,' she said. 'It's getting late.'

I marched down Emma Street, turned right and wound my way to Smith. I gritted my teeth at the tram stop, intermittently edging out into the street and squinting to discern slow-moving traffic from an oncoming 86 tram. Eventually, the bright lights trundled into view. I zipped up the stairs and claimed a seat.

The journey made me impatient. I'd taken pride in my twenty-minute commute before, but now it was an inconvenience. When the tram stopped, I ran down the stairs and let my body carry me the rest of the way. I wrapped my fingers around the keys in my left pocket and the fob in my right. I climbed the stairs two at a time. When I arrived, I could hear Kahli moving in the kitchen – I pressed my ear to the door and stopped, listening to her feet traipse across the floorboards as she doubled back on herself. She was cleaning, or cooking. Music played softly in the background. I slid my key into the lock and turned it as slowly as I could. RnB drifted out onto the landing. Kahli was humming along to the music, and as I tiptoed down the hall, I started to wonder if at some point along the way I'd lost my mind. Before I could really examine the thought, Kahli stepped into view. She screamed.

'What are you doing?' she said. 'What are you doing here?' Her expression moved between suspicion and relief.

'I live here,' I said. 'Remember?'

She took steps back towards the lounge room, as if I'd sprouted fangs. 'I texted you. I tried calling.'

'You called the police.' I stepped into the light and moved towards her.

'I was worried about you,' she said. 'I hadn't heard from you.'

I stood in line with the kitchen bench. From the corner of my right eye, I could just make out a chef's knife glistening on the drying rack.

'I was busy,' I said. 'We're spending more time at the office.'

'Marnie, you're being really weird. Are you okay?'

Kahli was standing at the centre of the lounge room. Her $2000 couch needed reupholstering. Her glass coffee table was smudged with fingerprints. I couldn't believe I'd spent so many hours waiting for Kahli to text me. It was such a low bar to clear.

'I'm fine,' I said.

'Okay.' She stood in the glow of the steel standing lamp, the base of which was starting to rust.

'I'll send movers next week. Rent is paid until the end of the month.'

'Are you moving in with . . . Luna?'

'No. We're all sleeping at the office. It's easier—'

'They can't ask you to do that—'

'Stop,' I said. It came out louder than I'd expected. Kahli took a step back. 'I'm fine. Don't tell anyone. Don't come looking for me. I'll just get some things and then I'll be off.'

She nodded, not entirely convinced. Then, tentatively, she said, 'Clea got in touch with Isabel, by the way.'

I gripped the side of the bench to steady myself. 'What did she say?'

'Something about going away for a while.'

'Right,' I said. 'Good.'

I went to my room and turned on the caustic downlight. Under its magnifying glass, everything was covered in a thick layer of dust. I slid open my wardrobe, pulled a puffer jacket from its hanger and threw it on the bed. When I returned to the rack, I caught sight of the three plastic tubs I'd stacked in the back corner of the wardrobe a year ago and proceeded to ignore. I was almost surprised to discover that they were still there; like running into a childhood friend whose life had unfolded entirely offline.

My mother was a fastidious record keeper. We were a team of documentarians, collecting evidence of each other's lives, until she died and I found myself surrounded by meaningless pieces of paper – trying my best to reconstruct a human body from the things it had left behind. In the months following her death, I was only really alive for the minute or so after I woke up; in the space between opening my eyes and remembering. Then, the crude facts arrived and I felt as if I was losing life-threatening amounts of something. I put the pieces of paper in plastic boxes and covered them with coats in the hope that it would stop the leaking, but even now – more than a year later – I couldn't seem to patch the hole.

Despite this, I pulled the first box from the stack and opened it on the floor. High school exam results. My Year Twelve yearbook. A poster I'd made as part of my media studies exam. The second box held three albums of baby photos, my birth certificate – good to know I still had it – and some abstract finger paintings. When I removed the third lid, a car alarm sounded down the street. I jumped, suddenly aware of my jittery fingers. I pulled a stack of paper from the centre of the box's concertina filing. *Marnie is a joy to have in class. I look forward to teaching her again in Year Three.* I flicked through the rest of its contents until my fingers found glossy photo paper. I pulled the first sheet. *North Park Primary All-School Photo, 2000.* The next sheet, 2001. 2002. 2003. I pulled out each of the photos and laid them on the floor in a semicircle. Hundreds of children in blue polo shirts smiled from each of the photos, and when I turned them over the white backing revealed a list of names. I searched from left to right, scouring the lists, scanning for a name I'd willed to appear on my own phone screen so many times before. But it wasn't there. I scanned the names of the staff members. Ran my finger over *Craig Lloyd.* Turned the pictures over again and held them up close to my eyes – examining his increasingly bald head, the selection of cargo shorts, the glint of his silver belt buckle. I wondered if he was capable of everything Luna had accused him of. But I didn't know him, and I never had. I was a child.

I returned everything to the boxes and stacked them in the wardrobe; slid my arms through the puffer jacket and turned off the light. As I went to leave, I heard Kahli sneer 'Enjoy your Kool-Aid' from the lounge room. I slammed the door shut behind me. When I got to the ground floor, something rustled in the bushes to my left. I stared into the darkness and, for a second, I thought I saw a face.

'Luna?' I said, but there was no reply. The leaves were still. I held my breath, waiting for signs of life. When I concluded I was alone, I turned in the direction of the tram and walked off into the night.

Thirty

I bounded down the stairs of the tram and charged towards *Emma*. Hordes of drunk people spilt out of Smith Street's restaurants, bars and clubs, and as I passed a group of people my age draped leisurely around an outdoor heater, I felt a pang of longing. As I rounded the corner of Emma Street, I heard footsteps shuffling behind me, but when I turned the street was empty. I continued towards the office, but as I passed the narrow laneway closest to *Emma* the footsteps returned, faster this time. Suddenly, sweaty hands were on my neck. Metallic cologne in my nostrils. I fell to the ground, and the weight of a man fell with me. He let out an exasperated cry as I rolled onto my back. He straddled me, and I looked up to discover that it was Antoni.

'Get off me,' I said, but his hands were on my neck again.

'You crazy fucking bitches,' he said, tightening his grip.

I kicked my feet against the pavement, trying to build enough momentum to push him off, but he was too heavy. There wasn't enough space in my throat to form a scream. As my vision began to blur, I heard the sound of a door, more footsteps, but a hazy glow had descended on the scene. For a moment, I was weightless. I heard Antoni cry out in pain. A woman's voice. He released my neck and I rolled to the edge of the footpath, coughing into the gutter. As quickly as it had arrived, the fog dispersed. I gasped for air, the shadow of his hands still clutching at my windpipe. When I sat up and looked over at Antoni, Luna was kneeling on his back, holding his arms in one hand and pressing his right cheek into the ground with the other. He was thrashing against her, but her hands were steady. A syringe lay discarded on the footpath beside him. The skin around his eyes was bright red and swollen.

'He was following me,' I said, although the effort required to speak left me breathless.

'It's okay,' Luna said as Antoni howled beneath her. 'Save your energy.'

Rose and Eva emerged from *Emma* and ran towards us. Antoni's movements were slowing. The tendons in Luna's forearms relaxed.

'Eva, take Marnie upstairs and make sure she's okay,' Luna said, her eyes glued to Antoni's skull. 'Rose, I need you with me.'

'I can help,' I said, but Luna didn't dignify this with a response. She just held Antoni's face against the concrete as she waited for him to lose consciousness.

~

'Are you okay?' Eva said, as she handed me an ice pack wrapped in a light-pink rytuał-branded gym towel. We were in Luna's office, me perched on the edge of the bed while Eva hovered stiffly a metre away.

'I'm fine.' I held the ice pack to my neck. It stung at first, but as my skin adjusted to the cold I came to like the way it felt. 'What will they do with him?'

'Antoni?'

I nodded.

'Oh. I'm sure they'll just keep him for a bit. Scare him. Until they know he'll . . . stay away.'

'Right.'

Eva fiddled with a strand of hair. 'I heard you worked at Ride On!. I love Steffani.' The words had lost their meaning – it was as if Eva had slipped into another language. 'She was really kind to me when I first met her. We did this yoga teacher training in Bali.'

'Oh. Cool.'

She nodded. We sat in silence until I heard Eva's phone vibrate in her pocket. 'That'll be Luna,' she said. 'Are you sure you're okay?'

'Totally fine.' I tightened my grip on the ice pack.

Eva's pink suede mules smacked against her heels as she walked away. I watched her golden hair bounce out the door and down the stairs, disappearing into the bowels of *Emma*.

When I was alone, I lay back on the bed and stared at the ceiling. I was starting to feel as if I wasn't real – as if none of this was real, and I was stuck watching a movie I didn't remember selecting. I pulled my phone from my pocket and checked my bank balance. More money than I'd ever had, but it was funny how quickly I'd come to see this as normal. At first it was everything, but now it felt like nothing. Everything had a way of eventually feeling like nothing.

I sat up and stared out the window. In an apartment building a few streets away, only one square was still light. I watched a figure moving around the room – tidying pillows, taking things to the kitchen – until eventually the square was swallowed by darkness, like all the others. My eyes returned to Luna's office, to the three framed pictures of her on the wall: smooth skin, plump lips, probing green eyes.

I lowered my gaze to the desk, to her computer. I remembered the last time I'd visited her office – how I'd asked her one question and received the answer to another. A thought crystallised as I moved towards the desk, the ice pack falling to the polished concrete with a flaccid plop. I sat in front of the screen and wiggled the mouse. Luna's staff portrait appeared above a prompt to enter her password. I stared at the blinking cursor, reminded of Rose's voice as she explained the story behind Coco's and my passwords. 'They always contain a woman's name,' she'd said, 'and your date of birth. We use the names of women we believe deserved a better story.'

Luna's birthday was the twentieth of July – 'a Leo, of course – so predictable,' she'd said, on a podcast or perhaps over lunch, and I'd slid it straight into the filing cabinet at the back of my brain. But there was still the question of the woman's name. I typed *CAROLINE2007* – after Caroline Flack, whom I now knew to be the bar's namesake. The rectangle jiggled. On a suspicious whim I typed Luna's own name, but it jiggled again. I looked around the room. There had to be one woman Luna identified with more than any other. My brain was straining under the events of the day – I was bone-tired. On the edge of the desk, I found a note Luna had left for me a few mornings before: *M, I'm working downstairs, can you proofread the next EDM? Love you. X L*

My stomach dropped. I returned to the screen and held my breath as I typed *MARNIE2007.* My heart began to race. I pressed enter. The rectangle disappeared. Luna's desktop was presented to me, full of folders and unsorted documents with titles such as *EVEBLUEPRINTV1* and *RYTUALSTYLEGUIDE_V9*. Her background was the rytuał logo, stamped on a hazy pink-and-red design. I opened a new search window and typed *CCTV*, but I knew it wouldn't work. The file would have a name made up of numbers and full stops and, judging by the messiness of Luna's desktop, she did not identify as a fastidious record keeper.

    I double-clicked on the photos app. When Luna's gallery appeared, I tried to select only videos but somehow found myself at the library's chronological beginning. And there it was. At first I thought I was hallucinating, but as I expanded the thumbnail its full resolution sent me staggering away from the desk. Luna's face was younger, much younger. She was lying in bed with a man – her head cradled in the nook of his right shoulder. The man must have been about thirty-six, which was disorienting in its own right. His hair was more blond than grey, his face achingly familiar. I heard footsteps on the stairs but I didn't flinch. As Luna appeared at the entrance to her office, her hair uncharacteristically askew, I looked up at her solemn expression and said, 'It was Spencer?'

~

'You planned all of this?' I said. 'You brought me here to . . . what? Kill me?' The feeling I'd had after Antoni tried to strangle me returned. I had to clutch the back of Luna's desk chair to stop myself from falling.

    'Kill you?' She laughed as she closed the door behind her. 'No! We don't hurt women here, Marnie. We help them heal.' She was grinning. She took a step towards me.

'Stop,' I said. 'Don't.'

She raised her hands as if I'd taken offence to something benign. 'Truthfully, I was waiting for you to piece it together,' she said as she sauntered over to the couch. 'I wanted you to figure it out for yourself.'

'Why did you lie? Why did you tell me all that stuff about school, about that teacher . . .'

She slumped into the couch and crossed one leg over the other. 'All true,' she said. 'All true, just not at your school.'

'I don't believe you.'

'His name was Kevin Mason. You can look him up.' She gestured to the computer, where her bright young face was still staring back at me. 'There was a case against him but he died before the trial. Such a shame, I would've loved to do it myself.'

I let my forehead rest against the back of the chair.

'I'm kidding!' she said. 'God, Marnie, I thought you were supposed to be funny.'

I looked up at her again. 'And Rose? You sent her to . . . find me?'

She nodded. 'I wanted to recruit you myself, but Steffani would have made a fuss. Rose could fly under the radar.'

'Why? Why . . . all of this?'

She uncrossed her legs and tapped the cushion beside her. I shook my head. She sighed.

'After it ended, I knew he wouldn't change,' she said. 'I knew it would just be another girl, then another, then another. When he married *her*, I had this brief moment where I considered that I was wrong – I was ready to be wrong, I wanted to be. But I couldn't let it go. And then, lo and behold, a few years later, you show up. And I knew what he was doing to you, how it would end.

So I started taking matters into my own hands. I started thinking about justice. About what it would look like, what it would feel like. I did this for you, Marnie. I did this for us.'

'How did you know about me?'

She laughed. 'You weren't exactly discreet. I saw he was a mentor for that program and I knew what would happen. After it was announced I just . . . kept an eye out.'

Under her impenetrable gaze, memory overwhelmed me. Outside the house in South Yarra, the smell of damp earth as I pressed my face up against the glass. I thought I heard my name, and when I saw a woman's face in the darkness I filled in the blanks. But staring at her, in the office at the top of the stairs, in the building called *Emma*, I now saw the woman's face clearly. It wasn't his wife at all. It was Luna.

'You . . . were there that night? At his house?'

She nodded. 'You and me,' she said. 'Cut from the same cloth.'

I pressed my thumbnail into my index finger. She tapped the couch cushion again, and this time I went to her. When I was sat beside her, she took hold of my shoulders and rotated my torso towards her. 'Do you want to heal?' she said. 'Or do you want to let him win?' She shifted her hands to my cheeks.

Luna was right. If I'd wanted to leave, I would have done it already. I would have done it on day one. Day three. Fourteen. There were so many off-ramps, and yet I'd stuck to the freeway, knuckles white against the wheel, careering towards this very moment. There was no other answer. I had nothing else to lose. I looked into her wild green eyes and said, 'I want to heal.' She kissed me, deeply, the full weight of our shared history binding us together.

Thirty-one

Autumn House was a five-star retreat perched on the edge of the Surf Coast cliffs. Rows of tea-tree obscured the view from the road, because it was a private place, for private discoveries. Our minibuses pulled up in a procession. The circular driveway hugged a lavish foyer where everything was white: the timber, the upholstery, the crockery, the artwork. Accents of beige peppered every room, but the retreat's predominant feature was blinding white. The only thing that wasn't white was the food, which was often tinged dark green. Luna was waiting at the top of the driveway when we arrived. As the buses pulled up, Rose emerged from reception behind her.

'Good morning, rytuałists,' Luna said as the bus doors flung open.

When I leapt from the last step she skipped towards me. I was wearing a lilac hoodie I'd found hanging on the back of her office chair, and the smell of her was thick along the neckline.

I huffed the scent of her like it was paint. She pulled me in, and I whispered, 'Is he here?'

'Mmm-hmm.' She took a step back and smiled at the rest of the group.

'I wish you'd let me help.'

'Too risky.'

'Where did you find him?'

'Later,' she said. 'I'll tell you later.'

Staff from the retreat centre tended to our bags in silence. This was part of the experience: none of the Autumn House staff would address guests verbally. The website said that this allowed for the deepest level of inward reflection.

In the foyer, Luna clambered up onto one of the white couches to make sure she could hold the entire crowd in her eye line. An Autumn House staff member winced beside me as Luna slammed her thick platform boots onto the linen, but it was all they could do. When I turned to look at them, they wordlessly offered me a sparkling water with lemon and mint.

'Welcome, all,' Luna said. 'I trust you're well rested and ready for what I'm sure will be a . . . transformative weekend.' Her eyes found mine. She winked. I sucked at my sparkling water, which was suspiciously delicious. 'First, an announcement of sorts. I know you've all been waiting to hear about our very special featured rytuałist, so allow me to put you out of your misery.'

From the other side of the room, Coco stared at me. Her face had lost its plump, spherical shape. I'd barely seen her in weeks. I'd barely seen anyone other than Luna.

'This evening, we'll host our first ever shared Friday Night Drinks. Your featured rytuałists will be myself and none other than my executive assistant, Marnie Sellick.'

Tame applause filled the room. I thought I heard someone say, 'We already did hers,' but when I tried to find the source of the voice I was met with vacant smiles. Supportive nods. Someone placed a hand on my shoulder.

'Get settled in, and we'll meet back here at twelve-thirty for lunch. This afternoon, Rose will lead a team-building session, followed by Eva's Dream Life workshop. Then, the main event. Any questions, ask the universe.' I watched all the tiny muscles in Luna's neck tense as she laughed. She jumped from the couch cushions to the floor and stomped towards the exit.

The staff dealt room keys like poker hands. I collected mine and followed the group down the hall, out the door and across the grass. They weren't rooms so much as they were cabins, and they weren't cabins so much as they were small houses. Gradually the congregation thinned as women filed into their allocated accommodations. Some were two or three bedrooms with a shared bathroom. Some were single occupancy. Number twenty-three was the closest to the cliff face. I followed a path that curved its way around the salt-caked courtyard. When I looked through the sliding glass door, Luna was already perched on the couch, smiling intently in my direction.

'The gym,' she said, once I'd slid the door closed behind me. 'We found him at the gym.'

~

Lunch was served in the main building. An impressively long table formed a line down the centre of the dining room – too long to be a single table, it had to be made up of several smaller ones, but covered by white linen it masqueraded as a woodworking marvel. Groups of women were scattered around it, gesticulating wildly as they performed intimacy with each other.

Staff members from the retreat centre wandered in and out of the oak doors bearing white trays: drinks on the way in, debris on the way out. A single rose petal floated at the top of each drink. Luna collected two glasses as we walked through the door, presenting me with one.

'It's sparkling water,' she said. 'They'll let you do anything here, as long as you don't serve alcohol.' She clinked the rim of her glass to mine and knocked her forehead against the space just above the centre of my eyebrows – as if it were some secret handshake we'd previously discussed. She stared at me, expectantly, when she was done. Before I could solve the puzzle, Rose appeared behind her.

'There you are,' she said. 'Just need to run a few things past you for tonight's session.' Rose held a terse smile that indicated I was not invited.

'Of course,' Luna said. She rolled her eyes playfully as Rose dragged her away, mouthing, *I'll be back.* I turned to stare down the length of the table. The crowd had multiplied – the spattering of women had become a swarm. I cut through them with my shoulders, moving to the end of the table, where a single square of vacant carpet was bathed in sunlight. I stared out the window, across the dry grass, to the space where the cliff gave way and all that was left was sky.

'Hey,' a voice said from behind me.

I turned to find Coco clutching a glass of sparkling water with both hands. She cast her eyes around the room and took a step closer. A whiff of body odour hit the air as she leant in, with her jaw sealed shut by a strained smile, and whispered, 'I need to talk to you.'

'Okay,' I said. 'What's up?'

Coco slapped my shoulder and laughed, as if I'd said something outrageous, and after scanning around the room again, she said – through tight cheeks – 'She's not Polish.'

'Who? Luna?'

'*Shhh*. Keep your voice down.' She waved at one of The Lauras, who'd just arrived at the entrance to the dining room. 'She just liked the spelling.'

We angled our bodies away from the crowd. 'Is that a big deal?'

'She lied. That's a big deal.'

'How do you know?'

'I did some stalking. Well, first I found the original business registration. Her name isn't even Luna.'

I waited to feel something, but my blood was cold. 'I thought Friday Night Drinks . . . *changed* you?'

'I was just . . . I wanted to believe it. I did, for a minute, but . . . I think Luna might have . . .'

'Luna might have what?'

She snuck a glance at the room's entrance. '. . . done something to my dad.'

The memory of Antoni's sour cologne flooded my senses. 'Why do you say that?'

'His texts are weird. Like, they're him, but they're not him.'

'I'm sure it's nothing,' I lied as a tight feeling spread from my chest to my throat.

Ruth and Noor walked towards our patch of carpet as Coco reinstated her smile. 'I'm going to confront her,' she whispered.

'No. Don't. Coco, just leave it—'

'Hey girl!' Coco said in Noor's direction.

'What was her real name?' I whispered as I applied my own demented grin.

'Laura,' she said. 'She's just another Laura.'

~

'Today, a different kind of Clearing,' Rose said. She was wearing a pale-blue two-piece yoga set, although yoga was not on the afternoon's agenda.

The Shala was a separate building to that which housed the foyer and dining rooms: a freestanding hall with a thatched roof that could be transfigured and transformed in any number of ways, although the name suggested its primary purpose was spiritual in nature. Yoga mats were set out in a circle, with a single chair at its centre. Rose stood behind it.

'We'll call this exercise Hot Seat. Like our weekly clearings, I want you to select a person – well, a man'—she gave a coy smile – like, *obviously*—'and for three minutes you'll imagine what it might feel like to be him. You'll answer questions in character. Does that make sense?'

I looked around the room. Two yoga mats were vacant, and as the women nodded I took attendance: Ruth, Noor, Laura, Laura, Laura. Victoria. Priya. Eva. Rose, obviously. Then, the faces I recognised but couldn't name. There were Sarahs somewhere, although none of them looked alike. A Rachel, probably a Maddy. I'd heard the name Alicia at one point. But I'd forgone the opportunity to get to know them in any great detail, in order to memorise the exact length of Luna's eyelashes. The curvature of her spine. I had given up so much to know her, and still I had the growing feeling that I didn't know her at all. Her face was missing from the circle. As was Coco's.

'I'd like to begin with one of our two featured rytualists,' Rose said as she extended an arm in my direction. 'Marnie Sellick.'

I stood up and moved towards Rose as if in a trance. When I got to the chair, Rose took her hands to my shoulders and guided me into the seat. 'This'll be fun,' she whispered, although nothing about the situation screamed *fun* to me.

'I can't see her,' a voice whined from somewhere behind my chair.

'You'll get your turn, Maddy.'

There was definitely a Maddy.

Rose walked to the edge of the circle formed by the yoga mats and positioned herself directly in front of me. 'Okay, Marnie. This exercise is about reclaiming the narrative, but more than that, it's about closure. If we can get inside the minds of those who have hurt us, we can break the cycle for ourselves.'

'Will Luna be joining us?' I said, eyeing the door.

'She's resting, but I'm sure she'll join us when she's ready.'

'Right.'

'Do you have someone in mind?'

'Well, yeah. Of course—'

'Good. Everyone, you're welcome to jump in whenever. I want to get to the heart of who this person is. Ask intelligent questions. What's his name, Marnie?'

I ran a hand over the back of my neck. I was starting to sweat. 'Spencer.'

'Spencer who?'

'Spencer Healey.'

She pulled her phone from her pocket and tapped its stopwatch app. 'Let's begin. Spencer, how did you meet Marnie?'

I felt the circle contract. 'I . . . I met her through a mentoring program.'

'Was she your mentee?'

'Yes, she won a prize.'

'What drew you to her?'

I tried to remember, which was pointless given I'd never actually known. I just remembered his laugh. The rosé. The sting of my own rabid desire. 'I don't know.'

'What's your occupation?' said green-eyed Laura from Rose's feet, directly in front of me. The other Lauras sat beside her.

I cleared my throat. 'I'm a producer. Sorry, used to be. Now I'm a creative director?'

'What was your childhood like?' said blue-eyed Laura.

'It was . . . ah . . . I don't know.'

'What's your rising sign?' Brown-eyed Laura smiled as if she was pleased with her contribution to the exercise.

'Rose, I don't know how this is supposed to help—'

'Do you hate women? Or do you hate yourself?' It was Eva's voice, from behind my chair.

In response, someone else whispered, 'So true.'

I looked up at Rose, but her gaze was cold.

'I want to ask you again,' Rose said, ignoring my desperate eyes. 'What drew you to her?'

'Um, she was young? Being with her made me feel young by proxy.'

'But what specifically was it about *her*?' Rose pursed her lips.

'She had a good sense of humour,' I said. 'She made me laugh, I think.'

'You can't build a relationship on a good sense of humour. You can't fuck a good sense of humour. What made you want to risk it all?'

I looked to all three of The Lauras, as if to ask if they were really hearing this, but the circle was blanketed in concerned expressions – they were taking this extremely seriously.

'I guess she was just special, Rose. I guess it's that simple.'

'Or the opposite. Maybe she wasn't special. Maybe she was just a warm body at the right time.'

'Do you identify as a men's rights activist?' a voice chirped as Rose tapped her phone again.

'That's time,' she said dismissively. 'Thank you, Marnie.'

I left the chair at the centre of the room and walked to the edge of the circle. 'I'm going to lie down,' I said, as I stepped over blue-eyed Laura's yoga mat. Rose didn't say anything, she just watched me leave. She was classy like that. If I were her, I might have pulled out a clump of my hair.

~

Luna wasn't resting. At least, not in our room. I lay down on the bed and tried to close my eyes, but my head was full of bees. After a few minutes I slid my feet back into my rubber sandals and went to find her.

A gravel path cut through artfully placed spinifex, snaking from room to room, eventually winding its way back to reception. From there, the path began again, leading to the Shala, and then on to the spa centre. It was the kind of early December day where the sun was masked by thick grey clouds but rain refused to materialise. Every once in a while, the clouds would part with a reminder that the sun was a prize fighter and human skin a poor contender.

When I arrived at reception, the hall was empty aside from two Autumn House staff members tapping attentively at their keyboards.

'Good afternoon,' I said, forcefully chirpy, as I crossed the floor. The staff members looked up from their screens but didn't say anything. 'I was just wondering if you'd seen my boss. Luna?'

From the furthest computer, a tiny blonde woman with disproportionately large lips nodded. She reached for a piece of paper and presented it on the desk. I walked towards her, shuffling on the balls of my feet. The piece of paper held a map of the grounds, and with a swift flick of her right wrist, the woman circled the square marked *SPA CENTRE*.

'Are you sure?' I said.

She nodded and handed me the map. With a polite smile, she returned to her screen.

I clutched the map in my right hand and edged backwards, towards the double doors that revealed the rest of the property. When the path reappeared, I followed it past the Shala to a white stone building with a flat iron roof. It was unassuming among the drooping eucalypts; the windows were tinted dark. A grey slab with steel trimmings presented itself as the door. I pressed against the coarse metal handle and watched as it sprang open with surprising agility.

'Hello?' I said. 'Luna?'

The spa reception was dark, and the windows were sealed with shutters from the inside. A desk sat unattended at the far left corner of the room, with a corridor leading to the rest of the building on the right. From somewhere down the corridor and far away, I heard a faint thud. Like a dog's head against glass.

'Hello?' I repeated, inching towards the corridor. I pulled my phone from my back pocket and held my thumb to the torch icon. The floor was dusty. 'Luna?'

I followed the corridor past rows of treatment rooms, all of them empty. I let my feet stumble to a jog, winding around corners, past more doors, too many doors. The corridor straightened out, and finally soft light glowed overhead. At the end of the hall, two doors remained. One was marked *Sauna*, and the other *Bath House*. The doors were made of translucent glass, speckled with texture. The sauna was dark, but there was a beam of light in the bath house. Inside, figures were moving. A scream reverberated out into the corridor, and I stumbled towards the door.

'Luna,' I said, but as the scene developed, I couldn't make sense of it. Low light. An empty bath house, each pool drained. Someone was lying on the floor, splayed out like roadkill – still twitching, eyes fluttering in and out of consciousness. Luna was standing, holding her phone torch. She was covered in blood. The roadkill was a woman. The roadkill was Coco.

'Don't move,' Luna said. 'Don't say anything.'

Thirty-two

Hers was the second dead body I'd ever seen, not counting my mother's. My mother doesn't count because when people died in nursing homes or hospital beds or a worn lounge chair they had 'passed away'. *Dead* was bright-red blood – striking even in almost complete darkness. Hers was the second dead body I'd seen in as many months, and it was, if I'm honest, two too many for someone with my gag reflex.

'What the fuck?' I kept saying. Over and over, like a chant. 'What the *fuck*?'

'I can explain,' Luna said, wiping the knife on the leg of her cargo pants, as if it were paint or chutney or nothing at all. 'But first we need to move her body.'

She said it as though it was something I'd already agreed to – as if I'd known this was where we'd end up. And at first it made me mad. But I was tired. In my body, yes, but also in a grand spiritual sense. And because I was tired, and I'd already sunk so much of myself into believing that this was the right place and the right time, I said, 'Okay.'

By the light of her phone torch, Luna deposited the knife on a tiled bench to her left – intended for jugs of water or pitted dates, something to reach for between baths. None of the pools held any water, and the sound of metal on ceramic echoed around the cavernous room; it was hard to believe we weren't underground. Very slowly, she moved to Coco's body and placed her phone torch face up beside it. I was still standing in the doorway when she looked at me and said, 'Hurry up.'

I tripped over myself to get to her. I didn't see the blood on the floor when I knelt down. Then, I couldn't see anything else: under my right knee, my left palm. I wiped my hand on my T-shirt, running it back and forth across the fabric until the skin was dry.

'Don't be dramatic,' Luna said. Her eyes glowed, and the impatience in her voice rubbed against my obedience. It was enough to spark a small fire, and in the glow of the embers I saw what she was asking me to do. I stood up.

'No,' I said, shaking my head, stringing together what might come next. 'What did you do to her?' The words were firmer in my head. When they left my mouth they wobbled like jelly.

Luna groaned, as she often did when I inconvenienced her. 'She attacked me. It was self-defence.'

I'd told Coco not to confront her, hadn't I? My sinuses stung. Luna hooked her arms around Coco's shoulders. She looked so small, her body deflated – the stillness was jarring. As Luna tried to drag her towards the door, I ran to the bench and grabbed the handle of the knife.

'Stop,' I said. 'Drop her.' The wound at the centre of Coco's stomach was still weeping. The knife was just a regular chef's knife.

'We both know you don't know what to do with that,' Luna said.

I edged closer. 'Do you want to test that theory?' My hand was shaking; the tip of the knife swayed wildly.

She sighed and released Coco's torso. Her skull hit the tiles with a gruesome crack. The back of my throat twitched. I took another step towards Luna.

'She was out to get me,' she said.

'What do you mean?'

She gave another melodramatic sigh. 'This is a place for people with big ambitions to thrive, but you have to follow the rules—'

'What rules? You've never cared about the rules.'

'She was going to go to the police. She was going to destroy everything, Marnie. Everything we've worked for.'

'Why would she go to the police?' I knew the answer, of course I knew the answer, but I wanted to hear it from her.

She stalled, casting her eyes around the dim room.

'Because I killed her father, okay? The man who tried to strangle you? Ring a bell?'

White spots clouded my vision. 'I didn't know—'

'Don't do that, Marnie. Of course you knew. Coco chose her father over us, and there had to be consequences.'

I dropped the knife. It clattered against the tiles, and the sound of it rang out for what felt like minutes afterwards.

'Let me show you something,' she said, as she moved to the door. I paused, willing Coco's sad little body to sit up and say something mildly irritating, but it was completely still. After a moment, I followed Luna's scent out into the hall. The lights were on in the sauna. 'Marnie,' she called, from inside. 'Come join us.'

As I pushed the door open, reality puckered at the seams – the sensation that I wasn't real, that this was all part of an extended fever dream, returned. When Luna's face came into focus, I didn't recognise her. But I recognised the man beside her. I tried to scream, but a creaking noise was all that left my shrivelled throat. Luna just smiled, her legs and arms crossed. She was sitting on the sauna's wooden bench seat. Beside her, a man was slumped over himself, hooked up to two IVs – one in either arm. Bags full of blood hung from hooks suspended over his head, and his wrists and ankles were bolted to the bench. His shoulders still sloped athletically towards toned arms and a small waist. He was wearing a blue gym shirt and shorts.

'They'll let you do anything here, as long as you don't serve alcohol,' Luna said. I backed out of the room. I fell backwards onto the stone floor, scrambling away as Luna followed me out of the sauna. 'Ta-da!'

'What—' I said. 'What are you doing to him?'

'Platelet-rich plasma,' she said. 'A miracle for the skin.' She looked down at the bloodstain on her caramel cargo pants, ran a finger across it, and returned her eyes to mine. 'But you know that already. You've seen the benefits for yourself.'

'What?'

'That's a terrible habit of yours, Marnie. Ask me a real question.'

'What are you doing with the blood?' I spat, shuffling further away from her, towards the edge of the light.

'Platelet-rich plasma,' she repeated. 'Other brands charge thousands, and all they do is stick a needle in your arm and call it a night cream. We'll be the first to use other people's blood. *Their* blood. To make something beautiful out of something so ugly. rytuał *Eve*.'

I raised my right hand to my cheek and dragged it across the skin there. I wanted to peel it away from my face. Luna laughed as she watched the thoughts lock into place. My heart rattled against my ears.

'Oh, come on,' she said. 'Why get squeamish now?'

'You killed them? You killed all of them?'

'No!' she squawked, as if I'd suggested something completely ridiculous. 'God, no. It was just a vial here and there to begin with. Then there was Justin . . . terrible accident. And Antoni. Well, that one wasn't really an accident, we just couldn't trust that he wouldn't try it again. I wanted it all to start with him.' She gestured to the sauna. 'But life just got in the way.'

I shook my head. I kept shaking it, as if I could dislodge the part of my brain that had thought any of this was a good idea. That had seen the good in something so rotten, in someone so sour.

'He'll never change,' she said. 'It's time to take matters into our own hands.'

Footsteps approached from the corridor behind me. My heart rate couldn't physically climb any higher without rendering me unconscious.

'Hello, Rose,' Luna said. 'We need to move Coco's body to the car. Marnie will help you.'

'Why the car?' I said, skipping over everything else.

'I think disposing of a body on the premises might be pushing it. Besides, we have the proper facilities at the Lab. Take her to *Emma*.'

I scrambled around to face Rose. 'You knew?'

'You didn't?'

I turned back to Luna.

'I'll leave this in your capable hands,' she said. 'I have to run. You might want to burn those clothes when you're done.'

I watched the soles of her platform boots strike the stone floor as she marched to the end of the corridor and disappeared. A light buzzed incessantly overhead.

'Come on,' Rose said. 'Is she in the bath house?'

'Why are you doing this?' I said as I stood up, steadying myself against the wall. White dots still punctured my vision. 'Why do you trust her?'

Rose snorted. 'That's a bit rich.'

'I didn't know—'

'Yes, you did. You were there, every Friday night. Surely you had an inkling.'

I turned to face the wall and pressed both hands into the stone. The white dots became large blobs. Rose paused, but eventually she placed a palm to my upper back. 'Coco didn't deserve this,' I said.

'When you decide to do things differently, sometimes there are casualties.' Then, she added, 'They're bad men. You know that.'

Did I? Rose wrapped her arms around me from behind. 'This is how you win a losing game,' she whispered. The words filled my head and came to a boil. The logic was flawed, but only in the same way that everything was flawed. They had found a way to turn the odds in our favour.

'Let's get this done before dinner,' she said, releasing her arms as she walked towards the bath house.

'Did you see the girl at the club?' I said.

'What club?' She was sifting through her memory in earnest.

'When you went to find Justin. There was a girl at the club, she was really drunk. Luna said he was trying to take her home.'

'We didn't go to a club,' she said. 'We broke into his house.'

~

The first drops of rain broke through the clouds as I ran. I took a sharp left at the Shala and ran towards the road. The rain made my sandals slippery, and my feet approximated their place as I threw them at the earth. Eventually, when reception had dissolved behind me, my right foot slid all the way off to the right, and I fell. The rain softened the impact – the ground was wet and warm, and I wondered if maybe I should just lie down for a bit. I'd left Rose in the spa centre, but my departure hadn't fazed her. She was mildly annoyed at the thought of moving a dead body on her own, but her lithe frame was deceptively strong. She was up to the challenge.

I pressed myself away from the earth and continued towards the gate – the overhead wire fence wasn't something I'd factored into the equation, but if I could make it there I could work out what to do about it. When the fence was close enough for my eyes to trace each individual wire thread, I saw something move in the saltbush. I kept running. I imagined the distance on a treadmill screen, counting down from two hundred metres, one hundred metres, fifty metres, ten. Someone stepped out from behind the shrubs, just as I was close enough to tumble into the fence. My heart jumped to my skull. I dug my heels into the wet leaves and took a step back. It was the tiny blonde woman from reception.

With an Autumn House umbrella held over her head, she stood by the fence, staring at me.

'What are you doing out here?' I said. She didn't respond. After a moment, she walked over to the fence and leant an ear towards the wire, keeping her eyes glued to mine. The fence hummed with electricity. I looked up at the woman, but something behind her caught my eye: in the distance, further down the fence line, there was another person with an Autumn House umbrella, and past them, even further away, another. Someone had sent them here. For this specific purpose.

'You have to help me,' I said, returning to the baby-faced woman with the swollen lips. Her skin was glowing, but was it *glowing*? I stared at the smooth, taut panel of her forehead. 'They're dangerous,' I said. 'Those women are dangerous.'

As expected, she didn't say anything, but I watched as her eyes dipped to rest on my torso. I looked down. I was soaked in Coco's blood.

The woman looked up at me again. 'It wasn't me,' I said, shaking my head, but her gaze was pointed. I let out a sob, doubling over myself as the rain intensified. I was soaked all the way through to my skin, and my wet hair dripped down the back of my body. The woman moved closer to me and held the umbrella over us both. 'It will be over soon,' she whispered, but I couldn't be sure if the words came from her mouth or the meat of my own brain. When the moment had passed, she took two steps back and returned to guarding the fence. I turned, which was when I saw Bibi and Liv waiting in the shrubs behind us.

'Marnie, this way,' Liv said.

~

Rytuał

After the fence, Bibi and Liv returned me to my room. I sat at the bottom of the shower as scalding hot water ran over my back. I changed into the only dress I'd brought with me, not out of respect for the evening's activities, but because if I was going to die I didn't want to die in lycra. I opened my messages and scrolled all the way to the bottom. I'd deleted his number, but I'd saved the thread. I returned to it routinely. The last message I'd received from him glared up at me.

> I wanted things to end
> differently as well, Marnie, but I
> think this is best for all parties.
> If you have any questions
> for me please let me know,
> otherwise I wish you well
> in your future endeavours.

My thumb scratched at the screen, returning to the first text he'd ever sent.

> Hi Marnie, are you free for
> a call today to discuss next
> steps for script development?
> Cheers, S.

I wondered if he'd considered the skin beneath my clothes when he sent 'S' instead of Spencer, when he'd decided to text instead of email, when he'd seen the pixelated selfie I sent accompanying my writers' biography. Or had it come later, once I'd passed some kind of test? I locked the phone and threw it on the bed. I left the cabin and walked out into the dying light, flanked by Bibi and Liv – like Luna and Spencer, a devil on each of my shoulders.

~

It was just like any other meal at rytuał. Luna held court at the head of the table, and even those on the opposite side of the room tried their best to win her favour. I could see how this energised her. Rose and I were seated next to each other, and I could feel her watching me, waiting for me to put a foot wrong.

My leg bounced incessantly beneath the table. At one point, Rose placed an open palm on my thigh and whispered, 'Tonight will complete the cycle. Once you're free from him, we will all be free.'

An Autumn House staff member leant over the table between us to collect our plates. Twenty other staff members did the same, rapidly clearing what was left of dinner.

'Sisters,' Luna said, rising from her seat. 'It's time.'

She rounded the head of the table and made her way to my seat. As she reached for my hand, the room grinned. She kept hold of it as we left the dining room and walked across the dark, damp grounds to the Shala.

Thirty-three

The yoga mats we'd waddled around earlier that day were laid out in a chequerboard. At the corner of each mat, a small bottle made from red glass was waiting. At the end of the room, a chair was poised amid an impressive altar. Flowers exploded from vases, candles lit up the space from various altitudes and crystals filled in any blanks. Two green fronds arched over the back of the chair like crossed swords. They were monstrous. Little silver cuffs were affixed to the chair's arms and legs – zip ties were so pedestrian.

'Marnie, this way.' Luna led me to the front of the room, gesturing towards the throne. Something had changed in her eyes. She was looking through me to an outcome; I was a means to an end. She deposited me in the chair as I eyed the Shala's two exits.

'Good evening, rytuałists,' Luna said, turning to face the crowd as they folded their legs up beneath themselves – some sitting on their shins, some cross-legged. Their faces shone towards Luna like a room of full moons.

'Good evening, Luna,' they said.

'Before we begin the official proceedings, I'd like to draw your attention to the vessels at the top of your mats. Say hello to our latest skincare offering, rytuał *Eve*.'

The full moons clapped, but none of them reached for the product. Not yet.

'This product signals the beginning of a new era for rytuał. With *Eve*, we will be granting our customers access to a suite of ingredients previously only accessible to the privileged few. In the process, we will be rewriting the stories of our own lives, as well as the collective feminine consciousness. We will be redefining what it means to break the glass ceiling. It really is very exciting.'

They clapped again, they cheered, while keeping themselves focused on Luna. A candle blew out somewhere to my right. The smell of it wafted over the giant fronds to fill my nostrils.

'Go on,' Luna said. 'Try it.'

The women swiped at the bottles, tearing off the lids and squeezing the dropper heads vigorously. They poured the gel into their hands, dispensed it however they could. The smell of frankincense filled the room. The women began to hum as they rubbed it into their skin – they massaged their temples, cheekbones and chins gleefully. As I watched them lather themselves in the product, the opulent, woody smell turned sour. The liquid turned bright red. They wiped rich, red blood over their faces and smiled, some of them licking at their hands to get the last of it. '*Mmmmmmmm*' reverberated from their mouths. I pictured Coco's stomach weeping blood, and Luna licking up what was left of it.

'Stop!' I said. The women looked at me like rabid dogs, but the blood was gone. From the back of the rows of mats, Rose stood.

'She's not the one,' she said, throwing her voice out over the other women's heads.

'She is,' Luna cooed. 'Rose, sit down.'

'Let me do it.'

Luna crossed the floor. The room was silent as her feet glided across polished boards, passing the rows of pink mats, to arrive at Rose.

'Your efforts will be rewarded,' she said, holding Rose's cheeks in her hands. 'Sisters, let's celebrate Rose for bringing Marnie to us.'

The women applauded. And when they applauded, they became one. Their individual features melted down to a vat of precious metals. I gripped the arms of the chair. Luna kissed Rose on the mouth.

'Everything okay, Marnie?' Luna said as she returned to the front of the room. Rose lowered herself back to her mat.

'They'll figure it out,' I said. 'Won't they?'

'Who is they?'

'People. The families. You'll never get away with it.'

'You'd be surprised.'

A sharp pain burrowed through the centre of my skull. Luna knelt down on the floor in front of me. Whispers shot through the crowd, whispers with sharp edges.

'We're doing this for the women who haven't met him yet.'

I couldn't get out in front of my breath. I started to cry. 'I don't believe you,' I said, between gasps. Rose's words echoed in my mind: *We didn't go to a club, we broke into his house.* 'I don't trust you.'

She pressed herself away from the floor and wrapped her arms around me. In my ear, she whispered, 'Through the power of the fallen woman we can return to the moment of genesis and write a new story.'

'What does that mean?' I pleaded, but Luna had already turned to face the crowd.

'We come together after a week of working to change the way the beauty industry operates, in order to change the way that we each operate. We come here to look inside ourselves, to examine the things we've accepted as truth from society and challenge these ideals. We come together to push out masculine norms and welcome in the divine feminine. We conspire together to overthrow destructive patriarchal standards, replacing them with the power inside each person present today.'

The crowd smiled. They returned to their positions on the floor, closed their eyes and placed their hands over their hearts. When had they learnt to do that?

Luna spun around to face me again. 'You will remain aware of everything we discuss and the events that take place this evening. At any point, you can end the session with the word "Set". Nothing that happens during this session will leave this room. You are safe here. Please confirm with the word "Prime".'

I shook my head. The crowd, my colleagues, these beautiful women with perfect eyebrows and festering holes in their hearts, began to chant. 'Prime, prime, prime,' they said. When I didn't join them, they got louder.

'Set,' I said. 'Set!'

But Luna didn't stop. She scooped me out of the chair. 'I've known you for so long,' she said, and then, 'Bring him in.'

'No—'

'Yes,' she said. 'Prime.'

From the back of the room, Bibi and Liv appeared. A frail approximation of Spencer hung from their arms. Luna nodded, and they dragged him across the floor towards us. He was only just conscious, drained of too much blood to put up a fight. As they got closer, I could smell him: cigarettes and oud cologne in my nose, my hair. They deposited him on the throne and fastened his wrists and ankles to the chair, although it seemed like overkill. He stirred as they stepped away, admiring their work.

'Thank you, two,' Luna said. They nodded and folded themselves into the other women, claiming their yoga mats.

I couldn't stop staring at him. I tried to find the glossy, untouchable man I'd once wanted, but now all I saw was the deep lines at the corners of his eyes. When he sat up and blinked, his one slightly swollen eye was all I could focus on. He looked sick.

'Marnie?' he said, shaking his head. His eyes were open but glassy. It was disappointing. I wanted to see him fight. 'What are you doing here?'

His voice frayed the ends of my nerves. It had been almost two years since I'd heard it.

'Laura, what is she doing here?'

There it was: Laura. Just like Coco had warned. At one point, she must have been Laura Healey. There was something so offensive about imagining Luna by any other name – she had made herself that kind of person.

I'd managed to tune out the sounds of the crowd, narrowing my awareness to hold only Luna and Spencer, but they were still there, a captive audience, purring with delight. 'Fallen woman, fallen woman, fallen woman,' they said.

Eva had been hovering on the sidelines, waiting to be summoned. When Luna turned to face her, she lit up. 'Let's get started.'

'Marnie,' Spencer said from behind me. While Luna and Eva fussed with a metal tray, I took a step towards him. His skin dissolved into the grey of his beard. 'I'm sorry,' he said. It was quiet enough to reach only my ears.

I had waited to hear those words from him for so long. Not because I wanted to forgive him, but because I wanted to know that there was something to forgive. It didn't matter how many times you told the story; you could never be sure that the way you saw things, the way you felt things, was right. Anger split me in two and pitted one version against the other. I had let it swallow so much of my life.

'I've changed,' he continued. 'Anyone who knows me now would agree.'

But he couldn't possibly have changed. *There was someone else after you*, Lily had said. *A production assistant.*

Luna appeared beside me with a silver tray. A pair of shiny hairdressing shears. Nothing else. 'The cycle just continues,' she said. 'Until we cut the cord.'

I looked at her. The line of her collarbones. Unearthly green eyes. Her delicate hands, like my own. Then, I looked to Spencer, and as I watched his face expand in fear, I saw god. Not a man in the sky, but the reality of what god was supposed to be – the idea that there could be order to the world. Because I was lying when I said I hadn't thought about it: that I hadn't imagined any number of ways I could harm a man, any number of ways a man could be destroyed. I just didn't think it was possible. I didn't think you could set out to change the world and actually succeed.

'I love you, Marnie,' Luna said.

The women on their mats, with their hands over their hearts, echoed after her. 'We love you, Marnie.'

I took hold of the scissors.

Acknowledgements

A large portion of this book was written on the unceded lands of the Wurundjeri and Boonwurrung peoples of the Kulin nation. I pay my respects to their Elders, both past and present, for caring for so-called Australia for over 60,000 years. Always was, always will be, Aboriginal Land.

This book would not exist without Yve Blake and Benjamin Paz. I know what you're thinking – authors throw that phrase around like it's home-brand table salt – but in this case I can assure you, it's the truth.

Yve, without your boundless enthusiasm I would never have believed I was capable of writing a book. Thank you for 'bullying' me.

Ben, without your gentle encouragement and narrative prowess I wouldn't have finished the damn thing. Working with you taught me more about writing than any course ever could. Thank you for changing my life, and ensuring the manuscript contained the appropriate number of croissants.

To Nikki Christer, the classiest woman in publishing: thank you for captaining the ship with grace, kindness and an excellent sense of humour. I knew as soon as you referenced the film *Death Becomes Her* that you were the woman for me. I feel exceedingly lucky to be your author.

Kathryn Knight, oh, Kathryn Knight! My editor and lead beauty industry consultant, working with you has brought me so much joy. I'm eternally grateful for your incredible mind and laser-focused attention to detail. You should be in Mensa. Thank you. Let's do it again sometime.

Thank you to Caitlan Cooper-Trent, Tara Wynne, Talia Moodley, Ruby Taylor, Amy Hardman and the team at Curtis Brown Australia, for championing *Rytuał*, and for championing me.

Thank you to the team at Penguin Random House Australia for their unwavering support, especially Hannah Ludbrook and Bek Chereshsky. I can't believe you're all actually penguins.

Thank you to Jo Porter, Rachel Gardner, Laura Nagy, Sami Swilks, Kim Wilson and the team at Curio Pictures. Although at the time I thought my brain might explode, the work we did on this story made it better in every way. Thank you for trusting me.

Thank you to Australians in Film, for allowing me to work on this book at *Charlie's*, despite the fact that it was not a screenplay. I have such fond memories of my afternoons at Raleigh Studios.

Thank you to my coven of witches for an inordinate number of things, but mostly for being my friends: Yve Blake (again), Michelle Brasier, Gillian Cosgriff and Virginia Gay. Thank you to Amy Taylor, for being my first author friend, and for reminding me repeatedly to do just one thing at a time. To Eilish Gilligan, thank you for teaching me what a D'Amelio is. I hope we're friends for the rest of our lives.

Thank you to the entire team at Shameless Media – fifteen of the greatest people you will ever meet. Thank you for welcoming me with open arms and an abundance of giggles.

To Sarah Soh, Helen Roberts, Lauren Ashman, Emily Rollis, Tan Trieu, Jessica Tomasino, Patrick Byrne, Jessica Paterson, Victoria Stamos, Liz Wilson, Abby Craw and all of my colleagues at Emeis Cosmetics: I trust this finds you well. None of these characters were based on you, and I treasure our time spent polishing amber bottles together.

Thank you to my parents, Jillian and Andrew, for always believing that I could do it, and for letting me live in their house while I wrote a lot of this book. I'm sorry for criticising the way you do laundry. I'm proud to be your daughter.

Thank you to my sister, Natalie, for reminding me to always be alive *and* amazing.

Finally, thank you to Hamish Patrick, for so many things, but mainly for teaching me that love can be easy. I would never nominate you for Friday Night Drinks. I promise.